Trigger Point

The Nicholas Ford Series™

Trigger Point

TONY ROTH

FULL BLOOM PRESS

Published by Full Bloom Press. First edition March 2022

This book is a work of fiction. Any references to historical events, real people or real places, are used fictitiously. Other names, characters, places and events are products of the author's imagination. While inspired by true historical events and public figures, all other macro events, places, or people—living or dead—is pure coincidence.

The Nicholas Ford Series™ is a registered trademark of Full Bloom Press

Library of Congress cataloging-in-publication data is on file with the U.S. Copyright Office.

PAPERBACK: ISBN 979-8-9852611-0-3
EBOOK: ISBN 979-8-9852611-1-0

Cover and book designed by John Lotte

Manufactured in the United State of America

Trigger Point: A specific point on the body at which touch, or pressure will elicit pain.

Trigger Point

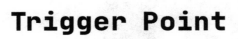

Chapter 1

The First Kill

Monday, September 15, 1986
Bogotá, Colombia

NICHOLAS FORD, better known by his CIA alias, Sean Smith, headed toward the river on his next lap through the winding paths of the Parque Nacional avoiding most of Bogotá's human congestion in the predawn gloom. Running always cleared his mind right before an assignment.

He quietly returned to the apartment and glanced into the bedroom. Gabriella was still asleep, her dark hair fanned across the white pillow. Nick slipped into the apartment's safe room to leave a coded message for his handler, Vincent. There would be no turning back.

JUST MONTHS earlier, Nicholas Ford had been given a code name, "Sean Smith." Recruited into the CIA by Vincent while in his junior year of college, he trained in secret and was assigned to Vincent's Clandestine Operations Unit. After graduation he began work as an operative with United States Agency for International Development (USAID) learning to funnel Congressional funds undetected through a money laundering operation, weaponizing the Freedom Fighters in Nicaragua. Nicholas reminded himself what he was doing was legal, even righteous, to suppress the evil Soviet Union and limit their infiltration into Central America via Nicaragua's president, Daniel Ortega. If all went well, his first official assignment would be completed by Wednesday.

Vincent's return message was simple: "Trust your suspicions. Be slow to take action."

Sean thought it sounded like a fortune cookie. But over the last year, he had learned quickly that Vincent was essential to staying alive. Vincent was highly intelligent, spoke five languages fluently, was a true chameleon, well-respected, aggressive, and loyal—as long as one proved useful.

By 8:00 a.m., Gabriella, Sean's interpreter, and Agency colleague, was awake and showering. She left the bathroom door open on purpose and he watched her as she stepped into the glass shower. Her athletic body, now glistening under the shower spray, was an unspoken invitation. Admiring her strong and sensuous curves, Nick joined her.

With an Irish American father and Mexican mother, Gabriella was an exotically beautiful woman. At twenty-eight years old, six years his senior, her confident sexuality and passionate warmth were an irresistible combination.

"Coffee and more coffee, please," she said as she walked into the kitchen still damp from the shower and wrapped in a towel. Reaching to plant a kiss on Nick's cheek, Gabriella barely came to Nick's chin even on her tip toes. She was all dark hair, big brown eyes, and golden skin pressing against Nick's lean, muscular frame. His blue eyes met hers and he smiled.

Sean poured her a cup of rich Colombian coffee and pulled a cinnamon muffin from the café bag. Gabriella fit perfectly into Sean's assignment "rodeo." Rodeo was the term for a perfect event that enabled every facet of Vincent's covert money laundering operation. Sean laundered Congressional funds through the USAID Rural Assistance Programs managed by Cartel fronts run by Fabio Ochoa, a notorious Cartel killer and long-time associate of Pablo Escobar. Most of the money was siphoned for purchases of weapons and supplies to support Nicaraguan Freedom Fighters. He sat down and laid out the plan for the rodeo presentation.

"It's a major fundraising event for the rural development fund and USAID's funding programs." Sean continued, "We have to make Fabio the star of the show and play off his entire Cartel connection. They need to be the promoters of rural Colombia."

"I know, Sean. I have made Fabio's prize horses part of the show with his personal trainer onboard. Fabio will like the idea," responded Gabriella.

"Excellent. The national police, DEA and all the political heads will hate it." Sean muttered sarcastically. They laughed out loud. They were ready.

They got in their car with their security driver, and headed to Fabio's home, The Ochoa Ranch. The Ochoa Ranch was home to the Ochoa Brothers, head of the Cali Cartel and principals of the Medellin Cartel. They arrived with ten minutes to spare; Fabio walked over to greet them. Sean and Fabio exchanged a big handshake and an even bigger hug.

"Bienvenido a nuestra rancho!" (Welcome to our ranch!)

Sean introduced Gabriella as a member of the USAID team and his interpreter. Fabio was a gentleman and a major flirt. He kissed Gabriella's hand. *"Bienvenido a mi rancho, guapa."* (Welcome, beautiful woman, to my ranch.)

Gabriella smiled, *"Es un placer conocerte!"* (Such a pleasure to meet you!)

They walked inside and were served iced tea. Jaime Leal and Rodriguez Gacha arrived at 10 a.m. sharp.

Leal was selected by the CIA to hold confidential informant status. He was a lifetime politician and friendly with everyone including the Communist Party and the FARC guerillas that controlled western Colombia. This made him a double-edged sword with political leaders. Sean, intuitively suspicious of Leal, needed him according to Vincent.

Gacha, a Cartel lawyer and accountant had been selected by Fabio as "the savviest businessman I know," and "essential for gaining trust among the leading Cartel families." Sean understood that the Cartels trusted Gacha and he would have to treat him with the same cautious respect as Fabio so money laundering assignments would be protected.

Sean presented the assignment: rodeo event, giving Fabio credit for hosting the meeting, and for assisting USAID. There were three basic requirements for the rodeo event to happen. First, securing Villavicencio as the premiere site.

Fabio immediately shouted, *"No hay problema!"*

The second requirement was the date. Gabriella took the lead and discussed the charitable attributes of the events, the need for a festival atmosphere that would draw men, women, and their families with *"musica y baile,"* (music and dancing). The men listened and watched her poise and passion.

"Por supuesto que tendremos eso," said Leal. (Of course, we shall have that.)

Then Gabriella proposed the date of February 13 through 15, 1987, and waited for their reactions.

Fabio spoke up first, *"Perfecto!"*

Sean was pleased. He loved watching Gabriella persuade men with the power of her intelligence and sexual energy.

"We need a strong committee," she said, "to coordinate operations, and all the logistics. We need to get sponsors. Public relations, security."

Leal stepped up and said he could chair, get sponsors and contributors, and build the team for the public.

"Gacha should be the treasurer," Leal offered. "Bring your ideas tomorrow."

Gacha was the best candidate for any accounting and legal work, and none of the others wanted to serve in that role. Gacha, a man of few words, nodded, and everyone agreed.

Sean took the lead again. He opened the briefcase and placed $10,000 on the table.

"This should get things started," he said, looking at Gacha. "We need to make some PR happen fast. We have to promote the USAID Rural Economic Development Funds."

"By when?" asked Fabio.

Sean said, "No later than Thursday."

The men groaned that Thursday was too soon, that it could not be done. Sean looked around the room, put another $10,000 down, and said, *"Hay que hacerlo. No es negociable."* (It must be done. It's non-negotiable.)

Fabio quickly deduced that the PR was there to create more cover for the money laundering operation. It would be helpful to keep the national police less interested in their undercover movements.

The men looked at each other and agreed to a Thursday morning press announcement. Sean was pleased and believed the PR could distract investigative interest in their Colombian money laundering operations.

Sean and Gabriella made their goodbyes and headed to their car.

"Adios!" shouted Fabio as they drove off.

LEAL LOOKED at Gacha. "Fifteen percent for me on everything I raise."

Gacha smiled. "And 30 percent for Fabio and me."

The committee would make their calls, acquire financial pledges, and secure the additional members needed for the rodeo event. In the car, Sean and Gabriella discussed their thoughts about the meeting. They agreed it went better than they could have hoped. Sean was convinced that Fabio, Gacha, and Leal were back at the house making plans to leverage the event for all sorts of criminal activity. But that was not Sean's problem.

Gabriella and Sean stopped at the Embassy to show their faces and spread the news about the USAID rodeo event. The Embassy had been in lock-down all morning, and the mood seemed a bit on-edge. Sean asked one of the affiliated managers of the agricultural division for coffee farming cooperatives what had happened.

"A killing took place just outside the entrance around 9:30 this morning. There was rapid gunfire. Two sicarios on motorcycles killed an unarmed USAID manager, and it is under investigation," said the manager.

Sean asked who was investigating.

"The National Police Colonel Ramirez," replied the USAID manager.

Sean shook his head and walked off, feeling the presence of Ramirez. He knew the Colombian Drug Enforcement Administration (DEA), and Ramirez were watching him. He was the new gringo in town with friendly affiliations in the Cartel. Sean muttered under his breath, *Might as well wear a fucking sign on my back.*

Gabriella and Sean made the rounds to update USAID managers and key executive directors at the Embassy. After informing the support staff with the news, they returned to the apartment. There were three messages waiting.

The first was for Sean, the other two were for both. Sean opened his private message from Vincent, "Discreetly arm yourself and be prepared for hostile behavior."

"There it is," Sean sighed. He knew too much was happening way too fast. Local officials combined with the Colombian DEA were on his tail. He could feel it in his bones.

Sean grabbed his knuckle knife. A gun was too much firepower to carry as a USAID representative if the DEA or National Police caught him. He burned Vincent's message in the kitchen.

Gabriella opened the other two messages. The first was from Gacha, requesting another $20,000.

Sean shook his head, "What a greedy asshole." The second message was from Leal, inviting them to the formation meeting of the proposed committee, to be held Wednesday at 5:30 p.m. at his home.

Sean said, "Call Leal and confirm the meeting. We will be there."

Then, as a dare, he said, "Let's shower and have each other for dinner."

Gabriella blushed and smiled in her most alluring way, "Yes, Sean, let's."

He knew he was not falling in love with her—he was engaged to Anna, his college sweetheart back in Illinois. But while in Bogotá, Gabriella had taken over his desires and the attraction was unstoppable.

They spent the rest of the evening in bed, ravishing each other.

Gabriella whispered, "You take my breath away, Sean. Are all farm boys this giving?"

"I'm just a hopeless romantic. I am taken by you." Sean ran his fingers across her thigh and kissed her neck again whispering, "Take me now."

By midnight they were famished. They put on robes and made omelets and toast. Gabriella whispered to Sean, "Let's eat in bed."

"Yes." Sean kissed her softly on the lips.

Tuesday, September 16, 1986

SEAN WOKE up before sunrise, grabbed his robe and took the dirty dishes into the kitchen. He made himself a *café con leche* and went for a run. Lately, running focused his mind and brought solace to his day, no matter the pressure. As he ran through the parks near the university, Sean reminisced about his track days at the University of Illinois, and simpler times on his family farm.

He and Gabriella spent the better part of the day at the USAID offices in the Embassy. USAID team members were assembled to plan for rodeo coordination and communications. Gabriella was a natural at persuading people to support the rodeo.

THE WHITE HOUSE was lobbying for freedom, while covertly directing the CIA Clandestine Units throughout Central America. Using apocalyptic terms, President Reagan was warning Congress of a "strategic disaster" if Nicaragua was left to the Sandinistas. Sean believed that there was heavy shit about to rain down on the current administration and these monies were helping to suppress Soviet Union infiltration. Committed to Vincent, he felt a deep swell of patriotism as part of the team strengthening Reagan's agenda, *Ortega must stop their Soviet Union alignment.*

Sean continued to operate under USAID cover at the Embassy. He was now planning the public rodeo event in plain sight. The National Police would participate in security, but there was always the risk of a leaker. Sean kept his eyes open, his ears to the ground, and his mind focused.

Near the end of the day, Gabriella whispered to Sean, "Ready when you are."

An Embassy clerk walked up to Sean and handed him a message. It was from Leal:

```
Committee planning meeting 5 p.m., Home of
Jaime Leal. Press meeting at 9 a.m. Thursday,
San Pablo Hotel Conference Room.
```

Sean nodded to Gabriella. "Let's go out tonight and see who's watching us."

His CIA training at The Farm with covert operatives taught Sean when it was wise to be noticed, and how to spot and identify potential threats. Being out in public would inevitably bring about information or even a confrontation that could reveal the enemy's plans or intelligence. *As long as you NEVER get caught,* Sean thought. Words to live by on The Farm.

That evening, Sean purposely told the driver to randomly drive around the city, allowing him to observe traffic and determine if they were being followed. Satisfied no one was following them, Sean directed the driver to drop them at a bar near the Westin Hotel.

He scanned the room and had Gabriella look for a booth or a corner table. He left to check the bathroom, and by the time he returned, she was sitting in a booth as their drinks arrived. He watched the room as he listened to Gabriella talk about her event planning details. He signaled the waitress and paid their tab.

Sean whispered to Gabriella, "Drink up. We're leaving."

Acting casual, she finished her drink and rose to leave. Sean threw some money on the table as they left to get a cab.

"There was a suspicious guy in the corner of the bar, carrying a weapon. He arrived just after us," he told her. Sean was taking no chances.

"El Barrio para cenar, por favor," Sean said, instructing the driver to take them to El Barrio Restaurant near the University

of Bogotá. It would not be crowded on a Tuesday night. It was a lower-priced restaurant, perfect for a USAID representative's modest budget if they were being followed. Again, Sean checked the bathroom, looking to see if anyone might have followed them. Gabriella picked a table.

When he came out, he saw two faces glancing his way: Gabriella's and the same young man from the last bar.

The waitress walked over, and Gabriella ordered a sangria.

"Que sean dos," said Sean. (Make that two.)

As the waitress turned, Sean touched her arm, handed her a $20 bill, and asked if she had cigarettes and matches. She smiled and came back with both. He stood, waived the cigarettes in the air as if he had struck gold, but whispered to Gabriella, "Don't order any food. We may be leaving. I'll be right back."

He walked to the door. *"Gracias,"* Sean shouted to the waitress.

Outside, he walked around the corner and into the alley. He lit a cigarette and waited. Footsteps came from the direction of the restaurant, creeping toward the alley. His heart beating faster, Sean opened his knuckle knife and tossed the cigarette. He leaned against the wall as if he had too much to drink. From the corner of his eye, he could see the stranger approach.

Sean sized him up. Young, twenty-something, about 5'7", dark, greasy hair, crooked teeth, decent clothes, and a tattoo of the mythical "evil eye" on his left hand. The evil eye was a curse said to cause harm in varying degrees, some harm worse than others. Sean knew that the tattoo was popular with law enforcement officers throughout Latin America. The stranger held a pistol close to his chest in his right hand.

"Para quien trabajas," (Who do you work for?) demanded the young man.

Sean looked him in the eye. "USAID," he said and grabbed the man's gun hand with his left hand while stabbing him in the lower left abdomen with the knuckle knife hidden in his right hand. The man dropped the gun and Sean slowly laid him down in the alley.

"Me apuñalaste en el estómago." (You stabbed me in the stomach.)

Sean knelt beside him and placed his knife on the man's throat. *"Para quien trabajas?"* (Who do you work for?)

The man attempted bravery, *"Que te den!"* (Fuck you!)

"Un intento mas! Para quien trabajas?" (One more try! Who do you work for?)

"Que te den!" repeated the man.

Sean heard voices on the sidewalk getting louder and closer. He pulled the man's jacket up to shield the blood from spraying as he pushed the knife deep into his neck, severing the carotid artery.

It was done. The man was dying. As the blood pooled on the sidewalk, reality set in. Sean felt sick. He watched the breath leave the man's body. Memories of his father's words penetrated his mind, "Never harm anyone's person or their property." The betrayal of his family's values seeped through his entire being. Reeling from nausea, he leaned away from the body to throw up.

"Focus, God damn it!" he admonished himself as he tried to pull it together.

Despite all his training, and rehearsing for this moment many times, he could not stop shaking. He had killed for the sake of killing. Whether it was the right thing to do or not did not cross his mind; at least not yet. Right now, he was physically shaking out of control as he desperately tried to get a hold of his feelings. It was done. He pocketed the knife and walked to the sidewalk, nearly bumping into three girls walking together.

He smiled at the girls using his most authentic farm boy smile, as if in character for a play. *"Hola, señoritas, ten cuidado al salir a caminar esta noche."* (Hello, ladies. Be careful out walking tonight.)

The girls, obviously in college, giggled and kept walking,

passing right by the alley. Pausing to collect himself, "Thank God they didn't see anything."

Sean paused, feeling regret for missing out on those carefree walks during his time at college. Vincent had recruited him mid-semester and swept him into the CIA clandestine program.

"Stay focused!" he screamed to himself.

He walked back to the restaurant, paid the bill, and gathered Gabriella. They walked for about 15 city blocks in silence. Gabriella knew enough to remain quiet. Something had happened, and she knew that Sean would talk when, and only when, he was ready.

"El Poblado is very close," said Sean. "Let's have something there, yes?"

It was all he could think of to say to Gabriella. He was not ready to talk about anything. Fear of what he had done was settling in. *Focus and stay on course Sean. What is essential for plausible deniability? Think it through.*

Gabriella observed Sean carefully as he processed whatever had happened and remained confident that he would talk at some point. They walked into El Poblado. Sean went to the bathroom to wash up, calm himself, and organize his thoughts. He took a long look in the mirror and saw small drops of blood that had splattered from his first kill.

He was shaking and breathing heavily, as if there was no more air in the small bathroom. He splashed cold water on his face and tried to clean the blood from his shirt.

"What did you do?" Sean looked in the mirror, and then down to the blood in the sink. "It was a necessary confrontation. It was self-defense."

Back at the table, he pretended to eat some of the grilled fish, though he couldn't taste anything. His nausea returned, and all he saw was blood, pooling on his plate, and the memory of his victim as he fought to take his final breath.

Gabriella sensed his distress and touched his hand. "Let's go home."

He was sure his actions would draw some unwanted attention very soon. He reassessed the altercation over and over in his mind. That man was clearly carrying a police-issued gun and was ordered to question and arrest, not kill. Sean dreaded the moment when he would have to answer to Vincent. It was not a designated kill; the man was asking questions while holding a drawn weapon. He had been sloppy, poorly trained, and inexperienced.

Sean's mind spun through the conversation angles, the operational chess game he would be forced to play when confronted by Vincent.

Sean grew determined to defend his first kill. "I was told to not to allow any Colombian Police, militia or foreign law enforcement to develop a profile on me."

No matter what, Sean knew deep down he made a mistake. It was a deadly one for the man in the alley.

Gabriella lay in bed next to him, her eyes trying to gently say something. No words came to her. She was afraid that her imagination might be far worse than anything that could have happened.

Sean looked deeply into her soul. "Can I trust you?"

"Yes, of course."

"No! Can I trust you no matter what?"

"Yes, Sean."

"It's Nick. I am still Nick Ford."

Gabriella spoke softly. "Yes Nick, I know you. I'm here for you, no matter what."

"I killed that man in the alley, the one who was following us. He might have been a policeman, or someone working for an agency, maybe the DEA."

His body was tense, and he shivered, full of anguish. "I was trained to never get caught and he caught me, so I killed him."

Gabriella held Nick tight and climbed on top, laying her entire body over his, whispering "Sssshhhh, ssshhhh, it will be okay, it will be okay. You did what you had to do."

Comforted by her weight, Sean passed out, exhausted.

Awakened in the middle of the night, Sean woke to find Gabriella curled next to him. Sean lay still in the moonlit room, absorbing the warmth of Gabriella's body.

He stared at the shadowy images on the ceiling, remembering the allure of Vincent's descriptions of the CIA. He had willingly, whole-heartedly stepped into the shadows of clandestine services. He was trained to analyze people and situations, collect intelligence, carry out missions, persuade assets, and terminate threats. Now in a foreign country, operating undercover to execute a mission designed by Vincent.

Who can I trust? thought Sean. Who am I, what am I becoming?

Chapter 2
The Debrief

Wednesday, September 17, 1986

SEAN BOARDED a flight from Bogotá and landed as Nick in Los Angeles. As he walked past the baggage claim doors, he saw a familiar face—it was Vincent. A handshake, a long hug, and a pleasant drive later, they were seated oceanside at The Ivy at the Shore Restaurant in Santa Monica.

Vincent whispered, "It's good to be alive. Let's enjoy the view."

"Yes, let's." replied Nick.

Cocktails arrived and Vincent began, "Tell me about the change in narrative."

Nick described the events of the days leading up to the kill, "I met with all three money-laundering principals the week before. The Calí Fund at Fabio's Ranch, The Banco Farm Fund, and The Rural Medellín Fund are all in agreement. It was at the group meeting at Leal's home where I first noticed suspicious behavior.

"When I arrived at the meet with Gacha, he glanced at me and immediately took a long drink of his coffee. I walked to the counter. There he was, Colonel Ramirez, live and in-person. I ordered a café con leche. Ramirez looked directly at me, paid his bill and left."

Vincent interrupted, "What did Gacha do?"

Nick flatly replied, "He dropped his pen and left a small note on the floor as he picked up the pen. It read, *"El rodeo esta apro-bado."* (The rodeo is approved.) Gacha left without even looking at me."

Vincent asked, "What is your suspicion?"

Nick whispered, "It was no coincidence. Fabio had warned me at the Fund Meeting that the DEA and the National Police were watching us." Nick leaned into Vincent "I saw the two DEA agents that harassed me in my first week in Bogotá. The agents approached me and said, "Don't get in over your head, boy.""

Vincent scowled at Nick. "Don't get in over your head, boy? Assholes. What did you say?"

Nick replied, *"Buenos dias, amigos mios."* (Good day, my friends.)

"And how do you feel about it now?" asked Vincent.

"My suspicions were at an all-time high with Leal and Ramirez, given their political and military connections," Nick confessed.

Vincent applied pressure to Nick's wrist. "Stop. We understand that, and we're intelligence gathering now."

Nick shook his head and finished his Bombay martini. Vincent called the waiter for another round.

Vincent lit a cigarette, took one long drag, and put it out in his water glass. "What happened in the alley?"

Nick breathed calmly. "The man was following us. We changed restaurants to verify. I let him see me buy cigarettes and stepped outside for a smoke." Nick paused to reflect and measure Vincent's reaction. "A minute or two later, the man approached me with his gun drawn."

Vincent interrupted, "Describe him"

"He was young, maybe my age, and demanded to know who I work for."

The waiter delivered drinks.

Nick waited for the waiter to walk away and continued, "His gun was standard issue National Police, but he wasn't police."

"Who do you think he was working for?" asked Vincent.

"Colonel Jaime Ramirez."

Vincent looked away, thinking aloud, "If that's true, Leal hasn't quite given you away yet."

This was a game of intelligence regarding the Communist movement in Colombia and throughout Central America, and more than just covert ops for money to fund the Contras in Nicaragua. The circles of politicians, Cartel leaders and the law Nick was now in the middle of were making more sense to him.

Vincent watched Nick's mind work through the angles, impressed with his process.

"Let's order lunch," he said.

Nick chose shrimp and grits concoction to absorb the gin he was starting to feel.

Vincent appeared to be in a progressively good mood. "Brother Nick, you must enjoy life, because it is fleeting," Vincent proclaimed as he ordered steak and eggs. It was turning into a three-martini lunch. Nick kept pace, but he was feeling the potent gin seeping into his relaxed mood.

IN A DARK basement below the streets of Bogotá, there was a secret room known as the inner sanctum. It was designed by Colonel Ramirez for his secret militia to serve his private wars. A meeting was in progress.

"Pedro is dead. I believe he was killed by the new gringo hanging around the Cartel." *Ramirez said.*

The men listened intensely.

"This Sean Smith is not who he says he is. He pretends to be a USAID Agricultural Specialist, but I believe he is with ties to the CIA and NOW HE HAS KILLED ONE OF MY MEN FOR NO REASON!"

Chapter 3
Nick's Cover

DEBRIEFING OVER lunch was complete. Vincent and Nick walked along the boardwalk. Nick enjoyed walking and talking. It reminded him of his father on the farm.

Vincent asked, "Are you thinking about your wedding?" It was a loaded question.

Nick paused, wondering if he should disclose his CIA career to Anna and recruit her loyalty.

"Yes," Nick replied flatly.

Vincent laughed out loud, "I bet you have. . . . Let's walk a little more."

Nick had become an expert at compartmentalization, separating his life in the States, including his fiancée, from his agency work. Anna Mayer, his college sweetheart, was a brilliant computer engineering graduate. Her sharp, tactical mind and small-town roots attracted Nick from the start. She was of German descent and naturally pretty, with strong features, dark wavy hair and deep brown eyes. At 5'8", Anna was slim, but not athletic, preferring computer code to almost anything else. She was at home in Illinois planning their wedding and life together.

"Remember that night after your first interrogation training exercise? When I showed up and we broke into the music building together, on campus?" Vincent said.

Memories flooded Nick. "It was 7:00 p.m. sharp, you rapped on my door, with a bottle of Glenlivet."

Vincent, just shy of six feet had a strong build with a defiant stance. His thick, black hair somehow appeared slightly wet, or even greasy, all the time. He was a mix of Irish and British, a "mutt," according to his own description. Despite imperfect teeth and mildly pock-marked face, Vincent managed to pull off a grin and a laugh that could spark a room. And he could be charming when needed, a man's man among the roughest, most macho guys around.

Vincent reminisced, "We walked all the way across campus, past Kirkland Performing Arts Center and picked the lock to enter the music building."

"You magically pulled out two small glasses from your jacket and we drank," Nick added.

Vincent broke in, "I asked you if you could still play piano."

Nick remained silent as they walked along the Santa Monica boardwalk.

Vincent mocked him. "You looked at the keys, sat on the bench, back straight, and laid your fingers gently on the keys with hollow palms to show off six years of lessons and high school jazz band."

Nick remained silent, thinking, *This is going to be painful.*

"You started with a chorus of Gershwin's 'Lady Be Good,' but when memory failed, you glided into a few phrases of Carol King's 'So Far Away' and then switched to Phil Collins' song: 'One More Night.'"

Nick interrupted, "Make your point, Vincent."

"You have a problem finishing," said Vincent.

Nick's small pride in his piano playing disappeared. Nick realized Vincent was pointing out a vastly more important issue. He took his time to reply.

Not waiting for a response, Vincent stopped walking, "What does 'finish the task' mean to you, Nick?"

Fueled with liquid courage, Nick blurted out, "FUCK YOU!"

Vincent laughed from his belly and put his hand on Nick's shoulder, "I tried to seduce you, remember? But it was too much for you to handle."

Nick escalated the bickering, "I pushed you off the piano bench!"

Vincent raised his voice, "And I wrestled you to the floor."

Nick bantered, "You thoroughly enjoyed yourself."

Vincent laughed, "I gave up and rolled over onto my back. I knew at that moment we would only be brothers"

"True," Nick said calmly, still relieved about that night.

They turned around to walk back to the restaurant.

Nick always believed that Vincent cared. *These mind games were tests designed by Vincent,* thought Nick. The only person Nick could really trust was himself.

Vincent shifted the conversation. "Back to Anna and your cover. Are you ready to debrief her after the wedding? Is there a plan to disclose and persuade her to join in secrecy with us?"

"I am worried about my plans. My long-term path," Nick stated.

Anna was already planning to work on classified and even top-secret computer engineering configurations for communication systems as a computer engineer. She was growing familiar with government agencies.

Nick continued, "I believe she will accept my news and agree to secrecy. She wants her own career in government-related work, communication system engineering is her dream."

"Nick, I will become a Deputy Director of Clandestine

Operations, and you will be one my case officers. Now, go get married and then WE will explain things to her."

Nick visualized his career ladder in the Agency and wanted to make an impact on the world—yet still be successful in the eyes of his family. Nick justified his lies and convinced himself he could have the marriage that his family expected of him. Approaching the restaurant, Nick remembered why he had decided to move forward in the Agency as a "married agent."

He grew up chasing his older brother's successes through the eyes of his parents. Graduate college, find a career, and then get married was the formula that his parents promoted and praised. The CIA published a study that showed married operations officers lasted longer (44 percent of field operatives were married), probably because station chiefs and case managers would take marriage into consideration for high-risk ops, and, most often, married officers climbed the political ranks more expeditiously. Vincent and Nick both sought a career in the Agency, and that meant becoming politically driven.

Vincent noticed Nick's heavy energy. "Go home, my Illinois farm boy. Dig those toes into that soil. Feel your roots and spend a night with Dad and Mom. It will all work out for the best."

"That does sound good," Nick replied. "I will."

Smiling, Vincent offered, "Being married is better for you."

Nick heard him but wasn't sure what to believe.

They approached Vincent's car, "Richard says hello. He's concerned about your first kill."

Nick knew that he should never be the one to bring Richard up first. Vincent had said it was too risky to discuss openly. While that could be true, Nick knew it could set off unnecessary hints of jealousy. Vincent was a bit of an egomaniac. To ask about Richard would make him suspicious or even jealous. Richard was Vincent's life partner and lover. Nick felt adopted by the two gay spies. Richard, a German Federal Intelligence

Agency spy, was 6'2", rugged, yet elegant in his movements with a smile that could charm a snake. Richard was lethal in his own right. Richard was an agent that CIA officials would admit to recruiting only off-the-record. Vincent approached Richard during his first assignment in Berlin many years earlier. Neither shared any more details. Nick admired Richard's bravery and sense of mission.

Nick turned to Vincent, "Richard likes the train to run on time." Half German, Nick appreciated Richard's pragmatic conversation style. It often annoyed Vincent. "Tell Richard I am okay." Nick replied with conviction.

Vincent smiled. "Enjoy the wedding party! I hear it will be quite the soirée."

They laughed.

As Vincent greeted his driver, he reached into his jacket and pulled out an envelope. "Here's a little something from Richard and me. Open it after the wedding."

Vincent had an olive cast to his skin tone that glowed when he gave someone a present. It also empowered him with chameleon-like capabilities. He was complex, almost bipolar at times, but true to his mission and friends.

Nick placed the envelope in his pocket, hugged Vincent and for the moment felt blessed to have his friendship, as well as a shared comradery.

DRIVING HOME, Nick's memories occupied his mind. Why did Merle Voigt profile him for recruitment? He was a mentor, junior high social studies teacher, and track coach.

Nick talked to himself to rationalize it. *After two years of junior high state track meets together, Merle lobbied the teachers for my American Legion Award, convinced my dad to let me pursue*

Eagle Scout, and became the high school track coach to stay close to me and my family. . . .

Nick remembered, "Merle once, and only once, let him know that he was part of the OSS and was there for the formation of the CIA." Nick always felt safe and valued by Merle.

Shaking his head, confused, Nick played out everything that Merle had done to help him. He medaled at the state track meets every year, won state basketball championships, achieved Eagle Scout and American Legion Awards. *He was profiling me for CIA recruitment.*

Then, Nick's painful memory of one regrettable night he had tried to forget became clear, *He saved me. He knew I would be loyal no matter what after that. I became his asset.*

Nick replayed the night. It was graduation night and his graduating friends invited him as a junior to the lake party after their ceremony. He remembered being unsure about the party—there were several assholes who hated him for taking their spot on the varsity basketball team, always trying to corner him and drag him into trouble.

Nick looked out the windshield, watching the traffic fly by on the 405, his mind replayed the fight.

He had only been at the party for an hour, it was still early, not even 9:30 p.m. He filled his beer cup, worried about drinking with this crowd. He wasn't quite 18 yet, and could get stopped by the local cops, which would ruin his reputation.

As he walked away from the beer keg, he was grabbed by three guys, two holding him and the third pushing him along. He struggled, tried to talk to them, but it did not work.

Nick could hear their words, "You don't belong here, asshole! You think you got the right to be here, you're fucking wrong. We're gonna beat the shit out of you, feed it to you and drag you out-a-here behind my truck for everyone to see what a pussy you are!"

They pulled him behind the small dock house and while two held him, the third began punching him in the gut. Still driving, Nick winced about what happened next.

Something snapped and rage took over. He instinctively leveraged the two boys holding him and kicked the boy who was punching him in the groin. As one of the boys let go, he spun out of their grip. He was free, but he didn't run.

I wanted to kill those motherfuckers.

He had spotted a small pile of two-by-fours stacked against the side of the dock house and grabbed one. Without thinking, he stepped into the fight, swinging and hitting the first boy in the knee. He went down in pain. The second boy came at him. Nick spun to maintain momentum and struck him in the kidney. The boy cried out and fell to the ground.

He was upset with the memory; one he had tried to erase.

All three were hurting. If only he had run, nothing bad would have happened.

I had to finish the fight and teach them a lesson, beating himself up.

Nick held the two-by-four tight, walked over to the puncher who was bent over. Nick couldn't resist. The puncher looked up at him, his face poised like a ball placed on a tee. Nick didn't hesitate. He swung the board like a baseball bat as hard and accurately as he could. As the board whacked the puncher's head, he heard a voice yell, "STOP!"

It was too late. The blow moved through his victim's skull like a tidal wave of energy. In Nick's mind, he could see it happening in slow motion. The face lost composure and his head was pulling his body to the ground. The puncher went down, convulsed once, in darkness and his body went still. The reality of the blow made Nick sick to his stomach.

A hand from behind grabbed the board from him. At first, he

tried to fight it, then he heard Merle's voice, "Stop it, Nick, you've done enough damage."

Nick looked around, the other boys had limped off, no doubt about to tell their side of the story.

"C'mon, let's report this now and we can straighten things out," Merle said.

They hurried to Merle's truck. Merle radioed the local police on his CB radio, reported the details of the "accident," and drove Nick to the police station. Merle stopped one block away and instructed Nick, "I need you to shut the fuck up, all you can say is there were three of them trying to beat the shit out of you, got it?"

Nick recalled saying, "I got it."

"Don't fuck it up, don't fuck your future. Let's go." Merle parked and walked Nick into the police station.

Merle explained to the police, he was at the lake to help chaperone the graduation party. He heard fighting and ran to see what was happening. He saw three boys fighting one and yelled, "STOP!" Two of the boys ran off, and third one had been just hit in the head with a board by Nick.

Merle told them that he grabbed Nick, called in the report on the injured boy to the police and asked for an ambulance, and then drove him here.

The police interviewed Nick for a statement and Nick repeated what Merle had instructed, nothing more, nothing less. They let him go that night.

Nick cried out loud in the car, now stopped on the shoulder of Interstate 405, "They fucking let me go!"

He could hear Merle's voice days after the fight, "You have good instincts Nick. But you don't know how to manage your rage. When to pull the trigger on that rage can be learned."

Nick collected himself and pulled back onto the Interstate. His thoughts went to the kid he had beaten. The boy suffered a severe concussion and cerebral edema and was out for nearly twenty-four hours. He required emergency brain surgery and later, medication.

Consoling himself, Nick remained defensive about that night, justifying the injury with *it could have been me*. He was relieved to later learn that the boy had taken vocational classes instead of college and became a self-sufficient plumber.

As Nick pulled into the garage, he placed those memories into their secret compartment. He still appreciated what Merle had done that night, but his job now was to move forward and provide results for his country.

He needed to pack, fly home to Illinois, and get married as per his life plan. His parents were so proud. They saw marriage as a solid foundation for becoming a responsible adult. Nick walked into his kitchen, poured a drink, and shook his head. *I'm not so sure...*

Chapter 4

Looking Back

Thursday, September 18, 1986
Illinois

NICK LANDED AT O'Hare International Airport in Chicago. He still had a four-hour drive down to the family farm ahead of him.

Peace, Nick thought. *Nobody to report to and only farmland past the city limits.*

In hindsight, Nick was exactly the kind of recruit Vincent was looking for. A talented athlete, Nick's long, lean muscles belied his power and agility and afforded him the element of surprise in a fight. At 192 lbs. on a 6'2" frame, his cool blue eyes and light brown hair added to the charm of his Midwestern farm boy appearance. But it was his quick, strategic mind that clinched him as Vincent's prized recruit. *And now I kill for information,* Nick scoffed.

1982: Fall semester at the University of Illinois

IT WAS Nick's freshman year. He pledged a fraternity and tried out for the varsity track and field team as a walk-on. He hated his major, pre-med biology. In high school, Nick was a state athlete in two sports, a top student, musician, and an Eagle Scout. Nick believed going to a Big Ten University would lead to something great.

He was introduced to Anna that year when he was invited to dinner at her sorority house as a friend of his "pledge mom" Debbie. Since Nick and Anna were from rural Illinois, she thought they might hit it off.

After dinner, Nick asked Anna to go for a walk. It was a fall day, leaves were changing colors, and the air was brisk—perfect jacket or sweater weather. Anna talked about her hometown, her parents, and her high school activities, including cheer-leading and Science Club. Once she realized that Nick had been an All-State basketball player and track-and-field competitor, she warmed up to him. They kissed that night and had a wonderful walk back to the sorority house.

Nick remembered all the parties they attended together during his freshman year and how they had grown into a couple. He spent so much time at her sorority that he was voted the House Sweetheart.

It was their sophomore year when Anna pointed out that school was most important to her and that she needed to focus on studies, so they stopped going steady. As their sophomore year flew by, they stayed in touch, even while dating other people. Nick accepted the time to focus on his own path.

Nick grew up with four brothers, all older, each one ex-tremely competitive. Nick shrugged to himself as he recalled his change in major. He hated pre-med biology and was searching for something more.

Late in the fall semester of Nick's sophomore year, Sandra, a guidance counselor, contacted Nick in response to his request for help changing his major. Sandra became a close confidant.

She guided Nick through his class schedule and subject se-lection. Nick had no idea of her role with the CIA. Nick's back-ground and profile was a prospective fit, referred for recruitment since high school. Nick successfully transferred to the College of Agriculture, majoring in agricultural economics.

Sandra's counseling was subtle. Nick grew fond of her supportive, yet firm, guidance. By the first semester of his junior year, Nick was in the best shape of his life, physically and mentally.

He and Anna dated seriously again that year and by the fall semester of 1984, they were discussing marriage.

NICK MET Vincent in spring of 1985. Merle Voigt called to see if an old family friend could spend a few nights at his apartment while he was visiting the campus. It was the week of break, so his roommate would be away. Vincent Connor attended Yale a few years earlier and was compiling research at the University of Illinois.

Nick shrugged. "Lies."

Vincent arrived. He was gracious, caring, and charming. They interacted extraordinarily little during the day but enjoyed long dinners together each night. Vincent was born in Liverpool, England, and moved with his mother to Connecticut at age 12. When she decided to return to Liverpool just two years later, he did not want to leave. He stayed with his aunt in New England. He graduated high school early with honors. He was a natural linguist, spoke four languages fluently at the age of 17, and was accepted into Yale on scholarship.

Vincent was secretive about his research at first.

Nick shook his head. "Manipulation."

Only thirty minutes from the farm, Nick wrestled with his choices to join the CIA, train in secret shrouded by lies, and kill. He felt sick. Stopping the car along the desolate country road, he stepped toward the ditch and threw up. For the first time in his life, Nick did not want his father to look into his eyes.

"Now I'm a liar and a killer!" Nick cried out.

Car door open, Nick sat on the driver's seat with his feet outside and breathed the clean country air.

The night he was recruited, Vincent brought two bottles of Glenlivet twelve-year-old scotch to his apartment, jokingly called the night, "Operation: Dinner In."

I wanted to know more, I wanted Vincent to understand I had skills, I wanted everything he was about . . . everything. Nick relived the evening.

Pizza, politics, economics, and scotch flowed. Vincent pulled out a confidentiality agreement. The terms "clandestine services" and "Central Intelligence Agency" excited Nick. Two consent boxes involving "classified" and "polygraph" leapt off the page at him.

Vincent spoke about Nick's life and prior choices intimately, disclosing things that Nick never discussed with anyone. Nick remembered the moment perfectly; words began to blur, and the room got smaller.

Nick lowered his head and tried to throw up again. He remembered Vincent's words: "Secret training, life-changing opportunities, and a bit of danger, all for the good of America."

"ENOUGH!" Nick yelled. He needed to compartmentalize his emotions. He closed the car door and drove toward the farm. Nick justified his decisions. His mother lost three brothers in prior wars. Nick decided to serve the country this way.

"Welcome to the family," Vincent declared when Nick signed.

Turning back is off the table.

The Cover Marriage

NICK FELT warm inside as he pulled into the farm. Despite his competitive relationship with his brothers and their mean-spirited treatment, his parents did their best to create a caring and disciplined home.

Like clockwork, his dad walked out to the car. Nick stood in front of his father to be inspected. His father gently gripped Nick's jaw with both hands, framing his face and slowly looked him over top to bottom, inspected his face, and then looked deep into Nick's eyes.

"Is everything going okay?"

Nick pulled down his father's forearms, "Yes, Dad, I'm doing okay." They hugged. This ritual had been performed dozens of times throughout Nick's youth.

His mom, Loretta, interrupted them. "Hey, you! I am going to need a hug, too!" Nick stepped toward his mom and gave her a kiss on the cheek and a long hug.

Nick followed his parents into the house and relaxed in the living room adjacent the kitchen so they could all share in the discussion. Loretta was preparing fried chicken and all the fixings for dinner. John, Nick's oldest brother, his wife Diana, and their two kids would be coming over soon.

Family night, Nick. *Normalcy.*

The next morning, Nick woke up early and joined his father for coffee and toast. By 6:30 they had walked the south 40 acres along the creek. Nick reminisced about the time he was flying a kite and the string had broken, and he had to walk along the creek in search of it.

"The wind was fierce that day," he reminded his father, "I couldn't hear mom calling for me."

Paul looked up to the sky in reflection, "I remember that day."

Nick went on, "I had just spotted my kite when I realized you were about 20 steps away, madder than a wet hornet, and coming at me strong."

Paul laughed out loud. "I grabbed you by the arm, dragged you to the house, bent you over my knee."

Nick stopped and looked at his dad. "You said, 'This is going to hurt me more than it hurts you.'"

Nick held his ground. "Did it? Did the spanking hurt you more than me?"

Paul looked at his son. "No, I believe you took the brunt of it." They laughed heartily.

Loretta rustled in the kitchen. John arrived to do chores. Nick loved the way time seemed to stand still on the farm. He needed to leave for Anna's house soon, so he absorbed as much of the farm spirit into his soul as possible.

Loretta interrupted his thoughts. "By this time next week, you will be married! Are you ready for it?"

Nick felt his mom, dad, and John staring at him, waiting for an answer.

"Yes, Mom. I am ready. We're both excited to be moving to California."

They were pleased.

Loretta packed chicken, dinner rolls, and small butter packs in a cooler for Nick to take with him. Nick hugged and kissed them goodbye. As he pulled away from the house, he was overcome with love for the farm and disgust about the lies and manipulation that now surrounded his life.

The wedding was just six days away. He lied to his parents about being ready. He stopped the car at the end of the driveway. He stepped out of the car and took off his shoes and socks off. As he walked through the front yard, his dad came out of the house and walked toward him. Loretta watched.

"Nick, are you sure you are okay?" Paul asked.

Growing up, he could never lie to his dad while his feet were planted on the soil of the family farm. But it was different now.

He walked to his father and looked him in the eye. "Everything will all turn out okay, Dad."

Paul looked deep into his soul and saw a disappointing realization. Nick could feel his father's concern. He knew Nick had not been truthful. He had lied about everything.

Nick concentrated on hiding his own disgust.

One more long embrace for his father, a wave to his mom, and Nick walked away from his dad. As he drove away from the farm, second thoughts swarmed through his mind.

WHEN NICK arrived at Anna's house, she came out to the car and hugged him long and tight. Anna's mom, Barbara, was waiting at the front door, much like his own mom did. It suddenly felt more real to Nick.

Nick believed in Anna and felt they were suited for each other, and that love would grow. Everything Nick heard about love while he was growing up led him to accept that it was something that took work and patience over time.

The next four days were a blur. Nick spent every day with

Anna. They visited friends and made final adjustments to the wedding plan.

Nick's orders were to prepare Anna for the disclosure of his CIA role. There was an agreed upon protocol in place about informing the spouse after the marriage. Nick tried to include his work when they dined alone. Anna, excited about the wedding, talked about the honeymoon, their townhome, and all the wonderful things they could do together. Nick failed to prepare her for the future and did not even hint about his work and the need to share more after the honeymoon.

Nick hated the way Anna's father, Jim, was behaving. He constantly declared aloud that the wedding reception was his gift. Nick called him *odioso de mierda,* (obnoxious asshole), under his breath.

Nick promised Vincent a check-in call prior to the wedding. So, just two nights before his wedding day, Nick called Vincent.

Vincent picked up almost immediately. "How is it going?"

Nick tried to share details, but Vincent interrupted him, "Glad it's on track, but we have picked up disturbing intel. Suffice it to say, you were right. I just want you to know that next Thursday evening, you will be on a flight back to Bogotá."

Nick tried to ask why. Vincent again interrupted, "There is a dangerous narrative brewing in the wake of your first kill. We must manage it immediately."

After a long pause, Vincent stated, "We are pulling together a team."

Nick sensed the severity of the situation, "I have not prepared Anna."

Vincent sighed over the phone, "Well, you are fucking up everywhere then, aren't you?"

Nick did not react.

"Just know we are coordinating meetings for you down here on Friday, October 1," Vincent proclaimed.

Nick understood. "I will make it happen." Then he realized that meant he would have to cut the honeymoon short by a full day.

Vincent said, "Prepare her," and hung up.

Friday, September 26, one day before the wedding, Nick awaited the arrival of his brothers with angst. Bradley, David, Frank and John, seven to thirteen years older than Nick, arrived by mid-afternoon around the same time as his mom and dad. The ceremony walk-through was scheduled to start at 4:30 p.m. with the rehearsal dinner to follow.

Nick's nerves were beginning to show. Anna was concerned. "I hate the idea of your brothers giving you stress on our wedding day."

Nick lied again. "It will all be okay."

Nick's brothers were not interested in the church rehearsal and were even rude at times to the pastor by not paying attention.

Anna whispered to Nick, "Why do your brothers have to be so negative?"

Nick responded, "When I do something to please my mom and dad, this is how they play it down." He shrugged and kissed Anna, "Want them to be happy and engaged? Wait till I get caught doing something wrong."

Anna, who had an older brother, replied, "I understand."

At the dinner, drinks flowed bountifully.

Nick needed an escape from the whole wedding show. The later the night went on, the more alcohol he consumed. Eventually, he passed out.

It was 8:15 a.m. when his brother rapped on his hotel door. "Everyone is looking for you at breakfast."

Nick looked at the time. "I have to be at the church for pictures by 9:30 a.m."

Bradley decided to take his best man duties to the next level. "Nick, if you are not ready to get married to Anna, it's not too late."

Nick responded, "What are you talking about?"

Bradley sighed, "We are all concerned about you marrying so young."

He looked at Bradley. "I can't do that to Anna."

"That's not the right answer," said Bradley, flatly.

Outraged, Nick yelled, "What the fuck are you talking about?"

Bradley could see the discussion was going nowhere. Bradley's wife, Jennifer, walked into the room, "Everything okay in here?"

Nick laughed, "Don't worry, Jennifer. How do I look?"

"Honestly, Nick? Pretty pale."

Family pictures went well. Nick's parents were happy. He felt their pride in him. Nick believed that marriage was the next sacrament in the Catholic faith that his parents hoped for after college.

It was time for the ceremony.

Once everyone was seated, Nick took his place to the side of the altar, awaiting a view of his bride at the back of the church. He looked out across the congregation of some two hundred guests seated in Anna's Methodist Church. The sun shone through the stained-glass windows, illuminating the altar. Anna and her mother chose exotic, vibrant, purple and white flower arrangements placed at the end of each pew.

Palms sweaty and still nauseous, Nick suppressed every thought about his secret life playing out in Bogotá. Thoughts of Gabriella, Vincent, and Richard—and the young man he had killed in the alleyway—swirled in his head. Nick gathered himself and focused, once again, staring at the back of the church.

Anna stepped into full view. She looked beautiful in her white lace wedding dress. Gripping her bouquet just a bit too tightly, Anna held onto her father's arm. She glanced nervously at Nick, smiled, and gave him a hopeful look. He smiled back reassuringly.

The ceremony was presided over by Anna's Methodist pastor, and Nick's long-time friend, Father Dean. The wedding lasted only about 30 minutes. Anna created a beautiful ceremony.

After more pictures, the reception was in full swing. Nick endured his brothers' backhanded compliments. He ignored his father-in-law's boasting about the expensive wedding. Nick shook hands with 200 people that he assumed he would never see again, danced when he was told, and shared some wedding cake with Anna for photos Then it was time to leave. Nick and Anna said their goodbyes to their parents, family, and friends.

Anna held onto Nick for three hours straight during the drive talking nonstop. *Can I really live this way?* he wondered. They dropped off the rental car, made it through security, and awaited their boarding time for the first-class flight to Reno, Lake Tahoe.

Settled on the plane, Nick sheepishly confessed, "I'm not feeling very well."

She looked at him. "Were you sick?"

Nick confessed, "I guess I drank too much last night. I passed out and missed breakfast."

Anna laughed, "Well, thank you for being a trooper and recovering so fast!"

They slept the rest of the flight. Nick arranged a limo to pick them up from the airport, and Anna was pleased. They checked into their luxury cabin on Lake Tahoe, put their bags down, and hugged each other. Nick allowed himself to relax and dream for just a moment, pushing thoughts of Gabriella out of his mind.

As Anna prepared for bed, Nick remembered the envelope he had gotten from Vincent and Richard. He grabbed it, ripped open the envelope, and $2,000 fell out. There was also a note:

"May your heart be light and happy. May your smile be big and wide. And may your pockets always have a coin or two inside. Love, Vincent and Richard."

Nick closed his eyes, *What am I doing here?*

Chapter 6

Reality Calls

Sunday, September 28, 1986

LAKE TAHOE was sunny, the water shimmering, and the high temperature for the day was expected to be 72 degrees. The Landing Resort was located on the south shore of Lake Tahoe, California—just under a one-hour drive from the Reno-Tahoe International Airport. It sat across the street from the lake and had a private beach. Nick and Anna loved the majestic lakeshore view outside their front door.

Heavenly Village and the marina were only a 15-minute walk. Nick had reserved jet skis for Monday and a boat rental for Tuesday.

Anna didn't wake up until nearly 10:00 a.m. Nick made coffee. The cabin was equipped with a small, but well-appointed kitchen tucked away just off the living room, comfy couches, a fireplace, and a king bed with a view of the lake. It was scenic and peaceful.

They spent the day walking along the lakefront.

Anna, so happy to be making plans proclaimed, "When we get to California, we will both be working and married!"

Nick decided to break the news about leaving a day early. "I received a message just before the wedding from Vincent, my boss, that our Bogotá fundraising plans are being threatened."

At first Anna was mad. But she quickly reacted in support, "Nick, I love you and we are in this together, right?"

"Right," Nick lied. His mind told him to sit down and prepare her for a meeting with Vincent and the news of his career choice and the code of secrecy. But his heart holding him back, Nick continued, "We will always work things out."

NICK'S MIND wandered back to December 1985. It felt like many years ago. Nick was living alone in a corner studio apartment on campus. His agriculture economics professor, who owned the apartment building, had taken Nick in as a "family member." Only later did Nick learn his professor was an asset of the agency. Vincent visited for several days and developed Nick' cover life.

Cover for clandestine operatives can be very thin or very dense, like a mosaic; every component of the cover could be intensely investigated and probed for veracity. Vincent and Nick crafted a cover story based on Nick's farm family background, his studies at school, and his interests in international travel. Nick would serve as a fully paid intern with Archer Daniels Midland (ADM). It afforded him travel throughout Central and Latin America while remotely attending Thunderbird School of Global Management. Neither the internship nor the schooling at Thunderbird was real. But his employee and student records would be kept in pristine order with the occasional course corrections. Flexibility was key. Nick's job included gathering information about trade, food, and farming throughout the Western Hemisphere. His projects would be humanitarian efforts sponsored by ADM and government aid agencies.

Vincent and Nick discussed Nick's personal goals and his family's expectations about marriage. The two decided that Nick should get married. His brothers all wed right out of college, and his parents had taught him that marriage was the most responsible and best way to start life. Marriage would deepen the cover and add more layers of deflection. A practical decision.

Nick wasn't sure if Anna was the one he could spend his whole life with. That spark and chemical attraction just wasn't there, but they had similar values and a common background. Anna was highly intelligent, attractive, and much more reserved than Nick. She had a cold and off-putting demeanor and was more career-focused than socially driven. Marrying Anna would help establish the kind of lifestyle that would be a perfect Agency cover.

Convincing himself it was the right thing, Nick asked Anna to marry him, and they planned a wedding for fall 1986.

Vincent flatly demanded that Nick and Anna live in Southern California.

"How do I get Anna to move there?" Nick remembered asking.

Vincent replied, "No worries. Anna will soon be begging you to move there."

And she did. Anna was scheduled for seven key interviews through the University of Illinois Computer Engineering College, where she was one of only a handful of female graduates. She graduated near the top of her class and interviewed well. The best offer came from the defense division of Northrop Grumman in El Segundo, California. It was such a great offer that even her overprotective parents had to endorse her long-distance relocation. She accepted the offer.

Nick remembered all the lies and half-truths, disgusted with himself. *How can I tell her the truth about our engagement and Vincent's career plan?* he asked himself. Nick convinced himself it would be better to wait, *Fuck the Agency protocols.*

ON SUNDAY evening, Anna and Nick shared a romantic dinner at Jimmy's, consisting of a five-star filet mignon paired with a hearty cabernet wine selection. The impeccable service anticipated their every whim. They ordered cherries jubilee for dessert, making for a delicious ending to the meal.

Happy about their first full day together as a married couple, they climbed into bed full of expectation. Nick touched Anna and felt a moment of hesitation rather than a passionate connection. Instincts took over and he kissed her deeply, closing his eyes and making love to his new bride mechanically. Nick's mind was elsewhere.

By sunrise, he realized that the foundation he was counting on to make the marriage work was already showing cracks. Gabriella's skin and smell were inside his head. He couldn't shake them free.

Monday morning came quickly. While Anna was still sleeping, Nick left to explore the fitness gym and have some time to himself. He returned about an hour later and found Anna making coffee.

"How was the workout?"

Nick gave her a kiss. "They have an awesome gym."

It's time to prepare her, he thought. "I checked in with work, and I have some bad news."

He explained the situation to her apologetically. His one big project as Director of the Economic Development Funds was in jeopardy. "I have to fly out Thursday evening to Bogotá for meetings all day Friday and Saturday, but I promise to be back home in time for Sunday dinner. My superior is on the Board of Trustees of The Forum for International Policy and was wined and dined by Reagan's cabinet members regularly," he bragged to Anna.

She was adequately impressed and wanted to be supportive. He made sure she understood the importance of doing a good job in Colombia and how it could further his career. Anna touched his arm. "I understand. There will always be circumstances we can't control." She switched the topic, "What time do we take the jet skis out?"

He grabbed a bottle of water, "Eleven o'clock."

It was a beautiful day. After nearly three hours exploring the lake on jet skis, they decided to eat an early dinner at the marina boathouse. They watched the sunset from their patio, drank wine, and talked about their townhome plans.

Anna was highly organized. Nick observed her thought process and could see her thinking through the timeline and goals she will accomplish before her job started on October sixth.

Nick woke up early again on Tuesday morning. As he laid in bed, he worried about his marriage. *There is no good time to tell Anna about my career choices and coordinate the sit-down with Vincent.* He decided to wait.

They enjoyed another relaxing day. "Nature walks and fireplace talks," Nick said, "what a beautiful honeymoon." Anna behaved like a newlywed bride, holding hands and sharing her dreams and plans.

Later in the day, they packed warm clothes and blankets for their private sunset boat ride. The boat was lovely in every detail and sparked romance. An authentic retired Navy skipper and his "first mate" staffed it. The skipper told stories about the lake, the wild parties that he had captained, and his encounters with celebrities, including Dean Martin, George Burns, and John Denver. They enjoyed the escape, the stories, the fine wine, and the excellent food, but as the temperature dropped, it was time to return.

Lying in bed, Nick couldn't help but feel a dark shroud of betrayal coming.

Wednesday, October 1, 1986

ON THE last full day of Nick and Anna's honeymoon, Nick opened his eyes and watched Anna breathe heavily in her slumber. He let her sleep in.

Sitting outside, Nick enjoyed the brisk air and hot coffee. Anna walked out through the patio door. She kissed him on the cheek, "Last day of our honeymoon. Let's go to Reno and shop, gamble, maybe see a show?"

Nick responded, "Sounds great!"

They relaxed outside for a bit and ordered a big brunch to enjoy with their cabin view for their last day. Anna went inside to get ready for Reno. Nick needed to check in with Vincent. He left a message on the secure line, "All clear for takeoff."

They arranged a car and headed to Reno, known as "the biggest little city in the world." Reno was famous for its casinos. It was the birthplace of the gaming corporation, Harrah's Entertainment. Their day went fast with shopping, gambling, dinner, and tickets to see Eddie Money. It was a great way to conclude their honeymoon trip by escaping into the busy scene and seeing a late-night concert together. They returned to their lake cabin, packed their bags, showered, and crashed into bed, exhausted but happy.

Nick closed his eyes and held Anna tight. He knew he could not trust her yet. She would not understand the decision, the lies, or his training.

Thursday, October 2, 1986

THEIR WAKE-UP call shook them out of bed at 7:30 a.m. Their flight was scheduled to depart at 10:45 a.m., which meant they had just enough time for coffee on the patio before heading to the airport.

By 2:20 p.m., they walked into their townhome in Torrance, California.

"Welcome home!" said Nick. Nick had been living there over the summer after graduation and Anna had only visited a couple of times when she helped him find the place.

Anna looked around and seemed a little disoriented. "This place needs a female touch."

Nick would have to head back to the airport in a couple of hours to catch his evening flight. Anna was not happy about his departure, and he tried to reassure her that he would be back for dinner on Sunday and home the entire week after that.

"I feel so alone all of a sudden," she said.

"You're feeling homesick, Anna. It's natural. I will be back in three days, I promise." She walked with Nick to the garage and waved goodbye.

An hour later, Nick had parked his car at LAX and cleared security. There was much to do, and he knew there would be a package at the apartment, full of critical intelligence. He tried to take a nap on the plane, but violent nightmares kept him from resting. He had bad feelings about the upcoming meetings.

It was after midnight when he landed in Bogotá. He walked into the apartment and peered into the bedroom. Gabriella lay still, sleeping heavy. He leaned over her and whispered, "I'm so glad you're here."

He quietly walked into the living room and opened the intelligence reports laying on the coffee table. A cover memo from Vincent read,

```
Sean, your cover is in jeopardy. Ramirez wants
to find the man who killed his squad member in
the alley and terminate him.
```

Nick stopped dead in his tracks and realized, *Ramirez won't stop. Everything and everyone are in danger.* He got up and went into the kitchen, made a pot of coffee, and began reading. It would be a long night.

Chapter 7
Tension Mounts

Friday, October 3, 1986

ATTACHED TO the intel reports was a schedule for the day.

    9:00 a.m. Jaime Leal at his home.
    10:30 a.m. Rodríguez Gacha at Devoción Café.
    12:30 p.m. Fabio Ochoa at the ranch.

Sean read these reports repeatedly, finishing a pot of black coffee. He sifted through the pages and catalogued the vitals of each report in his mind.

Report 1

The Patriotic Union (Unión Patriótica (UP)) is a leftist Colombian political party. The FARC and the Colombian Communist Party (PCC) founded it in 1985 as part of the peace negotiations that the guerrillas held with the Conservative President Belisario Betancur's administration. Several prominent FARC members were among UP's original founders, as well as members of the PCC. The PCC party was subject to political violence from drug lords, paramilitaries, and security forces agents.

According to internal FARC documents from the group's 1982 Seventh Guerrilla Conference, the FARC originally

intended for the creation of a group of clandestine
party cells to be its political branch for recruitment and
ideological propaganda purposes.

"Jaime Leal," Sean muttered, convinced this was the reason
for Leal's protective order and his placement in Sean's operation.
"This asshole will climb in bed with anyone."

Report 2

Jaime Ramírez was an official of the National Police of
Colombia, who led a fight against the illegal drug trade in
Colombia from the 1970s onwards.

He became the National Director of the Colombian Drug
Enforcement Unit, working with the Minister of Justice,
Rodrigo Lara Bonilla, against the Medellín Cartel. The
biggest blow against the Cartel was dealt by Colonel
Ramírez on March 7, 1984, in an operation involving the
DEA to locate and destroy a large cocaine production
camp in the jungle of the Yari River (between the
departments of Caqueta and Meta) known by the Cartel
as "Tranquilandia," the "Tranquil Land." It triggered direct
hostilities by the Cartel against the Colombian State,
commencing with the murder of Minister Lara Bonilla on
April 30, 1984.

"Ramirez escaped the Cartel's noose." Sean realized how dangerous he can be.

Colonel Ramírez's successes against drug Cartels got him
promoted to the position of Minister of Justice by the
Presidency of Belisario Betancur Cuartas (1982–1986). The
enforcement actions of Minister Lara against ringleaders
such as Pablo Escobar Gaviria, Carlos Lehder, Rodríguez
Gacha, the Ochoa brothers (Fabio, Jorge and Juan David
Ochoa), all known as the Medellín Cartel, made him a
target for assassination.

Colonel Ramírez and the DEA, with the agreement of
Minister Lara, also led the next and biggest blow to the
Medellín Cartel. It was the destruction of a huge camp
hidden in the jungles of the Yarí River, between the
departments of Caquetá and Meta. The *Tranquilandia*
(tranquil land), as the Cartel called it, was used to
produce cocaine. On March 7, 1984, the police seized 1,500
kilograms of cocaine (13.8 tons) and arrested 40 people in
what was called the "Yarí '84 Operation." The camp had
9 cocaine laboratories, 8 landing strips, health centers, a
communication center and basic services such as water
and electricity.

With the destruction of Tranquilandia, the Cartel declared
war on the Colombian State, starting with the murder
of Minister Lara on April 30, 1984, seven weeks after the
seizure of Tranquilandia.

Ramirez must be terminated. Sean believed he was the most
dangerous element to the mission and the connection between
Leal, Gacha and Fabio. Sean closed his eyes. *Surrounded by
snakes, evil, lethal snakes.*

Report 3

Guillermo Cano was born in Medellín. He started to write
for *El Espectador* as a reporter on bullfights, politics,
sport and culture. He had been leading the press agency's
management for 37 years.

El Espectador is a newspaper with national circulation
within Colombia. It was founded by Fidel Cano Gutiérrez
on March 22, 1887, in Medellín and has been published
since 1915 in Bogotá.

Sean shook his head. "Cano is the propaganda machine for
Ramirez and Leal." Determined not to become part of the politics of news and violence, Sean realized that time was not on his
side. He looked at the clock, *Almost 4:00 a.m.*

The coffee was wearing off, Sean needed sleep.

Three hours later, he was awakened when the phone rang.

"Hola," he said.

It was Vincent. "Be prepared today. Make it clear that the narrative around the rodeo would require fixing. We don't need press now. We need to clean up your kill."

Sean agreed. "I understand."

"There's a message coming later with travel details. Watch for it."

"Will do," and the two hung up.

Sean focused on "fixing the narrative." There was too much noise and too many enemies. The Cartel's movements in and out of Nicaragua were essential, with exchanges in Panama under Noriega's cover.

Sean believed his operation was simple. But the relationship between the CIA support for Contra Freedom Fighters in Nicaragua and the Cartel's movements had become very problematic with the DEA and Ramirez.

Sean sat down on the couch in the living room. He could hear Gabriella moving about in the bedroom. Clearly, he couldn't afford a Ramirez/DEA joint investigation, nor press coverage on a murder in the alley.

He knew what he had to do. The Cartel was his best asset, not Leal, for now.

Glancing at his watch, it was nearing 7:30 a.m. He got up to prepare. Knives, $30,000 in cash, and a healthy attitude.

He was ready.

ARRIVING PROMPTLY at Leal's home at 9:00 a.m. Sean noticed the armed guard count was considerably higher. He was welcomed onto the back patio for café con leche. The coffee, the weather, and the initial polite conversation were warm and friendly. Sean dug, clearly getting under Jamie's skin.

"What's the current objective of the Unión Patriótica political party?" he asked Leal. He leaned toward Leal. "Following the peace negotiations between the FARC and Belisario Betancur, the Unión Patriótica political party was formed, and you were called upon to be a senior advisor, right?"

Leal looked at Sean, sighed deeply, "Correct."

Sean continued, "At the time, you were also involved in the Colombian Communist Party and the formation of the Central Union of Workers of Colombia. And you still are involved, right?"

Leal sighed again, obviously annoyed. "Correct."

Sean could feel Leal's arrogance subsiding in favor of angst. "And when you ran as a presidential candidate for the newly formed UP, you ended up third behind Virgilio Barco and Alvaro Gómez Hurtado, with only 328,000 votes. Right?"

Leal collected himself, shifting in his chair, *"Cual es tu punto?"* (What's your point?)

Sean proceeded to plant worrisome thoughts into the conversation, "The UP party could soon become a target for paramilitary organizations. Local leaders could be targeted throughout the country. As party president, you might find yourself accusing the government of overlooking such violence, or even committing it."

Leal reacted visibly, and Sean knew he was reaching the core of his own concerns about Colonel Ramirez. Sean sipped his coffee, looked deeply into Leal's eyes, and asked, "What is your specific affiliation with Colonel Ramirez?"

Leal's answer was abrupt. *"No tengo ninguna relación con él."* (I have no affiliation with him.)

Sean accepted his response and poured more coffee. Leal,

visibly uneasy, appeared determined not to talk. Sean paused and changed topics.

"We're going to change the construct of the rodeo," Sean stated as a matter of fact.

"What exactly do you mean by 'construct'?" asked Leal.

"The committee will need to change. We don't need to be so close to Ramirez or the Press with our plans."

Leal leaned back into his patio chair, looked up into the sky, and said, "Okay."

Sean stood up. "Okay, then. I will be in touch. No discussions with anyone about this until we all agree, right?"

"*Correcto.*"

Sean left Leal's home and told the driver to go to Devoción Café. When he walked in he immediately saw Gacha sitting at a corner table with his back against the wall and a whiskey glass in his left hand. Sean knew Gacha was only interested in one thing—what's in it for him.

Sean sat down across from Gacha, and they exchanged pleasantries. Gacha voiced his concerns, "The Committee is no good." Sean sensed that Gacha was on the same page and wanted no complications. Sean also knew that Gacha essentially wanted Ramirez dead, but was under agreement not to act upon such an impulse at that time.

The meeting went smoothly. Sean took his jacket off and laid it on the seat next to Gacha before going to the bathroom. Upon his return, he picked up his jacket and noticed it was about $30,000 lighter.

"We are good to go to work on the rodeo," Sean said. "The goal is to appoint new committee members to best represent the communities being served." Gacha and Fabio would determine who that would be, but Sean demanded no more political or law enforcement members. The meeting ended.

In the back seat of the car on his way to the Ochoa ranch, Sean closed his eyes. *So far so good.* He handily scolded Leal, satisfied Gacha, and would now have a pleasurable business luncheon with Fabio.

His car pulled into the driveway of the ranch; Fabio watched from his chair under a giant shade tree. Sean stepped out of the car as Fabio stood and waved him to come sit. Fabio greeted him with a hug and a kiss on the cheek.

"Bienvenido! Me encanta ponerte nervioso!" (Welcome! I love to make you nervous!)

Sean just smiled. *"Gracias por invitarme a almorzar!"* (Thank you for inviting me for lunch!)

Fabio insisted that Sean try his favorite beer and homemade beef and cheese empanadas. It was Club Colombia Trigo's Cervecería Bavarian—a German Helles style beer. Popping the top, Sean inhaled a yeasty smell.

Sean raised his glass, "Very fresh-tasting. Great foamy head. Not too strong of a wheat flavor at all. Very refreshing and satisfying,"

Fabio loved the way Sean described food and drinks. In fact, he genuinely enjoyed his company.

As they drank and ate under the shade tree, Sean brought Fabio up to speed on the rodeo committee and asked Fabio for more advice on how best to proceed. Fabio saw it as respect and leaned forward in his chair.

"We will bring community leaders into the fold. Real Robin Hood-style men and women," said Fabio.

Sean liked his ideas and his enthusiasm. *"Fantastico! Realmente fantastico!"*

Fabio smiled and laughed, indulging in what must have been his fourth or fifth beer.

It was past 2:30 p.m., and Sean needed to get back to the

apartment, but Fabio was having a relaxing day and mentioned going for a horseback ride. Sean preempted the idea, saying he needed to return for the remainder of the workday.

Fabio waved over Sean's car, and they walked out onto the driveway. One more handshake and hug.

"*Cuando te volvere a ver?*" (When will I see you again?) Fabio inquired.

"Before the end of October, if all is going well."

Fabio leaned over and whispered, "*Si necesitas ayuda para arreglar cosas, solo silba.*" (If you need help fixing things, just whistle.) Sean smiled and nodded.

BACK AT the apartment, a message was waiting, detailing private plane instructions from Bogotá to Mexico City. The message provided details for contact upon arrival at 5:00 p.m. Sean glanced at his watch—it was already 3:30 p.m.

Onboard the flight, Sean looked forward to dinner with Vincent. He closed his eyes and replayed the day in his mind. There were no surprises, and in fact, the concessions from Leal were accepted with ease. Sean may have even noticed some relief in his body language. The decision to rid their op of any interference was now communicated; Ramirez was out.

VINCENT AND SEAN met for dinner in Mexico City, Sir Winston Churchill's, Vincent's favorite hideaway. Sean thought, Vincent loved telling stories of all the dramatic meetings held in that restaurant. It felt like a clandestine experience he shared with only a few trusted case officers.

Just as Sean relaxed, Vincent blurted out, "Oh. I almost forgot to tell you. When you return home, your in-laws will most likely still be there to greet you."

Sean looked at Vincent. "You're kidding, right?"

Vincent just laughed. "God, I wish I was." He breathed heavily, "In the past month, you have murdered someone, gotten married to provide cover, and broken protocol, even broken direct orders about disclosing your career and obtaining a secrecy statement from your wife."

Sean sunk into his chair. "What's the verdict?"

"Quite a rap sheet you are building. What's next, a private war in Bogotá to kill Ramirez?"

Sean looked deeply into Vincent's eyes. "Is that what you want?"

Vincent stood. "Let's get out of this restaurant."

As they walked out, Vincent's car pulled up.

"Get in," Vincent gestured.

Plans were set for a 10:00 a.m. debrief in the basement of the Mexico City American Embassy. They sat in the car, saying nothing. The car pulled up to Sean's hotel.

"See you tomorrow," said Vincent, and Sean stepped out of the car.

Sean checked into the Marriott in downtown Mexico City, exhausted.

At 8:30 a.m. the next morning, the hotel phone rang. "I am coming over to your room in 30," Vincent announced and hung up.

Sean rolled out of bed, showered, dressed, and threw the bed together. Moments later, there was a soft knock at the door. It was room service. Vincent had ordered a pot of coffee for two, English muffins, and fruit.

Nice work, thought Sean.

Minutes later, Vincent arrived. They sipped their coffee and devoured the English muffins. Vincent announced his intent.

"Today, we make a plan to control the narrative."

They detailed the increase approved for funding the Freedom

Fighters, when to make the drops, and how best to eradicate Ramirez, Cano, and any other interferences with the operation.

At 10:00 a.m. sharp, Vincent and Sean walked into the basement conference room of the Mexico City Embassy, determined to shake things up.

The over-arching theme of the meeting had three essentials: 1) Secure the USAID laundered monies for transport undercover; 2) Ensure that the funds and guns were properly traded in Panama undercover; 3) Monitor the Colombian political landscape, carefully observing the UP and its Communist-leaning affiliations for interference.

After the debrief, Vincent and Sean went to lunch at the Four Seasons and grabbed a table in the garden patio. It was already 1:30 p.m.

Vincent asked Sean, "Do you want to go back to L.A. tonight or tomorrow?"

Sean rolled his eyes. "Tomorrow."

Vincent replied, "Great! I have a surprise coming to dinner."

They took the next four hours off. Sean napped. He decided not to call Anna since he was certain she would be busy with her parents. He just wasn't in the mood to deal with all those domestic issues.

He was told to meet Vincent for drinks at the Marriott lobby bar before dinner. Vincent was with a man at the bar ordering drinks by the time Sean arrived. Sean immediately sized up the guest: 6'4", 220 pounds, medium-brown hair, European skin, possibly Italian—and familiar looking. As Sean approached, the guest looked directly at him, extended his hand, and said, "Hello, good to see you again!"

Sean shook his hand. "Frank?"

The two laughed. "Right. From the training mansion in Maryland. You can call me "Jon" now. Jon Robinson."

Vincent handed out Glenlivet's and made introductions.

"Jon is one of our black ops leaders," he said. Sean immediately recognized the term to mean a shadow agent, often referred to as Staff Division "D"—for "death" or "destroy."

"Good to meet you, again, Jon," Sean replied.

The three of them left the bar for a brisk walk to Private Quarters, a restaurant near the Marriott in the *Zona Rosa*, or the Pink Zone neighborhood. The neighborhood was officially part of the *Colonia Juárez,* or official neighborhood, which was located just west of the historic center of Mexico City. It was known for its shopping, nightlife, and gay community. Vincent was in his element.

The three of them bonded in the restaurant. It became clear to Sean that Jon would be involved in the Panama operation, and his squad would support Sean by fixing things, cleaning up messes, and killing or disposing of any threats. At that moment, Sean felt the weight of reality; the night had gotten deadly serious, given the current threats against his role and the secrecy of the mission in Bogotá.

Before the night was over, Sean shared his opinion of Colonel Ramirez and Guillermo Cano. By night's end, they had successfully hatched plans to deploy the personnel and resources to become far more influential across the Colombian landscape.

Vincent raised his glass, "Tonight we bond against any disruptors to our plans for Central America."

Jon chimed in, *"SALUD!"* (Salute!)

Sean stood, "To life, liberty and justice for all."

Vincent and Jon stood, raised their glasses, then finished their drinks slamming the glasses onto the floor. They placed their arms around each other and pledged loyalty above all.

Emotions were high. Sean believed he was part of something bigger, something impactful.

Chapter 8

Web of Lies

Sunday, October 5, 1986

NICK LANDED at LAX airport at 10:45 a.m. He deplaned and called Anna to let her know that he landed.

Anna could not contain her excitement, "Mom and Dad are here!"

Nick acted surprised. "What?"

Anna informed him that her parents had come on Friday night and would be leaving the next morning, but they planned a nice afternoon and dinner together.

"Oh," Anna said, "and we've been shopping for the townhome. You won't believe what we found!"

Nick broke in: "Sounds wonderful. Let me get on the road, and I will be there in about an hour, okay?" Nick realized there was no time to sit with Anna and break his news.

Anna said, "Can't wait!"

Nick stopped at the florist and picked up a bouquet. Then he stopped at the liquor store and picked up two bottles of Glenlivet, a six-pack of beer for his father-in-law, two bottles of Chardonnay, three bottles of Pinot Noir, and a bottle of Malbec from Mendoza, Argentina. He smiled, thinking about Gabriella and the night they drank Malbec and made love for hours. She satisfied something inside him that Anna never could.

He pulled into the garage, left his bag in the car, and walked in, bearing gifts. Anna and her parents greeted Nick with hugs, then set the table outside on the patio for a light lunch.

For the next several hours, Nick heard all about their shopping success. The shopping spree drowned out any negative vibes about his recent travel. And, of course, he had to listen to Anna's father describe his high school basketball team prospects.

Jim awkwardly asked, "Everything going okay with your internship and studies?"

Nick looked at Jim. "It's all very exciting. I am learning a great deal."

Anna planned dinner reservations at McCormick & Schmick's in Manhattan Beach so they could drop her parents off at the Marriott next to the airport. It was the best news Nick had received since landing at LAX earlier that morning.

The four of them enjoyed dinner with more talk of Anna's new job and her father's basketball team. Nick coordinated with the wait staff to hold his credit card for dinner and to only bring him the bill for signing. "It's the least I can do since you came all this way and bought so many housewarming gifts," he proclaimed to his in-laws. He and Anna dropped them off at the Marriott and hugged them goodbye.

Anna was already exhausted, thinking about tomorrow as her big first day of work. Nick was exhausted, too.

As they climbed into bed, Anna asked, "What is your day like tomorrow?"

Nick paused. He wondered what his day would be like, too. "I have studying to complete and two reports to write for my internship."

She kissed him quickly on the lips before pulling the blanket tighter around her. "Lucky dog. I love you."

He whispered, "I love you, too," *and* rolled over thinking, *Right, lucky dog.*

The alarm sounded at 6:00 a.m. Nick could hear Anna in the bathroom getting ready. He went downstairs, coffee had already been made. The townhome was on a tree-lined street just a couple of blocks away from Torrance High School and a beautiful park. He poured two cups of coffee, added some cream, and walked back upstairs to the bedroom. "Coffee?"

Anna was appreciative and gave him a kiss on the cheek. She sipped the coffee and focused on brushing her hair.

Nick asked if he could make anything special for dinner to celebrate her first day of work.

"I would love some sea bass grilled on those wooden planks like you made in college."

He nodded, "Done!"

Anna was ready to leave. She was dressed in something resembling a pilgrim maid's dress, with a wide black patent-leather belt and shoes to match.

He commented, "Dressed to kill."

She laughed and hugged him goodbye.

Looking around the townhome, Nick thought, *Time for a run.* He put his running sweats on and ran through the neighborhood park past the high school, dodging the dog-walkers, and circled back around the park. On his third lap, he noticed a familiar man in the distance, walking and smoking a cigarette. Keeping an eye on him, he decided to run directly toward the figure by crossing the park diagonally through the grass.

Halfway across the park, he started to distinguish the figure: It was Vincent. Stopping at the park bench, he sat down next to him.

"Good morning, sunshine," Vincent said. "The DEA has completely checked you out, and you are officially off the Persons of Interest list."

"That's good, yes?" asked Nick.

Vincent asked, while nodding in affirmation, "What's your gut telling you about Ramirez?"

Nick looked at the high school in the distance. The kids were hanging out before class, laughing and scheming. He thought about how far away his hometown and small high school felt, both by distance and time.

Nick said, "Right now, he is a dog who thinks Sean is the bone."

Vincent laughed at the analogy. "That's right, my brother. You are the bone he thinks he can have, no doubt."

Nick shook his head. "Well, what are we going to do about that?"

Vincent stood. "Let's walk and talk."

Vincent explained that the funding for USAID Rural Economic Development was substantially increasing. The next distribution was scheduled for the first week in December 1986. Congress approved new levels of funding, which were already in the works. In about 60 days, there would be $27 million coming in and $25 million going out to the three private funds.

"Even more money will be approved for the March 1987 funding," Vincent explained.

Nick looked at Vincent. "Well, that is one way to fund freedom."

They walked back to the townhome. Vincent made himself at home with coffee and toasted English muffins. Then he laid out his larger plan.

"There is a convergence among the separate Contra groups." Vincent's mission was to influence all Contra factions to become united into the Nicaraguan Resistance by early 1987.

Vincent described tactics and methods, illustrated his dark side and willingness to justify nearly any means necessary to achieve President Reagan's agenda. Vincent tested Nick's resolve and loyalty, grilling him on all types of scenarios that could occur as the operation grew in magnitude, "Killing to maintain secrecy and operational objectives will become commonplace."

Nick realized that the movement against the Nicaraguan government was escalating and that the Contras were committing numerous human rights violations, even terrorist tactics. The money laundering, weapons, and supply exchanges through Bogotá under his direction were systematically supporting Freedom Fighters illegally.

"Your involvement is not officially supported," Vincent emphasized.

Supporters of the Contras were constantly downplaying their violations, especially the Reagan administration, which had initiated a campaign of white propaganda to influence public opinion in favor of the Contras while covertly encouraging the Contras to attack civilian targets.

Vincent glanced at his watch. "I have meetings in L.A., and you have a new wife to cook dinner for." They hugged goodbye.

"Oh," said Vincent before walking away. "One more thing." He handed a pocket pager to Nick. "Check this out—it vibrates. Refresh your memory of our numeric codes. This is how I will reach out to you in the States."

Nick looked at the pager, hit the vibrator button, "Wonderful."

Vincent walked out laughing. "Anna will like it, too."

The next ten days amounted to formulating plans for November and December. Nick worked from home, read, and re-read briefs, worked out, and practiced at the shooting range regularly. His daily regimen was disciplined, but he could not bring himself to complete the agency's marital protocol to inform Anna and acquire the secrecy agreement. This was a problem.

Given the substantial increase in funding, producing documentation for all the fake expenditures to be approved by USAID at the Bogotá Embassy was time consuming. Fabio was taking a deeper role in acquiring support from local community leaders, so the rodeo event was gaining momentum.

Nick was provided with briefs and intelligence reports that included movements by the Cartels into Nicaragua, progress of investigations by the National Police of Colombia, traffic in and out of airstrips in Honduras and Panama, and the political environment throughout Central and Latin America.

He shared bits and pieces of what he learned in order to make dinner conversations with Anna appear intimate. Her work stories involved computer engineering systems for communication components that enabled encryption and analysis. She was completely immersed in her work. They were drifting. It was becoming obvious to Nick that they would have to find other things to talk about, *But what?*

Friday, October 17, 1986

NICK AND ANNA decided to go out for dinner and see a movie. They needed an escape. Over dinner, Nick shared his upcoming travel plans, "I need to leave early Tuesday morning for a professional speaker series at Thunderbird." He continued, "Then, on Sunday, I plan to fly directly to Bogotá for the economic development meetings and return on Thursday night, October 30."

At first, Anna didn't like him being gone so long. "That's a long trip."

It was fair to say that they both had become workaholics and somewhat disinterested in each other's work.

Anna sighed and reclaimed the evening, "Let's just relax and have fun tonight. Like we use to on our dates in college."

"Deal." Nick smiled.

They had a great Mexican meal at *El Torito Grille* and went to the movie, *About Last Night* with Demi Moore and Rob Lowe. They had fun that night, laughing, letting go, and enjoying each other's company.

Almost like an old married couple, Nick thought.

He woke up on Saturday morning and went for his run. His thoughts drifted to Gabriella. Her warm smile, subtle gestures, and encouraging touch made him feel different, more like a man.

The weekend was quiet. No messages from Vincent. He was growing anxious for strategy and tactics meetings with Jon. He was organizing the black ops unit in Bogotá.

His workouts became more intense, and his focus was laser sharp. *No room for mistakes.*

Tuesday finally arrived. Up very early to catch a flight from LAX, he kissed Anna goodbye while she slept. He arrived at LAX and was waiting for his boarding call.

Vincent paged a code: "123" (all clear). Nick sent the response: "123" (all clear).

Despite the "all clear" page, Nick could sense conflict. The intel reports and Vincent's communiqués raised dangerous questions around the secrecy of his operation.

Chapter 9

The Landscape Shifts

WHILE FLYING TO Phoenix, Nick was excited to see Gabriella. His cover story was solid, and he couldn't help smiling about their past. He closed his eyes and replayed how they met.

OUT OF COLLEGE only months, he had moved to L.A. in advance of Anna. He was being briefed by Vincent for his cover trips to Thunderbird and field operations in Bogotá.

One day, he received two airline tickets and noticed it was for someone named Gabriella Mendes. *Who the hell is Gabriella Mendes?* he wondered. Flipping the ticket sleeve over, he noticed there was a hand-written telephone number on the back.

Hmm. No instructions, no order, no certainty.

He thought about "Gabriella Mendes," but nothing came to mind. Just then, there was a knock at the door.

Another delivery? Great. More information, he thought. Nick opened the door, and there stood Vincent.

"I see you got the trip details," said Vincent, glancing at the kitchen table.

"So glad you could find some time for a visit." The sarcasm was completely lost on Vincent, but deep down, Nick was relieved to have him there to discuss everything in person.

For the next 48 hours, Vincent and Nick were inseparable. They discussed the details of the battle between the freedom-fighting Contras and the Sandinistas in Nicaragua, President Reagan's goals, and loyalty. Not a single major democratic government in the hemisphere—from Canada to Argentina—endorsed United States support of the Contras. It was risky and covert.

Reagan and his Secretary of State, George Shultz, apparently couldn't care less, at least that's what they secretly communicated. Vincent emphatically made the point that a Soviet base or a nest of spies was within two days' driving time from Harlingen, Texas. There was a clear and present danger that would authorize the rule of force.

Nick believed that this was heavy shit raining down on the current administration. Most remaining Contras had retreated to the relative safety of their Honduran bases. Now, more than ever, they threatened the stability of that fragile democracy whose moderate military leader was recently ousted because he resisted total American domination.

Holy shit! Nick thought.

Vincent's message was simple: If the Sandinistas refuse to negotiate with the already-defeated Contras, the U.S. will overthrow the Sandinistas. The $100 million demanded of Congress was only the first step toward that objective. A United States invasion of Nicaragua would be the second.

Nick opened his eyes, looked out the plane window remembering what he said to Vincent, "My mission is to support the president's objective, justifying all means."

Vincent placed his arm firmly around Nick's neck and pulled him close, whispering, "Now you are getting it."

Nick only had three days to contact and arrange a dinner meeting with Gabriella Mendes. Vincent only described her as the researcher who would be accompanying him to the Panama conference.

Nick tried to call Gabriella. Reaching her answering machine, he left a message with his name and a request to meet for dinner. That evening, he read briefs and drank Glenlivet until he drifted off to sleep. When he woke, there was a message on his answering machine.

The message was brief: "This is Gabriella. Let's meet tomorrow at Café del Rey in Marina del Rey at 8:00 p.m."

Okay, sounds good, thought Nick.

For some reason, Nick played the message over and over the next day in anticipation of his dinner with Gabriella. Then he began to grow paranoid. Vincent had given him a reasonably good description of her, some background information that might or might not be true, a code phrase to approach with, and a somewhat ridiculous response that only the right girl would know. When he pushed for more information, Vincent just told him to trust his instincts. "It will be fine," he said.

Arriving at Café del Rey 20 minutes ahead of the agreed time, he grabbed a seat at the bar. The restaurant was busy, even for a Tuesday evening, yet still had a relaxing and sophisticated ambiance. There was light jazz in the background and dim lighting. Enjoying his drink, Nick continued to survey the restaurant and take mental notes of the surroundings and movement of the staff and guests.

Just after 8:00 p.m., a beautiful woman walked in alone. Nick could only see her long dark hair from the back as she moved through a group of people to the host stand. She turned to survey the bar and their eyes met. Nick whispered to himself, "Maria?"

She walked slowly, with a sexy sort of confidence, straight to Nick.

Nick spoke first. "Maria?" he asked, incredulous. It was his Spanish professor from college. He had walked her home on numerous occasions and even gone to dinner to practice Spanish. He always had a thing for her. "What are you doing in L.A.?"

"My real name is Gabriella, and that's not exactly the look nor the line I was anticipating. After all, you are engaged to be married," she said looking up at him.

Nick shook his head and grinned. "Are you meeting someone tonight?"

"Only if you are my someone." Gabriella smiled like she use to when teaching Nick Spanish.

Nick hugged her close feeling the electricity spark between them. He whispered, "Let's sit down and catch up."

Gabriella explained that her assignment with the Agency was to teach Nick Spanish and assess his social skills. She'd be working with him now as an interpreter and assisting with tasks as needed.

Nearly three hours later, after sharing stories, catching up, and discussing the upcoming trip to Panama, Nick realized it was getting late. He needed to be at the airport in just a few hours. Gabriella noticed him checking the time and asked if they should leave.

"Yes. I have an early flight in the morning."

"Will you walk me home tonight, then?" she asked.

Nick paused and looked at Gabriella. Images of the nights they were professor and student sharing dinner flooded his mind and, before he realized what he was saying, he agreed.

"Of course," he blurted.

Gabriella smiled, knowing the feelings were filled with affection.

As they left the restaurant, he asked, "So, how far away do you live?"

"About 375 miles. In Phoenix," she said.

Through the entire dinner she never mentioned that she was a linguistics professor at Thunderbird University, where Nick's cover would assuredly be taking him. She watched Nick connecting the dots and smiled.

"Don't worry," she said, "my hotel is just down the street."

At the hotel, they got into the elevator together and Nick walked Gabriella to her room. She opened the door and stepped in, Nick paused, thinking, "this could be a problem." She placed one foot out of the room, her hands on his waist, and pulled him towards her for a kiss. She thanked him for the dinner and, with a flirty smile said, "Goodnight."

Nick whispered back, "Goodnight."

"Now go make your flight," and she closed the door.

As Nick approached the elevator, all thoughts led to one conclusion. This was going to be complicated.

LANDING IN Phoenix, Nick refocused and grabbed a cab to the hotel. The registration desk to the Speaker Symposium opened at 3:00 p.m. Then he would meet up with Gabriella at the reception area around 6:00, before dinner and the opening speaker.

He walked into the reception area and immediately made eye contact with Gabriella. He motioned in the direction of the bar while she spoke privately with the man to her left. As she glanced over to him, the man's eyes followed. Nick instinctively grabbed his drink and blended into the crowd of 150 students, young professionals and renown politicians, wondering, *Who is that man?*

"He's just a political science professor," she told him.

"Where from? He seemed interested in your eye contact with me."

Gabriella replied coyly, "New York, I think. He's not a spy Nick, just a friend. You know, like Anna."

She hugged Nick, allowing him no time to respond and softly said, "Meet me for drinks after dinner."

Nick nodded, and she left the drink line to mingle.

By 10:30 p.m., Nick and Gabriella were at the JW Marriott bar, sharing tequila and sexy banter. He left his extra room key on the bar and retired to his room. Less than 15 minutes later, she joined him in his room, and they were out of their clothes and in each other's embrace. Gabriella was insatiable, and Nick obliged without hesitation.

Nearing 3:00 a.m., Gabriella lifted her head. "I have to go home and get ready. My session starts in six hours." She slipped her clothes on and leaned on the bed.

"Eso estaba delicioso." (That was delicious.)

Nick sat up, and they kissed goodbye.

Over the next three days, Gabriella and Nick were inseparable every night, making love and talking into the early morning hours.

On the last night, Gabriella wanted an answer about Nick's goals.

He simply told her, "There are many things about my path that will not make sense to you now, but in the end, you will understand."

Nick had been trained to stay guarded, methodical, and in control. Gabriella accepted that, but Nick could feel her emotionally stepping back.

Saturday, October 25, 1986

IT WAS supposed to be a free day. Nick was up early and running in the cool morning air. He had found a shooting range nearby and wanted to shoot after breakfast. He had run nearly three miles to a coffee shop and was looking forward to an espresso over ice to re-energize. As he ordered his drink, the hairs on the back of his neck started tingling. He glanced around with his peripheral vision and instantly recognized the character in the doorway.

He called over: "Can I get you anything?"

Vincent took a step toward the open table by the window. "I'll have whatever you're having."

Nick collected the espresso shots and sat down. Solemnly, Vincent opened the conversation. "The situation is not as clear as we'd like. The rodeo idea is too loud. Removing Ramirez from the committee has prompted him to dive deeper into our rural economic funding. We cannot have that."

Nick listened and absorbed the magnitude of what was being said.

Vincent went on: "You have one chance to meet with Ramirez, and then you, and only you, will have to report back with a decision to terminate or not. Understood?"

"Yes," Nick responded flatly.

"That meeting will happen Monday afternoon at 4:00 p.m. You will meet Colonel Ramirez in the lobby of the San Pablo Hotel, less than 1,000 feet from the American Embassy."

Nick asked, "What about Gabriella?"

Vincent sat back in his chair and grinned at Nick. "You are smitten with her, my friend. Tell me, Nick, did you mark her for use in the field, or did she mark you for use in her career?"

Nick never took his eyes off Vincent's face, knowing he had been set up in some malicious sexual test of confidence and loyalty.

"It doesn't matter," replied Nick.

Vincent leaned in. "It does matter, Nick, and you passed the test yesterday by not answering her questions about your feelings, desires, and dreams." He paused. "Gabriella is on hold. You two are finished for the moment."

Nick rationalized, "It is becoming dangerous."

Vincent stood up and looked at Nick. "I fear it's becoming more dangerous than you realize. Stay clear and trust your instincts."

As they left the coffee shop, Vincent shook Nick's hand and pulled him close. "Always arm yourself on this trip, and don't worry about Embassy personnel one bit."

Nicked nodded affirmatively.

Vincent jumped in his car and left Nick to jog back to the hotel.

After spending three hours at the gun range, Nick was ready to relax and check in with Anna. He was relieved that Gabriella would not be on the trip to Bogotá, causing unneeded distractions. He ordered a Bombay gin and rocks, sat at the pool, and cleared his mind.

The final dinner was pleasant. Gabriella was absent. Nick had not seen nor heard from her since their kiss goodbye. When he returned to his room, there was a sealed envelope with his name on it. It was Gabriella's handwriting.

Nick opened the envelope and read.

My dear Nick, working with you, laughing with you, and making love to you will forever live in my heart. I have fallen in love with you. We both know that should not happen. Please be safe and stay sound in your judgment. Always, your Gabriella.

Nick read it several times and hoped she was leaving the door open for future friendship. He closed his eyes tight and thought he had best leave Gabriella alone for now—unless otherwise ordered to work with her again.

Sunday, October 26, 1986

SEAN LANDED at El Dorado International Airport in Bogotá, at 10:43 a.m. He called for a car and arrived at the apartment just before noon. He settled in and called Anna to catch up and get the call out of the way before taking his run and reading his intelligence reports.

He learned that Anna wasn't just sitting at home, bored. She discovered that a sorority sister, Laurie Miller, had moved to Redondo Beach, only 20 minutes away. They were planning to have dinner together. Her work was keeping her quite occupied during the week, and she seemed to genuinely miss him. Nick gave her a standard run-down on the educational facets of the symposium and how his work experience and master's work were so well aligned. The lies rolled off his tongue so well, Nick thought, *I am starting to believe my own lies.*

They said, "I love you," to each other and agreed to touch base later or in the morning.

IT WAS time to open the envelope with the intel reports. The cover message indicated a 4:00 p.m. meeting with Colonel Ramirez and a rendezvous at the Embassy immediately afterward for a formal cover debrief. Further instructions would be forthcoming after the meeting.

Damn, thought Sean. *Comando de Operaciones Especiales*, or Colombian National Police Special Operations (COPES), was a subdivision of the Colombian National Police. This Special Operations Unit functioned as a quick reaction force (QRF) for police operations and as a permanent training field for personnel.

"Ramirez is a bastard," Sean muttered.

Sean immediately began mapping out the overlapping

concerns of his operation and this so-called COPES unit. *Plenty of opportunities for mistakes,* Sean concluded. Colonel Ramirez was setting him up for a fall. Ramirez knew too much. Sean was standing in the middle of everything holding bags of illegal cash.

It was time for a run. Sean threw his gear on, concealing his gun. No more chances at this point. He could feel the heat all around him. Ramirez was now Sean's target.

Chapter 10

What Can Be Done

Monday, October 27, 1986
Bogotá

SEAN WENT on his usual morning run. After five miles and a good sweat, he felt renewed. He sat down at the table. No Gabriella. Sean focused on his meeting with Ramirez. He had contacted Leal for a late morning sit-down, then promptly at 8:30 a.m., the phone rang. It was Leal's assistant confirming Sean's request for 10:30 a.m. Sean confirmed.

Sean called for the car, mentally prepared for the confrontation. Upon arrival, the assistant greeted Sean and showed him to the back patio.

"Es un lugar encantador!" (It is a lovely setting!) Sean declared stepping out the patio door.

Leal rose and smiled, *"Bienvenido, toma asiento!"* (Welcome, have a seat!) The two sat down as tea was served.

Sean led the conversation, "The rodeo will be canceled. What have you told your associates and committee members?"

Leal looked at Sean. "What specifically do you want to know?"

Sean leaned forward. "Everything."

Leal led with his discussions with Guillermo Cano, the editor of *El Espectador.* Sean listened intently. The stories of dinners that included Cano and Ramirez were beginning to blur. It became obvious that Colonel Ramirez and Guillermo Cano shared a close relationship with Leal. They were a threesome that acted in concert to help each other manipulate the public through politics, law enforcement, and the press.

Sean asked Leal, "Why did you invite such high-profile investigators onto the committee supporting our secret Economic Development Funds?"

Leal became visibly uncomfortable.

Sean leaned back into his chair. "Let's plan on lunch together, okay?"

"What would you like to have for lunch?" asked Leal.

Sean spoke softly but directly, "The entire truth."

Leal looked at Sean. "Okay. We shall have chicken and cheese empanadas."

Leal explained his approach to building a committee that would add credibility, hence lowering the risk of investigation. Leal vigorously implied that they could trust Ramirez and Cano. He intended to leverage that trust to further the Rural Economic Development Fund project's "hide in plain sight" objective.

Leal said, "There is one problem."

Sean prodded him, "What is the problem, Leal?"

Leal spoke quietly, "Did you know you were being followed? Ramirez had you followed."

Sean maintained eye contact, "No." It was a lie, but Sean wanted Leal to believe he was one step ahead.

Leal looked away. "Ramirez had a COPES officer tailing you the night the officer was stabbed to death in an alleyway."

Sean shook his head. "That's not good."

Leal respectfully asked, "Did you or your people have anything to do with it?"

Sean said, "No." There was a pause in the conversation.

Leal's home staff placed the empanadas on the table with plates and drinks.

Sean again leaned toward Leal. "What do you believe?"

Leal did not look well.

"I believe you," said Leal. Sean detected strenuous breathing and speech patterns.

Leal continued, "I just know that Ramirez won't let this go until he finds the killer."

Sean said, "I see. What do you recommend?"

Leal looked genuinely puzzled and stared into the sky. Sean continued eating the empanadas as if nothing were wrong.

Leal didn't respond; he was in deep thought about his next statement.

This is becoming a mess, Sean thought. He pressed his radio signal. Jon Robinson had to be close. It was just after 1:15 p.m., and Sean would have to leave for the meeting with Ramirez soon.

Leal said, "I can speak to Ramirez."

Sean asked, "What would you say?"

"That you had nothing to do with the killing of his officer."

Sean just shook his head. "Don't be stupid. Right now, Ramirez trusts you. My associate is on his way. He will stay with you throughout the afternoon for your own protection."

Leal looked relieved. Sean was satisfied that Ramirez and Leal were not completely operating in concert—yet.

There was a firm knock on the front door. Leal's assistant walked Jon to the patio, and introductions were made.

Sean asked Leal, "Anything else you want to tell me before I leave?"

Leal earnestly replied, "No, Sean. Be careful."

Either he has become a damn fine actor, or he is truly concerned, Sean thought.

Jon said, "Sean, don't worry, we will be fine."

Sean said goodbye to the men. It was time to meet with Ramirez.

When they arrived, Sean had the driver circle the San Pablo Hotel twice then park in the alley for five minutes. Then they repeated the circle to detect anything unusual. Parked just 1,000 feet from the Embassy, there seemed to be little risk in this meeting. Sean was determined to stay calm, cool, and collected.

It was time. Sean decided to take off his holster and place it under the driver's seat. Then he told the driver to drop him at the front door, park across the street, and do nothing else but watch the door in case a fast exit was needed.

Just as he walked into the hotel lobby, Sean was stopped by Ramirez and two other officers. They insisted on frisking him.

Ramirez said, "One of our officers was killed recently. So, we frisk and search before meeting with people we don't know."

Sean replied, *"Buscas a todos tus nuevos amigos?"* (You search all of your new friends?)

Ramirez smirked and walked to the table in the corner, "Sean, your Embassy people called for this meeting. What can I do for you?"

Sean spoke firmly, "Colonel Ramirez, this is a personal meeting to let you know that we have decided to cancel the rodeo event."

Ramirez looked annoyed, "What a shame. Why?"

"The promotion is becoming too expensive. We want more of the money to go to developing agricultural communities and their legitimization." Sean paused to let that sink in with Ramirez.

Ramirez leaned back and folded his arms. "What does this have to do with me?"

Sean leaned closer. "We are no longer in need of your services on the rodeo event committee. Please accept our apologies for any inconvenience."

Ramirez was visibly unhappy, "Well, then. You have delivered your message."

Sean stood and stuck his hand out, *"Gracias."* He watched Ramirez. There was definite suspicion and anger in his posture and movements, but he stood to shake hands.

"Gracias por la reunión," (Thank you for the meeting,) grunted Ramirez. Sean walked calmly out the door and to his car, satisfied with the results of the exchange.

At 4:22 p.m., Sean walked into the Embassy and was shown to the secure room where Vincent and Jon were waiting.

"Where's your gun?" asked Vincent.

Sean replied, "It's safely stored in the car with my driver."

The three of them sat down to discuss what they'd learned. Sean opened up with three major pieces: First, Leal had to be kept on a short leash, given the interactions with Ramirez and Cano; second, although under suspicion, no one was aware of Sean's involvement with the killing of Ramirez's officer; third, Leal should never have allowed Cano so close to their cover with the Cartel. Vincent and Jon folded their arms smiling.

Sean looked at them, "What?"

Vincent took the lead. "One thing you must realize. We need Jaime Leal for just a little while longer. He is our mole inside the UP Communist regimes."

Sean nodded in agreement. "I assumed as much."

Vincent went on, "Ramirez and Cano are too close. Intel suggests they are threats to our cover and funding operation."

Sean and Jon listened intensely.

"Let's clean this up locally. No involvement from Langley," declared Vincent.

Jon and Sean simultaneously replied, "Agreed."

The next funding of development monies was to occur in mid-December. Both Ramirez and Cano needed to be terminated before then. Sean offered to collaborate with Fabio to ease the chore of staging the killings. Vincent agreed to make Fabio the backup, but he felt they should control the situation and maintain total secrecy. He offered, "Executing the kills in a manner that mimics Cartel hits may prove beneficial."

Jon spoke up. "That can be arranged. Our contact will provide the setup. Sean and I can handle the rest."

Everyone agreed on the operation.

VINCENT RECOMMENDED drinks and dinner at La Puerta Falsa, a traditional restaurant over a century old. Located in an old house, it had two floors. On the first floor, it had an area for dining tables as well as a counter where preparations such as *cocadas,* coconut confections, were offered to visitors. On the second floor, there was a private room with just two small circular wooden tables and barely any room to walk about. It was the Colombian version of European gastronomic fair: simple bar food.

Vincent handed the host a $20 bill, and they were shown to the private upstairs room. The menu included an array of simple tamales, soup with cheese and bread, and other baked goods. The Glenlivet was flowing.

While eating tamales, they quietly discussed the need to loop in Fabio Ochoa and Rodriguez Gacha. Sean would make that happen. Jon would gather more intel.

Congress had approved large sums of money.

Sean brought up potential problems, "We need new drop points and a more discreet exchange operation for the funds being laundered by the Cartel."

Vincent looked at his watch. "It's late and we have much to do over the next ten days. Let's get out of here."

They agreed to gather in Bogotá the week of November tenth to walk through intelligence and determine final plans.

Chapter 11

Ten Days to Plan

THE NEXT ten days were tense. Nick returned home to California, where he read intelligence reports under cover, and settled into marriage with Anna. Northrop was keeping Anna busy with computer engineering designs for the latest communication satellite systems. Anna loved to brag about her projects and how technical the designs were for government systems. Little did she know that intelligence communiques from those "top secret systems" over Central America might end up in Nick's hands.

Cryptic messages were routinely sent from Vincent reminding Nick that the Agency was displeased with the delay in disclosing his role with Anna. While there was no hard and fast rule, it was common to have the spouse sign a confidentiality and secrecy statement within the first few months of marriage. Nick decided he would wait until after the holidays to make that decision. Vincent would not be happy.

Halloween weekend was just around the corner. Anna made plans to attend a Halloween party. Her sorority sister, Laurie, would also be going to the party.

At the party, Anna encouraged Laurie and Nick to dance together. After several dances, in the middle of the crowded dance floor, Laurie leaned in and kissed Nick passionately. To make matters worse, Nick kissed her back before pulling away. The two of them knew instantly it was a mistake.

Anna had asked Laurie over to the townhouse for drinks after the party and by the time they had finished their second bottle of wine insisted that she stay over. The next morning, Anna told Nick she wanted to run to the store and pick-up food for lunch.

Nick went upstairs and showered. Laurie was waiting for him in a loose-fitting robe. She approached him and asked for a shower towel. When Nick reached into the towel cabinet, Laurie gently pulled on the towel that was wrapped around his wet midsection. He stopped her.

"What are you doing, Laurie? Anna and I are married."

She placed her hand in the center of his chest. "You may be married, but your heart is somewhere else."

In his heart, Nick agreed with Laurie. "That's not something that concerns you," he said.

She looked at him, took the extra towel, and left her door open as she slipped out of her robe. Their eyes met and he couldn't help but notice the curves of her naked body.

He closed his bedroom door and looked in the mirror. "That's not something that concerns you," reflecting on his response. He felt embarrassed for himself and his marriage. He heard the garage door and saw Anna pulling in.

Friday, November 7, 1986

NICK TOOK Anna out for dinner.

"My travel plans are going to be extensive before the holidays, honey."

Anna hated the late notice and uncertainty of Nick's trips.

"How do they expect you to be available to travel without definite dates?"

Nick had no good answer, "I will work on getting better plans in place for future trips."

She did not believe him. "Right. . . . Nick."

Nick observed her body language. He knew the problem was not going to go away. He reached out and held her hand, looked deep and long into her eyes.

"Anna, I promise to do better."

She smiled and Nick knew that his lies would soon catch up with him.

Chapter 12

Eliminating Investigations

Monday, November 10, 1986
Bogotá

SEAN LANDED in Bogotá and was greeted with a full set of intelligence reports, complete with recommendations from Vincent and Jon.

Led by Jon Robinson, Vincent's team in Colombia had been busy developing intel on Colonel Ramirez and the *El Espectador* Editor-in-Chief, Guillermo Cano. According to intel reports, the CIA indicated that new recruits were entering the guerrilla army and its urban militia units of the FARC. These guerrilla recruits were carrying out kidnappings and targeting regional politicians for assassination.

Ramirez was providing FARC and UP with political intel to help with their targeted assassinations, and Guillermo Cano was spinning the stories to blame the Cartels. In the meantime, Jamie Leal was in the thick of the game, burning his candle at both ends. Sean continued reading the reports; the intelligence was growing thick and complex. He soon realized that Ramirez was one of the heads of the Communist regime.

There may be three heads when you include Cano and Leal, thought Sean. Leal was an asset for now and could not be touched, just closely observed.

Sean leaned back in his favorite reading chair. Ramirez was digging into his Rural Economic Development Funds because he suspected money laundering. The reports indicated that Ramirez was not targeting Sean for the DEA, rather, Ramirez, UP, and the FARC were seeking information about CIA involvement in funding the Contras (Freedom Fighters).

Sean closed his eyes. *Vincent was right to have jumped into this situation,* he thought. *The situation was already unacceptable, given the timeline for the next wave of funding for guns to the freedom fighting Contras.*

The apartment door swung open. It was Vincent and Jon. "We have the opportunity pinpointed," Jon proclaimed.

Intel from inside Ramirez's staff revealed that he would be on a family trip to the country over the weekend. He would return Monday, November 17, without a police convoy.

Jon continued, "He will be taken out sicario style on his return from the country."

Vincent smiled. "Just brilliant."

It had become obvious to the team that Ramirez was using Leal to advance his political stature and ultimately to position himself to lead the Communist Party to either an election or revolution in Colombia.

Vincent poured a Glenlivet and sat on the couch facing Sean. Jon stood in front of the window, peering out over the walkway and park below.

Vincent looked at Sean. "Time for a meeting with Fabio. He will need to know in advance that he should do nothing, except prepare to take the blame. Cano will undoubtedly publish a story that the Cartel killed Ramirez."

"I will coordinate it as soon as possible," said Sean. "It will be important for Fabio to understand why we were taking the matter into our own hands."

"Tell Fabio we have reason to believe this is a personal matter, and we just need his help for cover with neither an admission nor denial," said Vincent.

Sean acknowledged the plan.

Tuesday, November 11, 1986

SEAN SAT with Fabio under the shade tree between the house and the barn. It had become the place for private talks. Fabio accepted the story of the assassination as a personal matter. He was pleased that Ramirez would be gone for good.

"You know what I love about you, Sean?"

Sean looked Fabio in the eyes, "What?"

Fabio took the last swig of his beer. "Respect. You have respect for your elders and for power. I appreciate you telling me this in advance, and I want you to know that we are here for you. Whatever you need when this blows up, I will be here for you, because I trust you."

Sean leaned over and touched Fabio's hand. *"Gracias, siempre seré un amigo de confianza."* (Thank you. I will always be a trusted friend.)

Fabio put his other hand atop Sean's hand. "I believe you will try, Sean. You will try." He released Sean's hand. "Do we have funding dates for the next Rural Economic Fund payment?"

Sean assured him that funding was being scheduled for the second week in December. Should any disruptions occur, he would personally inform him. This made Fabio happy. Sean stood and gave his respects to the Ochoa family and left the ranch.

BACK AT the apartment with Vincent and Jon, Sean had more movement intel on Ramirez and Cano to review. There were no surprises in the plan for Ramirez, but Cano was much less cocky, incredibly careful, and methodical about his self-protection. Cano had been receiving death threats for decades, therefore developed routines of commuting with an escort, maintaining unpredictable, last-minute schedule changes. All to never be easily anticipated.

It was a chore to find insiders willing to take a bribe, or angry enough to assist with gathering the intelligence needed to plan an assassination. As Jon explained the problems, Vincent's frustration grew evident.

Sean offered up Fabio. "We could ask Fabio to do something about Cano if needed. So long as the Ramirez hit goes smoothly."

Jon immediately liked the idea.

Vincent said, "Not yet. But Fabio is Plan B."

Vincent dismissed Jon for the evening and asked Sean to order dinner from La Monareta Pizza. It was a favorite for nights of laying low, drinking scotch, and analysis. Sean appreciated planning time alone with Vincent. It helped him understand Vincent's views and better understand his own role in the machine of America's freedom.

Planning to take a life—in this case, two lives—was new to Sean. Blood was already on his hands for the young policeman's death in the alleyway. He tucked that kill away in the back of his mind as "self-defense." In training, it was emphasized that "licensed to kill" also means "licensed not to kill." Maybe he acted too swiftly that night—or maybe he could be dead. Either way, Vincent had declared it Sean's first kill.

Vincent poured another round. "Stop over-thinking it. Ramirez and Cano are the bad guys. They are seeking to undermine Colombia and install communism. Our job is to stop them."

He paused. "Any questions?"

Sean took the scotch. "Thanks for the recap. No questions."

Killing was inevitable, Sean realized, and the good they were attempting to do by fighting the Sandinistas in Nicaragua was an important mission.

Wednesday, November 12, 1986

SEAN FLEW to Mexico City with Vincent to debrief in the basement of the Embassy. These sessions were designed to formally update the Executive Branch with operational missions, intel reports, and field observations. Vincent was trained to send taped briefs of such sessions to the Directorate in advance of an ops mission. This ensured that risk factors and alternative plans were clearly communicated in advance. It was a smart tactic. Stating the risk factors in advance was clearly the best way to alleviate second-guessing about any post-operational challenges.

The Ramirez and Cano assassination plans were fraught with risks and variables that could potentially spin out of control.

Once they completed the taping of the brief, Vincent and Sean went out for dinner. For the first two rounds of drinks, they said nothing. They were on the record that by November 17, Colonel Jaime Ramirez would be killed, and no later than December 17, Guillermo Cano would also be killed.

And so, it will be done, thought Sean. *Life and death.*

Wednesday, November 13, 1986

SEAN FLEW home to spend the weekend with Anna and planned to return after the Ramirez hit. Vincent was stationed in a nearby safe house throughout the operation and would direct last-minute changes or approve optional tactics as needed for Jon's squad.

Nick landed at LAX and drove straight to the townhome in

Torrance. He ran his laundry, including what he was wearing, cleaned his travel bag, and took a long shower. By mid-afternoon, he called Anna's work number and as always went straight to voicemail. He left a message. She never picked up her phone. Nick liked it that way because it allowed him to deflect calls and avoid any petty arguments.

Anna called back and was happy he was home. She asked if he would like to try an Italian restaurant in Redondo Beach. "It sounds like fun," he agreed. Dinner was lighthearted and an excellent escape from the activities underway in Bogotá.

Thursday and Friday seemed to last forever, with no updates or communiques from Vincent. Then, at 3:30 p.m., the townhome phone rang. It was Vincent.

"D is in motion. Clear?"

Sean replied, "Confirmed."

Vincent hung up.

Nick needed to escape the townhome and asked Anna to go out for dinner and a movie on Saturday night. He offered, *"The Color of Money* with Paul Newman is playing." She agreed.

He drank several tequila shots during their meal at a Mexican restaurant—so many shots, in fact, that Anna grew concerned and demanded to drive. By the time the movie ended, Nick was completely exhausted thinking about the plan to eliminate Ramirez. Anna tried to have a conversation with him, but he pretended to lie down and fall asleep. He wasn't in the mood to talk.

Sunday was a relaxing day for Nick. The weather was sunny and in the low 70s, so they hung out by the pool and grilled steaks. Nick imagined Ramirez with his family having dinner together for the last time. Once again, Anna could tell that Nick's mood was somber and troubled, but he would not open up to her, so she just sat on the couch next to him to give some comfort and peace. She told him that she had a big week ahead of her at work.

As they climbed into bed, a concerned Anna asked, "Could we have some quiet dinners at home together this week?"

"Sure," said Nick. "Just know that I'm on call and might have to go down to Bogotá to keep the development projects moving along."

Anna understood and hugged and kissed him good night.

Monday, November 17, 1986

As REPORTED in the newspaper:

> While returning with his family to Bogotá, Colonel Ramírez was shot at while driving over a bridge between the municipalities of Mosquera and Fontibón. It was reported that men in a green Renault 18 began to shoot at his car on a bridge, taking advantage of the fact that he was without a convoy. Colonel Ramírez lost control of his car and crashed against a rock, not far from a police station. The assassins approached his car and shot him dead in front of his wife and sons.

Nick was relieved that Ramirez's family was safe, but more relieved Ramirez was dead.

Tuesday, November 18, 1986

EL ESPECTADOR reported the murder of Colonel Ramírez this way:

> Just one act in a macabre war by the Medellín Cartel against the Colombian state in its attempt to outsmart it. But it was also a milestone that resulted in the fight against the Cartel being quickly strengthened with the international support of the DEA in order to hunt down the main ringleaders."

Nick read this and knew that Fabio was most likely smiling, drinking beer under his shade tree. Ramirez was dead. It was done.

Intelligence on Cano was heating up. Jon's insider was uncovering the trail that Cano was pursuing with Ramirez. The reports indicated that Sean was a person of interest.

Nick sat back and closed his eyes. He was in the middle of it all. *Who was Cano working with? How much does he know?*

Nick knew that Cano would be next.

Chapter 13

Vincent Opens up to Sean

Wednesday, November 19, 1986
Mexico City

VINCENT MET SEAN at the Marriott lobby bar in downtown Mexico City.

"Ramirez is dead. We terminated him." Vincent flatly stated.

Sean paused, "Yes, we did."

"This happened because you decided to kill his officer. You didn't follow protocol," Vincent scorned Sean.

Sean sat still and didn't offer a response.

Vincent spoke directly, "Will you follow orders for the Cano kill?"

Sean responded firmly, "Yes."

"Remember your training. It's that simple, get in, do your duty, get out."

SEAN THOUGHT back to his weapons training, just three months ago, *Am I ready for this?*

The coveted United States Marine Corp Expert Pistol Qualification Badge was a CIA weapons proficiency level that Vincent expected every recruit to achieve before they were placed in a position that could put them in immediate danger. Nick received his badge on August 1, 1986.

August 2, 1986, Nick was accepted into the ranks of Career Trainee and placed on the list for active duty. Vincent was proud to call upon Nick (alias, Sean) for his team in Central America that very day.

That same week, Nick learned that Gabriella would be traveling with him extensively. His Spanish fluency was weak, and she would serve as his interpreter.

Sean turned 22 years old on August 7, 1986. He celebrated it in Illinois with his family and Anna. Then he flew back to California alone to await his orders.

On August 14, Vincent showed up at Nick's door without notice, determined to go for a walk with him. Nick acquiesced. They walked the beautiful, old-fashioned tree-lined streets and circled the parks around Torrance. Vincent outlined details of the funding and flow of monies. He outlined the cover activities, including the people that Nick would be meeting, the actions he would need to take, and the monies he'd need to handle. Gabriella was to be by his side as a backup. Vincent informed Nick that the two of them would be inseparable; files presented for intel collection were safe with her.

That was the day Vincent first described Jaime Leal.

Nick remembered, "Leal sounds like a double-edged sword."

Vincent reassured Nick, "Don't get stressed out. You will know how to handle him when the time is right."

They finished their walk at the steps of Nick's townhouse, "Anything else you want to tell me about the op?"

Vincent's words never seemed more real: "Yeah. Don't get killed."

THROUGHOUT THE fall of 1986, Sean learned to "hide in plain sight." Working out of the U.S. Embassy, Bogotá, he allocated congressional monies for the newly formed funds, drafted instructions for exact sums to be pulled systematically from money laundering Cartel accounts and utilized to purchase weapons and supplies for freedom fighting Contras. These exchanges were executed in Hangar 63, at Panama City Airport controlled by Manuel Noriega. The CIA had nicknamed the hangar the "Fun Zone."

The funds were intended to prop up a lost cause, further indicating that the Contras had gained minimal popular support in Nicaragua and no international standing of any kind in the past few years. Millions of dollars had been poured down the most noisome sinkhole since Vietnam.

Vincent drilled the reality of the situation in Central America into Sean's head.

Many Contras had retreated to the relative safety of their Honduran bases across the border. Now, more than ever, they threatened the stability of that fragile democracy, whose moderate military leader was recently ousted for resisting total American domination.

Paving over Honduras with United States airfields (the sixth in three years was under construction) and pouring in thousands of U.S. troops (4,000 were in the plans for that year) for maneuvers on the Nicaraguan border was not the kind of aid that was needed by the poorest country in the Americas. The whole area was a mess.

In apocalyptic terms, President Reagan warned Congress that a "strategic disaster" was at hand if Nicaragua was left to the Sandinistas. Reagan's theory of Soviet bases or a nest of spies within two days' driving time from Harlingen, Texas, had a great deal to do with the administration's consistent favoring of the rule of force over the rule of law.

Yet not a single major democratic government in the Western Hemisphere—from Canada to Argentina—endorsed the United States' support of the Contras. No one approved of Mr. Reagan's refusal to negotiate an agreement with the Sandinistas that would protect both North American defense interests and Central American independence. As they demonstrated to the eight most influential foreign ministers in Latin America who had met recently with Mr. Shultz in Washington to press his Mideast peace initiative, Mr. Reagan and Mr. Shultz couldn't care less.

Sean believed in the CIA's narrative.

The message was simple: If the Sandinistas would not negotiate with the already defeated Contras, we should overthrow the Sandinistas. The millions of dollars demanded of Congress, along with the monies that Vincent's team would move, were only the first steps toward that objective. A United States invasion of Nicaragua might be required.

Sean was now more convinced than ever: *No one really knows where the 'point of no return' is in Nicaragua.*

VINCENT FINISHED his drink in the Marriott lobby bar. Memories from just a few months ago seemed incredibly distant to Sean and Vincent.

It was time for another drink. "C'mon, we have a suite upstairs," Vincent said.

"We?" asked Sean.

Vincent did not tell Sean, or anyone, that Richard was in town for the night. He ordered two bottles of Glenlivet and a bucket of ice and told the bartender to send a tray of cheese and crackers to the suite.

In the elevator, Sean thought about his parents and brothers. Despite growing up in a strict Catholic family, Sean accepted

Vincent and Richard's relationship as a whole relationship under God. He felt privileged to be trusted by Vincent and Richard, and a little envious given the cold relationship he experienced with Anna.

Vincent and Sean walked into the suite and were greeted by Richard with a hug. Vincent and Richard began catching up by speaking German.

Sean went into the bedroom and dialed Anna. She answered the phone on the first ring.

"Hello?" said Anna.

"Hi, I made it to Mexico City," said Nick.

"Thank you for checking in, honey. I miss you."

"Me too, honey. My boss is here, we are about to have dinner. I love you."

"I love you, too. Be safe and let me know how it's all going, okay?" Anna was searching for some connection.

"I will, I promise. Good night," said Nick.

Just then, Vincent walked into the bedroom, followed by Richard. Vincent was in a better mood already with Richard on his arm. Richard was lean and muscular with sandy, blonde hair that was military-style.

Richard knew that Sean was assigned his first assassination. The Cano operation.

Sean shook Richard's hand and gave him a warm but some-what formal hug, just enough to feel Sean's strength.

Richard sized up Sean, "How is your first operation going?"

"It has been challenging," replied Sean, "But nothing I can't handle."

Richard looked Sean over. "Fine, we don't have to talk about it now."

Sean shook his head, as they smiled while lifting their glasses high.

Richard and Vincent had met in Munich, Germany, on the

job. Richard was undercover for the equivalent of the CIA in West Germany. Richard and Vincent spoke many languages, and, as the night wore on, they would often converse in Spanish, German, and English.

Quite entertaining, thought Sean.

The night marched on. Both bottles of scotch were nearly empty, and a never-ending stream of melodic jazz selections played in the suite. Vincent paused and dedicated a finale to Richard, "Turn Out the Lamplight." Sean remembered their love story.

Very few agents or officers in the CIA knew about Vincent's sexuality or his life partner Richard. Richard closed his eyes and was mentally dreaming of a time and place far away. Vincent pledged his love to Richard with this song, declaring Richard as his home at the end of every journey. It was their secret love song.

Sean stood up and began a soulful slow dance to honor their relationship. He moved as if the music had taken over his body, gliding across the floor and leaning into the deep melodic chords as if he had a life partner of his own. Richard stood up, mirroring Sean with his own dance expression. Vincent was pleased. He loved Sean for being open to their relationship.

It was time for Sean to leave, Richard and Vincent walked him to the door. Vincent turned to Sean, "Get some rest, to-morrow is critical."

They all hugged good night. Sean retired to his room ready for the night to be over.

Debrief on Ramirez

Thursday, November 20, 1986

AT THE U.S. Embassy, Mexico City with Vincent and Jon, intelligence on Leal and Guillermo Cano proved to be remarkably interesting. Jon reported that Leal had been covering his tracks with Ramirez by meeting with FARC agents, and providing housing for the UP's Director Jaramillo Ossa since the night of Ramirez's death.

"Leal is a snake," said Sean.

Vincent laughed. "He will eventually provide the value we need to break FARC and upend the Communist movement in Colombia."

Jon was obviously proud of his team. "Leal has convinced himself that the Cartel assassinated Ramirez."

"What else can he believe?" Vincent snarked. "But, Jon, it was a job well-done." Vincent was genuine in his compliment.

"The highest risk is Cano," said Jon as he looked intensely at Sean. "We believe he has made the connection between Leal, USAID, and the Cartels that Ramirez was investigating. We also found enough information to allege that you support the Cartel's recent movements into Nicaragua."

Sean looked at Vincent. "So . . . they believe I am a Cartel plant within USAID, helping them move money and operations into Nicaragua to avoid the U.S. DEA?"

Vincent walked toward Sean, "Yes. But it's actually worse than that. They may be dangerously close to the Contra's fight against the Sandinistas."

Sean looked at Jon. "Well, hell, that cannot happen!"

"It won't happen, if we take out Cano now," Jon said.

For the record, they disclosed documentation that identified Cano as a Communist agent affiliated with the Sandinistas. Jon pulled out pictures and travel documents associating Cano with Nicaraguan leader, President Daniel Ortega. As a result, there was enough evidence and reason to declare Cano as a clear and present danger to the national security of the operations. Approval was granted to eliminate Cano along with any evidence.

Deep in the bowels of the Mexico City Embassy, a clear and present danger was identified and noted for the record. Ramirez had been eliminated, and his Communist propaganda would be systematically denied by eliminating the voice of Cano. After the morning briefing, Jon and Sean left for Colombia on separate planes at separate times. They would rendezvous at the Bogotá apartment after 10:00 p.m.

In the apartment in Bogotá, Jon illustrated Cano's comings and goings to his office at *El Espectador*. His movements were well-orchestrated, revealing no routine or specific habits. Sean asked if they had searched the premises, tapped his phones or bribed a janitor.

"We developed an asset. A reporter named Rodolfo Pérez," Jon revealed.

"Is he permanent or temporary?" asked Sean.

Jon replied, "He will assist with the assassination plan. After that we promised to ship him to the States."

Dozens of questions swirled through Sean's mind. "Let's get some shut-eye. We need the right cover story for Cano's kill."

Saturday morning came quickly, Sean went for a run at sunrise. Upon his return, Jon was sitting at the kitchen table, coffee made. Sean poured himself a cup.

Jon asked him, "Any brilliant ideas?"

"As a matter of fact, I do have an idea," Sean said, smiling.

Jon smiled. "Well, are you going to share it?"

For the next hour, Sean laid out a plan.

"Let's use your asset, Rodolfo Perez." Sean described a series of fake stories to leak salacious details about Pablo Escobar.

"Cano will eat it up!" laughed Jon.

Sean, thinking out loud, said, "I will let Fabio know about the plan in advance. He can loop Pablo into the assassination plan. Pablo should be pleased to know that Cano will be eliminated from his life as well."

"The stories, while fake, will be just credible enough to get printed." Sean continued, "The public will believe there is escalating tension between Cano and Escobar."

The inside mole, Pérez, would clean house of any USAID involvement or affiliation. Then, on an evening that Cano typically worked late, they would assassinate him, Cartel-style. Pérez would report the assassination as a Cartel hit.

"Are you in a position to devise a plan?" Sean asked Jon.

"I will need a little time, more access to his calendar, and we will have to work together." Jon said.

"There's one more thing." Jon paused and looked at Sean. "Vincent wants you to complete the kill but verify what he knows about the congressional money laundering and Freedom Fighter support before you pull the trigger."

Sean sighed, "This will take some coordination. Cano is so public. It will have to happen quickly if it happens at all."

Jon replied, "Let me design a plan. It will work. WE WILL MAKE IT WORK."

They said goodbye and Jon left the apartment.

SEAN CALLED Fabio to confirm a late afternoon meeting.

They sat under the shade tree at Fabio's ranch. It was a warm and sunny day. Drinking beer and nibbling on empanadas, Sean reported that Congress was on schedule for money movements. The larger fund payments were approved. The USAID program deposits would hit the bank accounts before Christmas.

"My dear friend, Sean, we will move the monies and deliver on our promise." Fabio said with resounding confidence.

Sean shifted in this chair, giving Fabio a direct look. "We have one more serious matter to cover today."

Fabio inquired, "What might that be, Sean?"

Sean told Fabio about the threat of Cano and the intention to eliminate him, Cartel-style.

Fabio laughed deep from his belly. "Pablo will love this!" he said. "No work, no risk, and all the glory!" Sean and Fabio laughed together. Deep down, Sean was relieved.

The plan was in place. Sean hugged Fabio and left the ranch for the airport.

Back in the states, Thanksgiving plans were in full motion. Anna had purchased airplane tickets for a flight back to Illinois, departing the next day.

Sean thought about Cano, *I am pulling the trigger. I will demand information from Cano and then kill him.* Sean's mind was reeling, *Will he beg for his life or make it easy?*

Sean hated knowing about the kill in advance. He closed his eyes to rest but could feel the blood of his first kill on his hands. It would never go away. Not now, not ever.

Chapter 15

Thanksgiving at Home

NICK PULLED into the garage Saturday evening just in time for dinner with Anna.

He walked into the living room, Anna asked, "Did you leave your bags in the garage?" She was concerned that he would bring insects into the townhome from his foreign travel.

"Yes," he said loudly, thinking, *It is good to see you, too.*

The relationship was strained at best.

Anna was finishing dinner preparations, making American goulash. Nick gave her a hug and set the table.

"Excited for Thanksgiving?" he asked.

"Mom and Dad are excited to host everyone and catch up." Anna replied happily.

Dinner was an exchange of lies. Nick believed Anna was just as dissatisfied in their marriage as he was.

After dinner they packed for their trip. It was well-planned out.

The first two days were with his family. Nick's parents were accustomed to celebrating Thanksgiving and other holidays early, so their son's wives could be home with their families on the actual holiday.

The next four days would be with Anna's parents. While he was packing, he thought about Jon, a bachelor in Bogotá, spying on Cano, and creating diversional stories about Pablo Escobar. He compared their life paths. *Jon was smart to have avoided marriage so far.*

The flight to Chicago was followed by the three-hour drive to the farm. Nick enjoyed the ride, decompressing and reminiscing with Anna. The season was shifting from fall to winter. The crops harvested. The skies were a blend of steel-blue and gray. Nick loved rolling the window down. Fresh air. Cold, crisp, clean air. He remembered pheasant hunting, long walks along the farm hedgerows, and the companionship of a faithful dog by his side.

Anna asked, "What are you thinking about?"

"Simpler days. Pheasant hunting and walking the fields," replied Nick.

Anna did not share Nick's romanticism of the countryside, nor his agricultural roots. The closer they got to the farm, the more nervous she became—and for good reason. Nick's brothers could be competitive, and even mean-spirited.

"Any family news to share?" inquired Anna.

"Nothing new," Nick said, irritated. Anna shook her head in disapproval.

Nick pointed out, "It's only been a couple of months."

"You have four older brothers, all married, one with their first child on the way, and your dad has had a minor heart attack with continuing health issues" Anna responded.

"Thanks for the briefing on my own family." Tired of the line of questioning, he pointed out: "It's only been two months since our wedding."

Anna often criticized how little he seemed to communicate with his family.

Nick confessed, "I am ashamed about not calling Mom and Dad more often."

"Why don't you call them more often?"

Nick looked straight ahead. "I don't know."

"You don't know, or don't want to tell me?" Anna prodded.

"It's a mystery. Talking with Mom is never easy. She compares everyone and no matter what I am doing, it's not good enough," Nick confessed.

Anna reached for Nick's hand, "I understand."

They arrived at the farmhouse, pulled into the driveway, and parked the car. As if on cue, Nick's father, Paul, walked out to greet everyone and inspect his son. Nick stood tall and looked his father in the eye, "Dad, it's so good to be home."

"We worry about you," said Paul.

Nick interrupted without blinking, "Don't. It's all going well."

They hugged tight.

There was a father-son bond. Nick could feel his father's presence long after his visits. Nick's mom, Loretta, embraced Nick and Anna, and the rest of the family came out to participate in the greeting. Nick's brother, John, who was thirteen years older, and his wife, Diana. David, a Chicago lawyer, eleven years Nick's senior, along with his second Chicago-raised wife, Carol, were there.

Nick's remaining two brothers were already in town: Frank, nine years older than Nick, and his wife, Jennifer. Lastly, Bradley, seven years older than Nick, and his new wife Theresa.

Carol picked up Anna's purse, "Whose Gucci Ucci purse is this?"

Anna was angry, but unsure what to say or do as the newest wife to clan of brothers.

Nick responded, "Why? Do you want one just like it?" He

walked over to Carol and put his arm around her. "We can help you get one." With that, David and Carol were pissed, and Nick had empowered Anna.

Nick walked back to Anna, and whispered, "Let the competition begin."

The next day about 25 people arrived between 11:00 a.m. and 12:30 p.m.—mostly uncles, aunts, and cousins from Nick's mother's side of the family. Then Nick's dad, Paul, returned after picking up his mother, Geneva, and her third husband, George. She had outlived her first two husbands. Nick observed his grandmother and noticed her mental decline and physical frailty.

The meal was fantastic: spiral honey baked ham, vegetables galore, sweet potatoes prepared with marshmallows baked on top. In the country, things didn't seem to change much.

Anna was already glancing at her watch; it was nearing 7:00 p.m. Others were leaving for their long drives home. Anna knew it often took an hour just to say proper goodbyes. There were last-minute chats and promises to come back and visit more often.

Nick made the rounds. He gave his mom a long hug and a kiss on the forehead, then waved at his brothers and their wives; it was time to leave. His dad followed them out to the car.

Anna gave Paul a nice hug and kiss, then jumped in the car.

Paul turned to Nick, "I'm not sure I understand what you do for a living, but I hope you are safe, and it is what you truly want."

Nick hugged his father with strength. That was the most his dad had said about his career during the whole visit.

"It's a fulfilling job, Dad. I am learning so much."

Paul replied, "Careful out there in foreign lands, it can be dangerous."

"I will be careful. It's all part of growing stronger and smarter, right?" challenged Nick.

"You are growing stronger. I will have to trust you on growing smarter," chuckled Paul.

Nick laughed, leaned in and whispered, "I love you, Dad."

"I love you, too," his father said.

It was a quiet drive to Anna's home. Anna was tired and napped on the way. Nick was tired of talking and visiting, so he played soft music and enjoyed the drive. Nick pulled into Anna's driveway and he gently woke her. Anna spotted her mom at the front door, jumped out of the car and went in the house, leaving Nick to gather the bags.

He shook his head, thinking, *The princess has returned with her mule of a husband.*

At the door, Anna's mom, Barbara, greeted him with a loving hug. Her dad, Jim, walked over and shook his hand aggressively. Then, Anna's brother, Brad, seven years her senior, and his two-year-old son, Christopher, came into the entry. He and his wife were separated. Brad, a pharmacist, had been in trouble with recent allegations of his drug use and potential dealings.

Jim gave directions to Nick, "You and Anna will be sleeping in the basement."

There were two twin beds in the finished basement that doubled as couches for a playroom. *Ah, of course,* thought Nick. *A conspiracy to keep me from sleeping in the same bed as the princess.* Jim explained that it would be better for Brad to have the second bedroom on the main floor for managing Christopher.

Jim pointed out, "No stairs and the bathroom close by."

"No problem," Nick blurted.

On Wednesday, November 26, the weather was cold and gray. Nick's attitude was turning colder by the minute. Anna's parents had decided that they would pick a Christmas tree together and bring it back for a family decorating party.

Nick knew it would be a full day of "follow-the-leader." Jim had clearly decided he was the leader. Barbara could sense the tension and tried to warm Nick up throughout the day.

The tree made it back to the house and the fireplace was roaring. Nick poured himself a Glenlivet scotch on the rocks from a leftover bottle he had purchased for a party months earlier. Anna's father was a beer drinker.

One drink after another, Nick tried to numb his brain into submission. He wrestled over his relationship with Anna and her family. He sat in the chair nearest the fire, warmed his bones and thought about his life: *I hate this.*

Nick would never live up to the expectations of her father. The animosity between them was becoming palpable.

That night, as Anna and Nick laid in separate twin beds, Anna tried to get Nick to understand her father.

Anna positioned her father, "His questions and constant probing are just his way of trying to learn more."

Nick laid still in the dark, thinking how hypocritical it all seemed. Jim was a poor student, attended a lesser college, and had only recently become a more notable high school basketball coach.

Nick offered, "Your dad has worked hard to build a good landscaping business."

He could hear Anna breathing heavily but saying nothing.

Nick went on, "It's natural for him to want more for his daughter."

Nick thought about Jim's business of collecting cash payments as often as possible to avoid taxes so he could live a lifestyle above his means. *What bullshit.*

Anna responded wearily, "Thank you for understanding, I love you."

"I love you too. Good night."

Thanksgiving Day finally arrived. Nick started quietly

drinking at noon. Brad noticed how great Nick was with his son Christopher. He asked Nick about growing up on a family farm. Nick looked at Brad, who was obviously as high as a kite on something.

"Hard work and discipline. Does that sound like fun?"

Brad laughed, "Fuck, no."

The day proceeded in a predictable fashion. The mid-afternoon turkey dinner, football on TV, followed by more turkey plates from leftovers for a late supper. Jim spent most of the day sleeping in his living room chair. Barbara, Anna, and Nick played cards and quietly talked about Brad's problems with drugs. He had recently purchased a Porsche 911 Turbo and Barbara was worried.

The next day, Jim invited Nick to basketball practice. Jim coached the team. Nick threw on his sweats, sneakers and embraced the chance to get some exercise. Coach Jim introduced him to the team as an Illinois All-State high school player from 1981. One of the team leaders asked if Nick could still play. Jim said, "Let's try him out."

For the next two hours, Nick played full court hard press basketball and ran his team as the point guard. Nick took pleasure in the workout, but thoroughly enjoyed schooling his father-in-law.

Jim refused to acknowledge Nick's superior play, but the high schoolers repeatedly praised Nick with high-fives and slaps on the back as their team won the scrimmage.

Nick was going to enjoy dinner. He had thoroughly stuck it to Jim on the court and was ready to travel back to L.A. the next day.

Dinner was approaching, Christopher was playing with his toys in the living room, Jim was in his office, when the phone rang. Barbara picked up the call and went running to Jim's office. Anna looked at Nick, "It's Brad. He must be in trouble."

Barbara came back to the kitchen, visibly shaken, "That was

the bar manager at the Ramada Inn restaurant. Brad is high. He's with men that they don't recognize."

She was now crying. "Your dad is going to go get him."

Anna, hugged her mom, "Nick will go with him."

Nick put his drink down and went to get his jacket.

Jim was in the garage, getting into the car. He looked at Nick in anger, "If he is high, we are taking him to rehab tonight. Are you prepared for that?"

"I understand," Nick firmly replied and jumped into the car.

Jim and Nick walked into the Ramada Inn bar. The manager was a friend of Jim's and immediately explained, "Brad is out of his mind. There were two men with him, and they were upset."

"Where is he now?" Jim interrupted.

"They walked out maybe just five—ten minutes ago."

Nick asserted, "His car is still out front."

Jim and Nick began looking for him. They walked out of the hotel and split up, each walking around opposite sides of the building.

Jim ran into the men first. Brad was beaten, laying on the ground and bloody. Jim confronted the men loudly, "Stop! The police are on the way!"

Nick heard the commotion and ran around the back of the building. Nick peered around the corner of the building. The men were now walking toward Jim.

The only weapon Nick could see was a baseball bat in the hands of one. The second man appeared to have no weapon drawn. Nick shook his head, thinking, *Here we go.*

"Freeze," Nick commanded.

The two men stopped. They turned to look at Nick. Nick walked slowly toward them.

Jim walked toward the men, but Nick commanded him, "Stay put, sir. Back-up is on the way."

Determined to inflict as much damage as possible, the man

with the bat turned back to Brad and began swinging the bat into his bleeding body. The second man pulled a gun from his coat and pointed it at Nick.

Nick's training took over. He walked slowly and began talking, "Clearly you two believe you have good reason to beat the shit out of this guy."

Jim screamed, "Leave him alone. Stop hitting him!"

Nick inched his way closer to the gunman, "That is his father. Cops are on the way, and you now, you have only two choices."

The gunman replied, "Really. Why don't you enlighten me asshole?"

"Well as I see it, you've made your point here and you should leave," Nick said quietly inching his way into the fight, standing now just few feet from the men.

The man with the bat looked at Nick, "Maybe we should beat the shit out of you."

"That's not an option," Nick responded calmly, but with a firm edge.

He turned to the gunman, "Or you can stay. . . . suffering your consequences tonight."

The man lifted his bat to strike Nick, drawing the attention of the gunman. Nick leaped at the gunman, pushing his gun hand away and grabbing his throat on the way to the ground. As the man's head violently slammed the concrete, his gun dropped. In a microsecond Nick was firing the gun at the bat man's legs, toppling him with multiple bullet wounds. Both men were on the ground in pain and Nick was holding the gun on them.

Nick looked peripherally at Jim, paralyzed by episode.

Nick called back to Jim, "Call the police. Now!"

Jim ran back inside the hotel.

Nick, shook his head. "Errand boy."

While holding the gun on two men, Nick checked on Brad,

who had a possible broken jaw. He was beaten badly but would live to see another day.

Nick had mental images of his kills, as he watched the blood pooling onto the concrete. But, empowered, he maintained control of his emotions, and applied his skills gracefully.

It was a long evening of hospitalization and police reports. Jim was shocked at how Nick had managed the armed men, but he was even more appreciative that he had stepped in to save his son from a worse beating. Barbara was crying, thankful and full of remorse that they had not demanded help for Brad sooner.

Anna was proud of Nick, but full of questions.

"Nick, why did, how did, I mean—"

Nick interrupted, "Blind luck honey, they were high as kites and I was showing off in front of your father."

Anna hugged Nick, "Well, I am proud of you."

Nick smiled. Anna leaned back and smiled, "And Dad is still speechless." They laughed and climbed into bed. The dark basement kept Anna from seeing Nick's face. He laid wide awake for hours.

The next morning was quiet and surprisingly calm. By 10:30, it was time to make the drive to Chicago. Anna and Nick needed to make the 5:00 p.m. flight. During their drive to O'Hare International Airport, they talked about Brad's addiction and their family differences. Anna reached over and placed her hand on Nick's leg, "I want you to know that I am proud to be your wife."

This was the moment that Nick thought he was waiting for since college. But it was unfulfilling. He half-heartedly responded, "Thank you."

"What's wrong?" Anna asked with concern.

"I don't know how I am supposed to feel, I mean, I just shot a guy," replied Nick. Of course, this was a little white lie compared to the killing in the alley. More lies upon lies.

Anna quietly responded, "Thank God you did Nick. No telling how that could have ended. And we don't really know who those guys were or what they wanted. My brother must be in bed with some serious people for this kind of thing to happen. It is not the movies".

"Well—" Nick began to reply but Anna cut him off.

"I don't want to talk about it anymore. As far as I am concerned, you saved my brother's life. So, thank you."

They slept on the flight and made it home without talking much at all. Anna and Nick went to bed that night, understanding there were problems in their marriage, but neither of them wanting to open the discussion yet.

Maybe it was a phase they need to grow through. Maybe it was a reaction from the family visits and threatening situation with Anna's brother.

Maybe they didn't trust each other to be open and honest. Maybe they were afraid to walk down the path they were on, knowing where it would lead.

Chapter 16
Prep Time

Monday, December 1, 1986

NICK WAS called to meet Vincent for lunch. Nick pulled up to the Ivy at the Shore in Santa Monica. He walked in at 11:30 a.m. sharp. Vincent was seated at a corner table in their front porch section looking at the ocean shore and boardwalk.

"Sit down and order a drink," Vincent instructed as Nick approached.

"Well, hello to you, too," replied Nick.

The waiter appeared.

"Bombay martini, very dry, with two olives," ordered Nick.

Turning to Vincent, he asked, "Where are we now?"

The situation in Bogotá was unstable at best. Congressional approval was in place for the monies to be moved through USAID to the Rural Economic Funds in December—it needed to happen before December 31 so they would not be required to obtain new approval.

Guillermo Cano was now identified as a target. He had knowledge—rather, "alleged" knowledge—of USAID involvement in laundering monies for the Medellín Cartel. But technically, Vincent and Nick were laundering monies through the

Cartels to fund the Contras' fight against the Sandinistas in Nicaragua.

To make matters worse, Cano was secretly supporting the FARC and UP Communist underground through his propagandized newspaper coverage. That trail led back to President Ortega in Nicaragua and Soviets' desire to build out their presence in Central and Latin America.

"We have to fix this and change the narrative," said Vincent. "The name 'Sean Smith, USAID' has been listed as a potential information source or be further investigated."

Nick suddenly felt ill.

Vincent went on. "We will take care of this, and then you will end it. And we will not include Langley, understood?"

Nick nodded his understanding and took a drink of his martini.

"We will call it 'Operation: Narrative,'" Vincent continued. "You understand that we need to cleanse or remove everything that can be linked to you. Jon has an insider, but you will need to ensure the job is complete. Verify who Cano works with and who knows about this research. It's your career, hell it's your life."

"Do we have a timeline and logistics?" Nick asked.

Vincent explained that Cano would not be back at work until December 15; his typical workweek included working late into the evening on Wednesdays. Therefore, the plan would evolve around that week.

First, Jon's insider, who had been working closely with Cano on the story, would cleanse the office of all documents and notes. Second, Jon would ensure that Cano was grabbed for questioning Wednesday evening when leaving *El Espectador* offices. Lastly, once satisfied, Nick would terminate Cano. Jon's insider would report on the shooting, and Cano would be reported DOA at the hospital.

The USAID Rural Economic Funds would launder monies as planned, and Nick would escort the funds to Panama. This would all be completed by the nineteenth of December.

Vincent flatly said, "We report back to Mexico City for a debriefing on Saturday, December 20."

Nick was processing the plan in his own mind.

"Are we clear?" asked Vincent.

"Yes, sir."

Vincent ordered another round of drinks. "Ready for lunch?"

"Yes, let's order food," said Nick.

There was only silence as they pondered the menu for a few minutes. Vincent gave Nick time to process the operation and the magnitude of the operation.

"You understand this kill will not be in self-defense; it will be an assassination."

Nick looked at Vincent. "It's for a greater cause."

Vincent took a drink of his martini. "That's right. That's exactly right."

Their food came, and they talked about Anna and Richard for a while. Vincent commented that Richard would be back in L.A. for the week of New Year's Eve. They would rent a bungalow at the Beverly Hills Hotel and would expect to have a boy's night out together. Nick assured Vincent that he would make that happen.

Nick planted the seed of distrust in Anna, "I do not believe I can trust Anna with my career."

"Well, we will have to figure out a remedy for that," Vincent replied without even looking up from his plate.

When they finished lunch, Vincent said, "Walk me to my car. I have reading material for you."

They paid their tab and walked to the car. He reached inside and pulled out his briefcase. He quickly toggled the combination to unlock it, reached inside, pulled out an envelope, and handed it to Nick. It was filled with the intelligence reports for Bogotá, Panama, and Nicaragua.

"Over the next few days, you need to absorb the details in these reports and assess—then reassess—and plan to spend the entire day with me next Monday at a secure location to be provided later. Understood?"

"Yes. I understand." They shook hands, and hugged goodbye.

The luncheon had taken more than three hours, and it was already 3:00 p.m. Nick replayed the discussion in his head during the drive home. He felt as though he was on the outside of his body looking in, the way his father would look at him. *Who was he turning into? Could he complete Operation: Narrative? Or, worse yet, what would happen if he did not complete it?*

He was driving the speed limit, but it felt as though he was suspended in time. He had scored well in the psychological training exercises for just such moments. He was trying to utilize the compartmentalization tools to better manage his emotions before arriving home. It was going to be a long and trying week with no one around, except Anna. She already accused him of not paying enough attention to her and their marriage.

Focus on what you can control, Nick told himself as he pulled into his garage.

Operation: Narrative Is a GO

Tuesday, December 2, 1986

NICK OPENED the intelligence package after sending Anna off to work. There were details surrounding the successes of Guillermo Cano throughout the initial reports. His published bio stated that he was born in Medellín on August 12, 1925. He started to write for *El Espectador* as a reporter on bullfights, politics, sport, and culture. He led the press agency's management for 37 years. For his leadership and vision, he had most recently received several acknowledgments, including the National Journalism Award of the Bogotá Circle of Journalists on February 10, 1986, in honor of his column *"Libreta de Apuntes"* (Notebook) that he published in his Sunday columns.

Cano and *El Espectador* had officially become targets of the Cartel bosses on August 25, 1983, when the newspaper's front page had the sensational headline: "Pablo Escobar Incarcerated for Narcotics." Cano's column also put his life at risk. In it, he routinely reiterated the idea that drug trafficking was a factor in the social corruption that reached sectors of politics, discouraged honest businesspeople, and canceled out any good examples set for youth. Pablo Escobar hated him.

Nick studied intelligence reports by day but spent evenings making dinners and relaxing with Anna. They had fallen into a pattern that enabled them to sustain their friendship, but it was not a whole marriage or loving relationship. Their weekend plans included dinners out and activities like movies or live music venues. They were beginning to behave like the partnership they talked about in college.

Nick was consumed with Operation: Narrative; it took all his energy. At the same time, Anna seemed more satisfied and happier with her focus on work and career advancement.

Monday, December 8, Vincent called to instruct Nick about the meetings for the week. On Tuesday and Wednesday, they would meet at a secure room at One Wilshire to determine exact money movements, procedures, and alternate plans for issues that might occur during the operation. It would be a strategic session to flush out all probabilities of "what could go wrong."

On Monday evening, Nick laid his lies for Anna. He told her of his plans for the rest of December, explaining that he would have to attend Thunderbird for semester exams December 14 through the 20, and then return home on Sunday the 21.

Anna accepted the lie as fact without any resistance and asked Nick if he had been thinking about Christmas gift ideas. She had already purchased tickets to go back to Illinois for the holidays. Nick thought, *Hopefully, not a repeat of the Thanksgiving week trip.*

He replied, "Gifts. Hmmm. I will give you a list if you give me one."

Anna smiled. "Sure! You will have mine by tomorrow."

On Tuesday and Wednesday, December 9 and 10, Nick had half-day sessions to review intel reports and walk through the routes, timing, and maps for Operation: Narrative. He and

Vincent then reviewed the details for the USAID Rural Economic Fund payments and drops to the safe house for transfer to Panama. By 2:30 p.m. on Wednesday, Vincent declared him, "ready to roll."

Vincent encouraged Nick, "Let's have a drink to relax."

They walked a couple of blocks to Seven Bar, sat down, and ordered drinks. Vincent watched and measured Nick's mental preparedness while, in turn, Nick took note of Vincent's pointed questions.

At 4:00 p.m., Nick declared cocktail hour complete; he had promised to be home for dinner on time.

Vincent said, "It's a nice routine you have now with Anna, yes?"

Nick did not look at Vincent but acknowledged it to be true. Then he asked, "Will you be in Bogotá next week?"

Vincent sighed and took a deep breath. "You know I won't answer that. But I will tell you that I am always with you." Nick accepted the answer per protocol.

Nick made it home in time to have dinner with Anna; he had picked up their favorite Mandarin take-out food as a surprise. Anna walked in shortly after he got home.

"Perfect!" she exclaimed. "You read my mind."

They were both famished, so they sat down to an early dinner. Anna suggested a shopping trip for Saturday to Rodeo Drive in Beverly Hills.

"Christmas time on Rodeo Drive, sounds fun," said Nick. He was pleased that they had planned something enjoyable on the day before his flight to Bogotá.

On Saturday, during breakfast, Anna handed Nick her entire gift list. They spent the late morning shopping Rodeo Drive and had a light lunch at Mr. Chow's. Nick enjoyed the Christmas spirit in the air, people-watching and feeling normal. That evening, He surprised Anna with a reservation to dine at Spago on the Sunset Strip in West Hollywood. She was the happiest he had seen her since their wedding day.

Nick knew that Anna would never understand the world he had allowed himself to enter with Vincent and the Agency. Watching her enjoy the day of shopping and dining out, he realized that he might never be able to offer her the life she truly desired. It was the beginning of the end.

On Sunday morning, after coffee, Nick kissed Anna goodbye and headed to the airport. She thought he was headed to Arizona for school and finals week, but he was already mentally in Sean's skin, and his mind was in operational mode as he approached LAX for the flight to Bogotá. He rested on the flight and arrived at the apartment around 4:30 p.m. Shedding his Nick persona, he was ready for the operation.

That night, he checked the safe locker in the apartment for weaponry and protective gear and then looked in the fridge to take inventory for meals throughout the week. He pulled maps out to reorient himself with the mission sites: *El Espectador;* the abandoned building exactly five blocks from the bookstore front and safe house; and the private airstrip in El Dorado. Feeling fully prepared and ready, he poured himself a stiff Glenlivet rocks and laid down to relax, drifting to sleep while he watched television.

On Monday morning, December 15, there was a knock on the door at 10:00 a.m.

It was Jon. "I've arranged a private meet and greet with our insider at *El Espectador,* Rodolfo Pérez, tonight."

"Excellent," said Sean.

They sat down to prioritize their most critical questions about the intelligence they needed for the assassination plan. They also created another list of possible related topics that Rodolfo would need to search for when cleansing all notes and materials of Guillermo Cano. The meeting was set for drinks at 8:30 p.m. at Tomate, a local bar, near Rodolfo's neighborhood.

Sean would meet with Rodolfo alone, and Jon would remain in the shadows for reinforcement as needed. Sean was pleased that the insider appeared to maintain a serious commitment to assist with the operational narrative.

Sean walked into Tomate at 8:30 p.m. and noticed Rodolfo at the bar. Sean took note of two men at a table in the corner and three couples in the booths along the wall. The bar was small. Sean sat at the end of the bar and awaited an all-clear signal. Sean ordered, and by the time he was served his first drink, the two men at the corner table were leaving. At that moment, Rodolfo walked over to Sean and introduced himself as if he were seeing someone he recognized. They agreed to sit at the now-vacant corner table.

"What do you want?" Sean asked Rodolfo.

Rodolfo explained that he had been threatened in the past, and he wanted out of Bogotá. For the next 20 minutes, Rodolfo reassured Sean of his access and close working relationship with Guillermo Cano. They agreed on which key topics and associated files and notes were to be collected or destroyed Wednesday night. Sean made it clear that they would assist with getting Rodolfo and his family moved to the United States immediately, but if there was ever a double-cross, Rodolfo would be jailed for life, and his family deported back to Colombia.

They agreed on all counts, and Sean left for the apartment.

On Tuesday morning, Sean went for a run at dawn, armed and ready for anything. His nerves were completely honed into a state of battle. Jon would stop in around lunchtime for a walk-through. The schedule for Wednesday appeared to be solid, no anticipated changes. He showered and prepared sandwiches and iced tea for lunch.

Jon showed up at 11:40 a.m. Sean pulled out the sandwich meat, cheese, toppings, and bread. They both made plates and sat at the dining table to run the plan and discuss any last-minute steps or possible variables. They outlined their positions and confirmed signals that would be given by Rodolfo. Jon will drive by sicario style on a motorcycle and open fire. The shots will derail the automobile and they will then detain Cano. Sean would enter the vehicle to question Cano and complete the assassination. They both agreed that they were ready. Jon left, and Sean was completely prepared mentally and spiritually.

In fact, Sean decided to take a nap.

When he woke, it was almost 5:00 p.m., and a message had been left for him under the apartment door. Sean opened the envelope and felt the bottom right-hand corner for Vincent's secret embossment. It was there. The message simply read, *Operation: Narrative is a go. I am with you.* Sean smiled, then burned it immediately and decided to make himself another sandwich for dinner. To stay focused, he left Anna a voicemail to avoid any discussions, and laid in bed to stay rested.

Sean slept soundly and woke up fresh at 6:15 a.m. on Wednesday, December 17. He looked in the mirror as he brushed his teeth and thought, *Today is the day, I pull the trigger for the greater cause.* He was ready. He could feel the blood pumping through his body, passing the fear and engaging the energy he knew he would need to perform and survive. He put his running clothes on, strapped on his gun holster, and affixed his ankle knife. His run was fast as he only went half the distance of his usual course.

Operation: Narrative was simple in design, but Jon had told Sean that the simple plans often find the most interesting ways to get fucked up. All day, Sean played scenario after scenario in his mind. Following his training for assassinations, he ate only small amounts of simple food. Nibbling on peanut butter and toasted English muffins throughout the day, he reread the intelligence reports on Cano's typical movements. He visualized Cano in the most vulnerable positions to ensure he'd be able to question him before terminating his life.

At 5:00 p.m., Sean dressed for the operation in his military boots, stashing knuckle knives, a belt with four spare magazines for his Walther PPK, and a vial of VX. VX was the most dangerous known chemical nerve agent. Just 0.4 milligrams of the substance were enough to kill an adult. He wore dark gray parachute pants, matching gray shirt, and a custom-made, soft leather Italian jacket. The jacket fell slightly longer than typical waist-length and was made with full sleeves and custom holsters for two Walther PPKs. There were three front buttons that barely held the coat together for easy access. Sean slipped it on, thinking that only Vincent would have such extravagant taste in operative attire. He checked the weapons and loaded both guns with special armor-piercing ammunition that could pierce most automobile doors and even bulletproof vests. They were nicknamed "cop killers" back in the States.

By 5:45 p.m., Sean and Jon were in place. Sean was seated at the café on the corner with a view of the parking lot exit that Cano would have to use upon leaving work. Jon was on watch at the opposite end of the street. While reading the morning edition of *El Espectador*, Sean was intrigued by Guillermo Cano's editorial column. Near the end of the piece, it read: *"El Espectador's story is one of never having backed down to any threat and of never having interrupted its struggle for the responsible freedom of press and its right to exercise it."* Sean thought to himself, *Well you have not felt the strike of our threat.*

SEAN NOTICED Rodolfo leaving the building at 6:53 p.m.—the reporter was to circle the building as a lookout—Sean took several deep breaths to settle his nerves and heart rate. He ordered one more café con leche and laid some money down for the tab. As the time drew close, Rodolfo came walking around the opposite corner of the building, removed his hat, and scratched his head vigorously. Jon and Sean understood the meaning of the signal: it was an all-clear signal, and the operation was a go.

As he often did after work, Rodolfo Pérez wandered into Bar Ama across the street, where he would wait for the kill.

All eyes watching, it was now 7:12 p.m. Cano's Subaru truck stopped at the parking lot exit. As Cano pulled the truck onto the street in Sean's direction, Jon, riding a motorcycle and dressed in a flashy shirt and black helmet, opened fire right into the car. He shot through the driver's side doors with an AK-47, Cartel-style, and had clearly hit Cano, who had lost control of the car and driven right into a street post not more than 50 feet from Sean.

Out of the blue, there were shots coming from behind Jon. It was the goddamn security guards at *El Espectador*. Jon went down. Sean stood, measuring Cano's truck wrapped against the street post and Jon's situation. Jon opened fire at the security guards, and they retreated for cover. As Jon climbed onto his bike, firing crazy at the guards, he sped away. Sean ran to the car and, in his peripheral vision, saw Rodolfo recognize the security guards and then run into the street, waving for them to call for an ambulance. Sean took advantage of the diversion and climbed into the car, where he found Guillermo Cano with multiple bullet wounds to his legs and midsection, but still conscious.

Cano opened his eyes and looked at Sean, blurting out, *"Quien eres tu?"* (Who are you?)

"Eso no es importante!" answered Sean. (That's not important!) Then he leaned over Cano and looked deep into his eyes.

"Answer this to live."

Cano looked desperately back into Sean's eyes with hope.

"Who else knows about your story to expose USAID's support in fighting the Communist movements?" Sean waited for only a moment and then placed his gun into Cano's neck and asked for a final time. "Who else knows!"

"No one. No one!"

Rodolfo was standing beside the car as lookout. Satisfied with Cano's answer, Sean leaned back, pulled the trigger, and shot Cano close range in the chest. He pulled Cano to the passenger side, looked at Rodolfo, and instructed him to drive Cano to the hospital.

Sean walked away as Rodolfo started the wrecked Subaru truck and sped away. Sean's car and driver were less than a block away. He hoped to see Jon at the rendezvous hangar at El Dorado in under 30 minutes. The reporter, Rodolfo Pérez, took the 61-year-old journalist to the Caja de Previsión Clinic, where he was declared dead.

Sean arrived at the El Dorado private plane hangar just 20 minutes after his assassination of Cano. He waited with the pilot for another 20 minutes for Jon.

Sean instructed the pilot, "Jon must be tending to his wounds. Let's go."

"Yes, sir," replied the pilot.

Landing in Mexico City, Sean was instructed to not contact anyone. He couldn't get Cano's face out of his head. He had seen pictures of Cano, but when he was face to face, he saw the similarities to his father's face and expressions.

The shot to Cano's heart was fatal and nearly instant, thought Sean. But he could feel Cano's body squirm when he pulled him to the passenger side. *Should I have shot him in the head?* Sean wondered.

He laid down in his bed, haunted by both Cano's face and his father's face grimacing at him. Throughout the night, Sean found himself looking into the bathroom mirror, asking God if he did the right thing.

Was it for the greater good? Please God, help me understand.

Chapter 18

A New Narrative Begins

Thursday, December 18, 1986

THE STORY IN *El Espectador* described the killing as:

ASSASSINATION OF EL ESPECTADOR
EDITOR-IN-CHIEF GUILLERMO CANO

Wounded by four gunshots, Mr. Cano lost control of the vehicle and crashed into a post. The newspaper's security guards, alarmed by the gunshots, opened fire against the attacker and wounded one of them. A reporter who also witnessed the attack, named Rodolfo Pérez, took the 61-year-old journalist to the Caja de Previsión Clinic, where he passed away before 8:00 p.m.

VINCENT HAD been in the basement of the U.S. Embassy in Mexico City since dawn, preparing for the post-kill briefing on Guillermo Cano. The newspapers in Mexico City were covering the story, and all had taken the same lead that Pérez had written and submitted as his last story in Colombia.

Sean walked into the room promptly at 8:54 a.m. "Any word from Jon?" he asked.

Vincent replied, "He's alive. He took a bullet in his butt."

"Any permanent damage?"

"None that we know of, yet," offered Vincent.

No sooner had he said the words, Jon hobbled into the room.

"Well, Jon. You made it." said Vincent, smiling.

Sean shook Jon's hand, "That was fine work."

Jon appreciated the sentiment, "We got our man."

For the next two hours, they taped their briefing, outlining the purpose for the kill, the plan, and the execution. During the briefing, Jon and Sean learned that Rodolfo Pérez had left the hospital, submitted his story around 9:15 p.m., and was on a private flight with his family to an undisclosed city in the U.S. by 10:40 p.m. Awaiting him was documentation for a new identity and a job.

The kill was successful. Sean felt satisfied that the operation was completed, but as if a part of his soul left with Cano as he bled out in his truck. The assassination was affecting his recovery time, creating a cloud over his thought process.

It was lunchtime. Jon left the Embassy to rest and recover. Vincent and Sean went to the Four Seasons Garden Café to walk through the Economic Development Funding Plan.

Vincent leaned in, looking Sean over, "What's up?"

"Cano's face is haunting me. I see my father's face in his," Sean confessed.

Vincent leaned back, folded his arms, "Do we need to arrange for a counseling session?"

Sean interrupted, "No, no, of course not."

"Do you have any questions?"

Sean paused, then answered thoughtfully, "No questions."

Vincent, not looking completely convinced, nodded affirmatively, "Okay."

In approximately 24 hours, there would be three Cartel drop point meetings to sign off and secure the cash for transport to

Panama. A total of $11.8 million was approved by Congress, and after the laundering split and delivery fees, there would be $10 million for the purchase of weapons, ammunition, and supplies for the Contras. Sean was ready.

Vincent was unrelenting, "Now that we have taken the action to clear up the narrative around USAID and our rural economic development cover, we need to go back to our plan for hiding in plain sight." Sean nodded in agreement. Vincent continued. "There will be a keen interest in Leal's movements from this point on."

"I don't know how much longer Leal will be of use to our intelligence gathering," Sean remarked.

A slight grin appeared on Vincent's face. "Correct."

There was going to be more work in Bogotá. Vincent outlined the details for the original rodeo event that would be scrapped and detailed a more focused approach to the event. Sean needed Gabriella.

Vincent glanced at him. "You're thinking of Gabriella, aren't you?"

Sean replied, "Yes. Someone will have to coordinate the event, PR, work with Fabio, and—"

"And cover your back." Vincent broke in. "She could be essential to your safety."

This was good news for Sean. He missed Gabriella.

"A spring rodeo would be best, maybe April." Sean suggested.

"We'll see," replied Vincent, "Will you be able to move past Cano's assassination?"

With that simple question, Sean realized just how alone he felt inside. He had to search for words and sort through his feelings. Vincent asked a simple, yet achingly personal question, "Will you be able to move past Cano's assassination?"

He looked at Vincent. "I don't know how I am supposed to feel."

Vincent leaned toward Sean, and in a soft voice said, "Richard wants you to know that when he completed his first assassination, he became distraught with overwhelming sadness."

Sean leaned in, too. "And this knowledge will help me how?"

Vincent sat back in his chair. "It won't. That is exactly what Richard wants you to know. Feeling sad about the choices outside your control in this line of work will never help."

Sean sat back in his chair. "That puts it into a perspective I can manage."

Vincent smiled, "I thought it might."

Sean left for the private airstrip. Vincent went back to the Embassy. Jon was resting in the Mexico City apartment on the Square near the government building and the hospital team was tending to his wound care.

Another big day awaited Sean. He called Anna from the Benito Juárez International Airport while his pilot was en route. She was happy to hear his voice and could not wait to share her good news. Her project team won a major contract with McDonnell Douglas, St. Louis. She would be traveling to and from St. Louis to work on communication systems in test production.

"That's wonderful news," Sean said.

Anna declared, "It is wonderful. I can see my folks from time to time." Then she asked completely out of the blue, "What's new down in Bogotá?"

Sean replied, "It appears they still want to do a rodeo event in the spring . . ."

Anna responded, "Great! We both have major projects to keep us busy."

Sean felt the distance between them. He knew something was wrong, but he had no time to worry about it.

Chapter 19
Moving Money for Weapons

SEAN LANDED back in Bogotá, where his car was waiting for him. His regular driver peered at him in the rear-view mirror. When he arrived back at the apartment, he was restless and couldn't stop thinking of the money collections scheduled for noon, 1:15, and 2:30, the next day.

He sat on the couch with nothing but his thoughts about Guillermo Cano. Cano had a fatherly look about him, Sean recalled, and was about the same age as his own father. He had given the man an ounce of hope. . . . just to retrieve an honest answer to a single question. Then, with no hesitation, he killed him. Sean sat motionless, consumed with an overwhelming feeling that he had turned into a killer.

"NO!" he cried. Then he pushed those feelings into a box marked NO CHOICE, reminding himself, *It was him or me.*

His mind began to focus on the next task at hand. He checked the safe for weapons, took a shower, and went to bed.

Friday, December 19, 1986
Money Day

SEAN WAS awake by 5:40 a.m. He made a pot of coffee, slipped on his running shoes, holstered his gun, and pulled on his sweat-shirt. It was daybreak and quiet on the running paths. He ran through the parks and across the campus of the University of Bogotá. Managing a healthy, detoxifying sweat, he turned around to head back. He had run nearly four miles further than his usual workout, and it felt good.

Back at the apartment dressed and ready, he noticed an envelope inside the door. He picked it up and opened it, immediately feeling the bottom right-hand corner for the small emboss-ment of Vincent's mark. It was there. The message read: "Funds landed. All meetings confirmed. Coverage in place." Sean took a deep breath and glanced at the clock, 10:23 a.m. He figured that the car would be there in about 45 minutes to pick him up. He went to the closet, pulled out the leather jacket he had been wearing since the killing of Cano and noticed that he had missed some blood splatter on the inside of the left sleeve. He took the jacket to the kitchen, ran some water, and used a little soap on a dishrag to wash the blood away. He threw the dishrag in the trash with vigor.

In the car, Sean was watchful of the movements around him as he was driven to the abandoned building for the collection meetings. The city seemed extremely quiet. He told the driver to drop him approximately three blocks from the selected building, an old manufacturing warehouse with an open floor plan on the main floor with offices on the second floor. He walked the building perimeter and noticed the back entrances had all been boarded up, leaving the front door as the only entry and exit. He walked up to the second floor and found a table with three chairs, several bottles of water, receipts for money, and agreement letters for each fund.

He would collect the funds in large travel bags. There was a secure closet on the second floor, and he would place the cash bags in the closet until the team arrived to transport the money to the safe house.

The noon meeting with the Banco Farm Fund went smoothly, and the 1:15 p.m. meeting with Cali Rural Fund went down without a hitch. At 2:35 p.m., there was still no sign of the Rural Medellín Fund. Sean waited patiently, but he knew that Jon and the transport team would be arriving promptly at 3:15 p.m.

This is not good, Sean thought to himself.

At 2:53 p.m., Sean heard heavy footsteps entering the building. As the footsteps marched up the stairwell, Sean drew his Walther PPK and sat still behind the metal table, playing out the possible threat scenarios in his mind. As the footsteps reached the top, he heard a winded, but familiar voice.

"Sean, *soy Fabio!*" (It's Fabio!)

Sean peered at the doorway and saw Fabio peeking around the doorframe, smiling.

"*Siento mucho llegar tarde,*" (I'm very sorry I am late) proclaimed Fabio. He walked in, and Sean holstered his weapon.

"*Que paso?*" (What happened?) asked Sean.

Fabio set the moneybags down, quietly informing Sean that the banker had an accident. Sean knew better than to ask. He provided the forms to Fabio and stood up to greet him with a warm handshake and professional hug.

Fabio looked at Sean. "I will sign as the fund manager."

Sean nodded approval. Fabio signed and took the receipt from Sean.

Sean whispered to Fabio, "*Vete ahora.*" (Go now.)

Fabio left immediately.

Sean pulled all six bags to the top of the stairwell, and, right on cue, he heard a truck pull up outside. He stepped away and drew his weapon.

Then he heard Jon's voice laughing, "Don't shoot me!"

Sean peered down at Jon and his helpers, "Right on time."

They loaded the bags into the SUV and drove swiftly to the safe house through the back alley. The gate opened for them, and they pulled in and switched vehicles. There would be three SUVs in the caravan to the private hangar at the Medellín airstrip. The drive was fast and direct. Military escorts were both comforting and nerve-wracking at the same time. He felt like a target in the caravan, but he also felt well-protected.

The driver said, "We will arrive at the hangar in 12 minutes, sir."

Sean nodded affirmatively.

They drove into the hangar, and the doors closed behind the last SUV. The helpers jumped out and transferred the bags onto the plane. The flight would transport the pilot, Jon, and Sean. The hangar doors opened, and the pilot taxied the plane out and signaled to the small tower that they were ready for takeoff. Within three minutes, they were airborne and on their way to Panama, Hangar 63—the "Fun Zone."

Jon closed his eyes for a 20-minute rest. Sean could see he was still in pain from the bullet that sliced his butt just 48 hours earlier. The plane touched down on Noriega's private airstrip and quickly pulled off the runway. Sean noticed a private aircraft being fueled, and the paramilitary traffic seemed heavier than the last trip. As the plane approached Hangar 63, the wide doors of the hangar opened, and field men were awaiting their arrival. They quickly and efficiently closed the doors behind them.

The pilot looked back at Jon and Sean. "We've got company," he said.

Jon pulled the lever and opened the plane door. Six Panamanian militia greeted them with automatic weapons drawn and aimed directly at them.

Jon whispered to Sean, "Stay cool."

They walked down the steps of the King Air. Out from behind the guns, a familiar face appeared.

"Darryn Morales," said Sean calmly. They approached each other, shook hands and shared a warm, professional hug. Morales ordered his men to stand down. They walked over to the cargo door, and Jon pulled out the bag earmarked for Noriega.

"*Toma.*" (Here you go.)

Morales took the bag and disappeared into the hangar office. Sean signaled the crew to check the money for the trade. The other plane was already loaded with weapons, ammunition, and supplies. Morales stepped out of the office and saluted Sean. Jon shook his head in disgust, and Sean waved back as the paramilitary militiamen exited the building.

Jon walked past Sean. "What an asshole."

Sean looked back at Jon, rolling his eyes. "Just stay cool."

They laughed. The trade was complete.

They reboarded their plane, and the pilot looked back and said, "Mexico City."

As the plane pulled out of the hangar and onto the runway, three tactical military trucks blocked the plane, bringing it to a stop. Jon looked out the window and saw ten or more heavily armed soldiers surrounding the plane.

"Those are not Noriega's military," Sean said.

The soldiers pounded on the door.

"*Abre o disparamos!*" (Open up, or we will shoot!)

Jon pulled the lever to unlatch the door, and the stairs fell out. Soldiers stood at the steps.

"*Sal ahora!*" (Get out now!)

Jon, the pilot, and Sean deplaned. Two soldiers climbed in and inspected the empty plane. A leader stepped forward and began to ask questions.

"Vas a hacer en este aeropuerto?" (What are you doing at this airport?)

Jon answered, *"Hemos dejado a un amigo en el Hangar 63, para Morales."* (We dropped a friend at Hangar 63, for Morales.)

The soldiers spoke among themselves. The leader walked up to Sean and peered at him closely. Then he looked at Jon, *"Vete de aqui echando ostias."* (Get the fuck out of here.)

The three of them climbed back onto the plane. The pilot pulled the plane onto the runway as the military trucks allowed them through. Within just a few minutes, they were airborne.

What bullshit, Sean thought. *Noriega was allowing our trade to occur at the same time that Ortega was transporting through the same goddamn airfield to Nicaragua.*

Sean looked at Jon, "That militia squad was Nicaraguan."

The situation was more dangerous than it had appeared. Sean didn't like being identified by anyone from Nicaragua, especially with a gun drawn.

The plane touched down in Mexico City, and the pilot looked back at Sean, "Thank God," he said.

Jon and Sean jumped into their car and met Vincent at Winston Churchill's for drinks and dinner.

VINCENT LISTENED intensely as Jon described the militia squadron in grave detail including the attitude of the leader. Sean waited for a reaction from Vincent.

"Good work getting out of there clean."

Sean reacted. "Had they stopped us inside Hangar 63, there would be hell to pay—"

Vincent interrupted him. "—but they didn't. Besides, even the Nicaraguans don't want to fuck with Hangar 63."

Sean thought, *Well great, now they know I'm CIA.*

Vincent could see Sean mind-fucking himself. "Stop thinking about that for a moment. Let us toast to the freedom fighters and our successful day."

Sean realized he was famished; he had barely eaten all day. He decided that low protein was part of his hyper nerves. The three men devoured their dinner. Afterward, Sean and Jon got dropped at the Marriott downtown. They both needed to decompress alone.

"See you both at 9:00 a.m. sharp," said Vincent. They waved good night.

On Saturday, at 8:54 a.m., Sean walked through security at the U.S. Embassy in Mexico City and then down to the secure basement. Vincent sat at the head of the table, Jon was getting his coffee, the pilot looked even more nervous than usual, and an Agency recorder was present. Sean walked over.

"Good morning, everyone." Everyone mumbled, "good morning" back. Sean felt a bit out of the loop. Vincent began the meeting by stating they would work backward for the briefing. "Let's hear from the pilot."

The pilot, Steve Anderson, started as if he'd been rehearsing all morning.

"Just before we took off from Panama, there were three, heavily armed military trucks alongside dozens of militia troops blocking us from the runway." He paused and watched Vincent for a signal.

Vincent looked up. "Did you notice any other foreign aircraft in the vicinity?"

Steve began a long reply. He rambled on and on about several prior flights to the airstrip and militia that appeared to be funded by the Soviet Union. The secret airstrip was being leveraged for both sides.

Sean began to piece together the magnitude of the chance

meeting on the airstrip. The Agency had worked feverishly behind the Iron Curtain and throughout Euro-Asia, alongside President Reagan and his executive branch, to make Mikhail Gorbachev the last Soviet premier.

Now more aware of the global impact, Sean realized *We could empower Gorbachev and make him universally popular.* It was ultimately the Agency's goal to end the old Communist rule and provide an acceptable landscape that would embrace a more modern relationship with the United States.

Sean took a breath and realized that Vincent was staring at him.

"Now you know what we are doing is helping the world by advancing improved relations while beating down old guard Soviet Union footholds. It's real," Vincent said. He turned to focus on Steve. "Thank you for your observation and intelligence. Now continue with your version of the drop and the pickup."

After Jon and Sean recounted their versions and observations of the mission, Vincent concluded with a summary of the normal risk factors, variances from the operational plan, and the success of the operation to date.

Jon left for his trip home, and Vincent signaled Sean to wait. He leaned in as everyone else was leaving, whispering, "Be at the Four Seasons in 15 minutes." Sean nodded and left the secure basement room.

Fifteen minutes later, they were at the outside garden patio of the Four Seasons.

"Sean, you have been identified as a USAID Director, but, unfortunately, a potential spy by the Soviet Union."

Sean was not entirely certain where this intel was going. Vincent went on to explain that Noriega and his entire organization were not trustworthy and there was infighting happening within the White House and Executive Branch about what to do with him.

"That means that Darryn Morales, Noriega's top aide, is most likely playing all sides against each other for more money," said Vincent.

Leaning back in his chair, Vincent continued, "I will ask around the State Department about Morales, maybe we can turn the tables on him, too."

"Yes." Sean looked into Vincent's eyes. "What are we going to do about my cover?"

Vincent tried to reassure Sean, "We will strategize, place you where its most effective with enough cover and firepower to squash any plan. So, don't worry about it for now."

Sean did not look convinced.

Vincent laughed to lighten the moment, "You're coming to our weekend long New Year's party in Beverly Hills. Richard and I are hosting. You will lose the wife for a couple of those nights, right?"

Sean finished his coffee. "Of course. But right now, I need to go to the airport and get home to Anna, or it will be more difficult to get away later."

The two of them stood and gave each other a quick hug goodbye.

"Merry Christmas, my friend," said Vincent. Sean echoed the sentiment.

Sean walked toward the gate leading out of the garden patio and turned toward Vincent, "See you in Beverly Hills."

"See YOU in Beverly Hills." Vincent smiled.

As Sean boarded his flight back home, he felt secure in his mission. There was a plan to protect and expand the greater good. On his better days, he thought he was becoming an integral part of something impactful that would make the world a safer place. On his bad days, he was not so sure.

Chapter 20

Christmas Time 1986

NICK ARRIVED home a little late for dinner Saturday, after a long week. Anna was annoyed. Anna talked about the holiday schedule, and Nick made the mistake of saying, "It feels like we are spending our entire holiday with your family—"

Anna broke in. "Don't give me a hard time for wanting to see my parents."

"I just want to get on with our own lives. . . ." Nick felt himself rambling.

Anna raised her voice, "We don't have a life! You travel all the time! I am beginning to think you have someone else in Bogotá."

"Why would you say that?" Nick asked calmly, staring into her eyes.

Anna softly said, "You don't really love me."

Nick stood up, defused the situation, "Go upstairs, get comfortable, I will clear the table and we can spend the evening in bed, reconnecting."

Nick hugged her from behind and could feel her shaking, and he kissed her cheek, "I will kiss those tears away. You are my love."

"Okay," Anna leaned into his embrace.

They spent the evening in bed, talking about Anna's career and her dreams for advancement. Nick listened and lied about the pressures of his internship and uncertainty of his career choice. They made love, but Nick could only think of his own complicated situation. The distance between them was now even greater.

Vincent was demanding agency protocol be met. But Nick, convinced he could not trust Anna to hold his status secret, could not bring himself to follow protocol disclosures.

Anna slept soundly. Nick was awake most of the night and got up at dawn to take a run.

After running five miles at dawn, Nick had a plan.

He told himself, *Just get through the holiday and then end the marriage.*

Nick walked into the kitchen to make coffee. Anna surprised him, "I made coffee already."

"Thank you. You are up early," Nick said while pouring himself a cup.

Anna suggested, "I thought we could spend the day together, maybe go up to Beverly Hills, have lunch and finish some shopping?"

"I love people watching. Let's do it." Nick said enthusiastically with a smile.

Sunday became a shopping day on Rodeo Drive, and a late lunch at Barney's.

Driving home, Anna was happy, "That was a fun day. Thank you for shopping for so long, you must really love me."

Nick replied, "I do really love you." They laughed.

Inside, Nick had waves of guilt. He knew it was over. He also knew she had no idea.

It was a quiet night; Monday was a workday for Anna, and they were planning to fly to Illinois on Tuesday morning. They would stop by the farm and then go to Anna's parents' house for Christmas day and through the weekend.

Anna wouldn't stop talking about the plans her parents had put in place for Christmas. Nick sensed a big request looming. He poured himself a scotch-rocks and interrupted.

"So, what is the question?" Nick asked.

"Can you stay some extra days in Illinois? I will understand if you want to see your family some more, too." Anna looked at him with sincerity.

"How long are you thinking?"

She sheepishly said, "I was thinking we could return on Sunday, January 4."

Nick thought for a moment before he responded, "New Year's Eve is on Wednesday. I have a work function I need to attend in L.A. on Friday, January 2. Why don't I fly back on the first, and you can come home on the fourth after your family events?"

At first, Anna was not happy. She stared at Nick, measuring his words, and looking into his eyes. He could feel her testing him.

Nick offered, "That way we have New Year's Eve together."

"That sounds good." Anna agreed.

Nick felt their marriage slipping away, but he didn't want to acknowledge it. Not yet. Things in Central America were heating up.

TUESDAY, DECEMBER 23, came fast. Nick and Anna pulled into the family farm, the tires grinding along the gravel lane. It was snowing, the sky was a dark gray, and the wind had picked up. The sun was setting. As they got out of the car, the wind blew snow in their faces. It was difficult to see between the gusts of swirling snow. Anna grabbed her bag and ran to the side door of the house, which Paul held open for them. Nick grabbed the luggage filled with clothes and presents for the holiday and slammed the trunk on the rental car.

The windy, snowy night was turning colder. As he stepped out from behind the car, his arms fully loaded with bags, his dad hollered, "Need any help?"

Nick yelled back, "All good!"

Within moments of stepping inside the house, Nick's dad had firmly gripped his face, to inspect him.

"You're looking hardened," he proclaimed.

"I have been ridden hard and put away wet, Dad." Nick pulled his dad's arms down and gave him a big hug. "But all is okay. Merry Christmas."

"Merry Christmas, son."

They walked into the kitchen where Nick's mom stood awaiting her hug, a beautiful Irish grin on her face. Nick gave her a big hug and kiss on the cheek, and her grin turned into a big smile.

"I believe you are still growing and getting so tall!" she declared. At 6'2" Nick towered over his mom, who was barely five feet.

"I will try to stop growing, Mom, but it might be out of my control." They laughed and settled in for the evening.

There was a cozy fire in the sitting room off the kitchen. The aroma of holiday cooking, baked goodies, and a homemade pecan pie made especially for Paul filled the air. Dinner was devoured and everyone proclaimed exhaustion, so bedtime came quickly. The peace and quiet of country life, the snowy winter outside, and the warmth of the farmhouse made sleep easy.

The next morning everyone slept in. As Christmas Eve unfolded, gifts were opened. Nick missed the big Christmas celebrations of his youth.

Paul was happy to have time with Nick and Anna. After a big

lunch, Anna was anxious to pack up and drive to her parent's home.

Paul cornered Nick, "Everything okay between you and Anna?"

"She's just anxious to see her parents Dad. . . ."

"That's not what I asked," Paul said sternly.

"Okay, Dad, we are doing well. Just a long week, stressful." Nick said convincingly.

With the car packed, Anna gave Nick's parents an extra-long hug and kiss goodbye, thanking them profusely for the gifts. They were appreciative. The house would be full of family the next day, brothers and children. Nick, regretful about leaving, told his parents, "I love you."

"We love you, too," proclaimed Nick's dad. His mom hugged him tight. It comforted his soul.

Nick hugged his dad and whispered in his ear, "Thanks for everything, Dad."

"You're welcome. Call more often, your mom would appreciate it."

"I will try, I promise."

THE DRIVE to Anna's was quiet. Nick concentrated on the dangerous country highways, passing cars that had collided or slid off the road into the ditches.

Arriving Anna's home, everyone was gathered in the living room with a fire blazing in the fireplace and *Holiday Inn* with Bing Crosby and Fred Astaire on the TV. The snow was still falling, and the wind howled.

Jim and Barbara were happy to have Anna, Brad and Brad's child home. But Nick never felt completely welcomed. He was somber through dinner and observed Anna's interactions with her parents and brother. He knew he didn't belong.

After dinner, he poured a tall scotch straight-up and grabbed one of the lazy-boy chairs by the fire. He drank as memories creeped into his mind. He could hear his farmhouse attic creaking in the wind. The 1863 wooden peg frame farmhouse he grew up in was full of character. He had Christmas Eve memories from when he was only four years old. His brothers would sneak into the attic and try to make him believe that Santa had landed on the house.

Nick felt a hand on his shoulder and nearly jumped out of the chair.

"You fell asleep," Anna said.

"What time is it?" Nick asked.

"After midnight, let's go to bed," Anna said caringly.

As Nick lay in bed next to a sleeping Anna, he thought back to all the nights he listened to the winter winds. His mind ventured back to the times he had to shovel snow and complete his early morning chores before school. Nick remembered those five a.m. hog lot chores—filling the feeders, cleaning the stalls, and checking for eggs in the chicken coop. Nick fell into a deep sleep.

MORNING CAME, and Nick looked out the window. The wind had stopped, and the sun was coming up bright. Fresh snow sparkled like diamonds in the sunlight. He was back on the farm.

What a beautiful sunrise, he thought.

He quietly left the bedroom, making sure he did not wake Anna. His dad was sitting at the kitchen table, looking out over the south 40 acres that lay between the house and the creek. He was drinking Folgers Instant Coffee.

"Good morning! Want some coffee?"

Nick turned the stove burner on to reheat the water and plunged his spoon into the large can of Folgers. "Absolutely."

As they sat across the table looking out at the snowy landscape, Paul looked at Nick. "Anything you need to talk about, son?" he asked.

Nick deflected the opportunity. "I'm so busy with work, I'm not sure where to begin."

Paul chuckled softly. "That's the way it usually goes." They smiled at each other and enjoyed the quiet for a bit longer.

Nick broke the silence. "How are you and Mom doing now that everyone is grown and out of the house?"

"We bump into each other a lot more often, but good news, we still like each other."

Then, like clockwork, Loretta walked into the kitchen. "Now, what are you boys talking about this morning?"

Nick answered quickly: "Dad says you guys are bumping into each other a lot, but it's a good thing because he still likes you."

Paul smiled.

"Oh, my God! He still likes me!" said Loretta.

After breakfast, Nick and his dad decided to take a walk along the hedgerow near the creek. As they walked through the snow, Nick grew concerned about his dad's breathing. "Everything okay, Dad?" His dad had survived a heart attack when Nick was in high school, and then he had quintuple by-pass surgery just two years later.

Paul grunted. "I am feeling my age. Closing in on sixty!"

Nick decided not to push the walk. "We should think about turning back."

They stopped. Paul clasped his hands around Nick's face and asked, "Will you tell me about your job and how the marriage is really going?"

Nick looked into his dad's eyes. "That's a hard one, Dad. We are still trying to figure it all out."

Paul was looking into Nick's soul, "I'm going to pray for your marriage, but a little harder for your happiness."

Nick mustered up a response, "Thanks, Dad. I love you."

"And I love you, too," Paul replied in kind.

December 25, 1986

"Wake up honey, it's morning and you were talking in your sleep," Anna said leaning over him.

"I was dreaming about my parents," Nick said barely awake.

Anna offered, "I'm sorry we didn't get to visit with them longer. Maybe you can drive back over and see them before you leave?"

"Maybe," said Nick.

"Get dressed. Let's have coffee with everyone. You'll feel better."

They shared the morning with Anna's parents, catching up with small talk. Nick told stories of Bogotá and Central American travels.

Several friends and family members arrived around noon to help with the Christmas party set-up, bringing finger foods and drinks. As Nick wrapped a couple of last-minute gifts in the spare bedroom, Anna's old room, he looked around and was amazed that it had not changed at all since they moved to California.

Then he noticed a picture that was partially hidden in her bookcase. It was from one of Anna's high school formals. At first, he felt a little odd about even noticing the picture. Then Anna walked in. Nick pointed to the picture. "What's this?"

Anna clutched the picture, looked at it for a moment. "That was prom my junior year."

Nick inspected the young man in the picture. "High school sweetheart?"

Anna laughed, "You're jealous."

Nick scoffed, "Mostly curious. He actually looks familiar."

Anna laughed again. "Well, he should. It's Stan Franklin." Stan was a year ahead of them in school. He was also an All-State basketball player two years in a row and played for Indiana State in college.

Nick started to feel slightly threatened, but wondered, *Was Anna required to marry someone that would please her overbearing, basketball coaching dad?*

Anna interrupted his train of thought, "What's going on in that brain of yours?"

Nick muttered, "Nothing really, nothing at all."

Anna put the picture back where it was. "Okay. When you're done wrapping, Mom wants to have a toast with just us before everyone starts arriving."

Nick grunted, "Okay."

As Anna's parents toasted the holiday, Nick started drinking. He kept drinking as he listened to all the gloating questions from Anna's dad about her computer-engineering career and interactions with the Department of Defense. He felt alone, not enjoying any of the party.

As people arrived, he made a few sporadic appearances, taking time in the bathroom, hiding in Anna's room, but never letting enough time go by during his disappearances to upset Anna. He could not wait until January 1. He was ready to leave after the first night.

The next few days were a blur of visits with friends, basketball practices for exercise, and dinners with Anna's family friends. All Nick could think about at times was the question his dad had asked in his dream: Are you happy in your marriage?

No, Nick realized, *I'm not happy.*

On Wednesday morning, December 31, he woke up and rejoiced deep inside. *Thank God the visit is almost over.*

Anna knew it had not been a fun visit for Nick. But deep

down, she didn't care, and she was not going to allow his distaste for her family dampen her time.

"Happy New Year," she whispered.

Nick rolled over and kissed her on the cheek. "Happy New Year."

He listened to Anna plan out the whole day and evening. He felt as though she was the cruise director, and he was a mere passenger awaiting the next activity. On the inside, he was completely fed up with all of it, but on the outside, he wanted Anna to be happy. It would make his departure easier.

Then, out of the blue, Anna asked, "Nick? Do you think we have a good marriage?"

Nick immediately responded, "Yes, Anna. But we are both ambitious in our careers."

She hugged Nick, "I hope so."

Nick hugged Anna extra tight, with as much as love as he could. After all, he wanted to leave the next morning with as little guilt as possible.

By the afternoon, both Anna and Nick were feeling exhausted. Anna suggested a nap, and Nick agreed immediately. They disappeared into Anna's bedroom and laid down, both instantly nodding off.

About an hour before dinner, Anna's mom came into the room to wake them.

Nick looked up at Barbara and said, "Happy New Year!"

She laughed, "It's not quite the new year yet."

Anna and Nick got ready for the dinner party. Nick focused on being engaging and loving. He behaved unusually nice and respectful to Jim, Anna noticed suspiciously. They counted down as they watched *Dick Clark's Rockin' New Year's Eve* special and the ball dropping in Times Square. Then they welcomed in 1987, with hugs and kisses all around.

By 1:00 a.m., the last of the guests were leaving. Nick retired to bed ahead of Anna, and immediately fell into a deep sleep.

Nick rolled out of bed around 8:00 a.m. and sat in the kitchen with Jim. He observed Jim's slow movements; and enjoyed watching him wince in pain due to his drunken evening.

"Rough morning?" Nick baited.

"Good party," Jim offered up.

"Maybe too good . . . I'll take it easy on you," said Nick.

Jim was still recovering. "Thank you, I appreciate that."

As everyone else woke up and dragged themselves to the kitchen, Nick hopped into the shower and then completed his packing. Barbara insisted on feeding him and decided to make pancakes and sausage. Nick was hungry and appreciated the food before his drive to Chicago and flight to L.A.

After eating, he threw his bags in the car and gave Anna a giant hug and a Happy New Year's Day kiss in front of her mom and dad. She was a little taken back and embarrassed, but he knew it was the right thing to do, given his departure.

Anna walked Nick to the car, "Thank you for spending so much time here. Can we find time together when we get back to California?"

"Absolutely we will. I love you," Nick replied confidently.

Anna smiled, "Let me know that you get in okay. I love you."

He pulled out of the driveway and looked back for a wave, but she had run back into the house to escape the cold. He was content to be on his way to the Beverly Hills Hotel to party with Vincent and Richard.

BEFORE PULLING onto the highway, Nick stopped at a gas station. He found a payphone, called the Beverly Hills Hotel, and asked for Vincent's room.

Vincent and Richard yelled into the phone, "Happy New Year!"

Nick responded in kind: "Happy New Year!"

"We are going to the pool this morning to get some sun," Vincent told Nick. "Drive and fly safe. We have an amazing surprise for you when you get here."

"What is it?" Nick questioned.

Together, Vincent and Richard said, "You will like it!"

Vincent continued, "We have an extra bedroom for you, so just come here when you land."

Before Nick could ask another question, Vincent hung up.

Nick sped onto the highway thinking, *Happy New Year, Sean. You love surprises.*

Beverly Hills Rendezvous

January 1, 1987

NICK LANDED at LAX around 7:30 p.m., jumped in his car, and drove to the Beverly Hills Hotel. Once there, he left his car with the valet, and called Vincent's room from the front desk.

"Hallo!" said Richard in German.

Nick smiled. *"Ich bin es, ich bin an der rezeption."* (It's me. I am at the front desk.)

"Excellent. We will come down and fetch you. Go to the tower elevator and wait," Richard replied.

"Okay," Nick answered.

As he walked to the elevator, Nick began thinking about his situation. Tempers were rising in Central and Latin America. Nicaraguan forces had just taken a snapshot of him, and as January unfolded, there would be increasing risks to the operation. He prayed that his cover was not blown.

The elevator doors opened. Nick looked up. There was Gabriella, radiant. Her captivating smile, engaging eyes, and smooth tan skin.

"Nick," she said breathlessly.

Nick pulled her from the elevator and kissed her long and hard as her body melted into his. Her hair was a bit longer than he remembered, and her red dress covered her shoulders, but not her strong, shapely arms. The silky fabric draped across her voluptuous body, catching her curves in just the right way, and grazing her thighs. Nick wanted her, he needed her, in more ways than he realized.

Nick just held her close, without saying anything.

"Happy New Year, Nick. Are you happy to see me?" Gabriella said tenderly.

"Very," Nick said.

The elevator doors opened again, Nick and Gabriella stepped inside. They slowly ascended to the fifth floor, tasting each other's kisses, bodies pressing against each other, filled with desire. They caught their breath as the elevator doors opened.

Vincent and Richard, dressed in hotel robes, greeted them in the hallway, *"Feliz Año Nuevo!"* (Happy New Year!) Everyone cheered and the party was officially started.

For the next few hours, into the early morning, they toasted their love, the bonds that tied them all together, and the New Year with music and dancing.

Eventually, Nick's energy faded. He looked at Vincent. "I'm turning in for the night."

Vincent muttered in a drunken fashion, "Turn into what?"

Gabriella, sensing the dark side of Vincent was awakening, walked up behind Nick and placed her hands around his chest, "C'mon. Let's get ready for bed."

Richard looked at Nick, "Happy New Year, brother."

Nick gave Vincent and Richard a hug and thanked them for the invitation and the present.

Nick stepped outside of his conscience to let go of his marriage, thought of himself as Sean, and took Gabriella to bed. They made love and pleasured each other in every way imaginable. But they refused to declare their love. That would place them on dangerous footing when operations needed top priority.

Gabriella was being assigned to Sean in Bogotá once more to help manage the rodeo for Fabio's team. She would be his interpreter, his attaché, and his liaison in Colombia.

"Tonight, was a beautiful surprise," Nick softheartedly said.

Gabriella placed her hand on Nick's chest, "What are you thinking?"

"This is going to be complicated."

They laughed into the early morning.

It was January 2. Nick woke up at sunrise, despite the lack of sleep. Gabriella lay next to him, the sheets only half covering her toned body. As his eyes scanned her curves, he noticed a small new tattoo on the inside of her right ankle.

Nick took a closer look. It was an eagle, the one bird that is shared by the U.S. and Mexico. The eagle featured on the Mexican coat of arms is referred to as the "golden eagle." He smiled and thought, *A true patriot.* He appreciated her loyalty, intellect, and heart.

Slipping out of the bed, Nick went to the kitchenette inside the suite to find coffee. There was Vincent sitting on the balcony adjacent the kitchenette, drinking his percolated coffee, reading the paper, recovering.

"Good morning, Nick. We have a great deal of debriefing to accomplish over the next two days."

Nick poured himself a cup, "Thank you for the surprise last night."

"I paired you two years ago during psych evaluations in college," Vincent said, smiling. Nick did not always believe in such evaluations but agreed with this assignment. He sat down on the chair next to Vincent.

"How are we?" asked Nick.

Vincent rambled through numerous intel highlights. The gist of it revolved around how Noriega (Panama's president) was playing all sides against the middle. He was becoming a liability and even a greater risk than the U.S. State Department ever anticipated.

Bottom line: if the hostile exchanges and, worse yet, hostile behavior, toward U.S. diplomats, agency officers, and military leaders continued, Panama would become an enemy of the CIA.

Vincent summarized the Panama situation: "It's beginning to look more and more like Noriega will continue to disregard our wishes. He appears determined to cannibalize civil government throughout Central America, and we will not allow that to happen."

Nick looked at Vincent. "This is becoming a grave matter."

Noriega sided with the U.S. rather than the USSR in Central America—notably by sabotaging the forces of the Sandinista government in Nicaragua and the revolutionaries of the FMLN group in El Salvador.

For doing so, Noriega also demanded that the U.S. increase his pay to $200,000 per year. Although he worked with the DEA—Drug Enforcement Administration—to restrict illegal drug shipments, he was known to simultaneously accept significant financial support from drug dealers. He would facilitate drug money laundering, and, in return, he helped provide protection from DEA investigations, all thanks to his special relationship with the CIA.

Vincent looked at Nick, "This vicious power cycle is going to Noriega's head and endangering CIA clandestine direct operatives. More specifically, endangering YOU."

"I will let you absorb that Nick, it's not good." Vincent continued, "Let me give you some more color on the situation."

Over the past year, President Ronald Reagan began negotiations with Noriega, requesting that the Panamanian leader step down after his scandals were publicly exposed in *The New York Times*. Reagan pressured him with several drug-related indictments in U.S. courts; however, since extradition laws between Panama and the U.S. were weak, Noriega deemed the threat not credible and refused to submit to Reagan's demands.

Nick thought, *Vincent hates anyone who would dare disregard the wishes of President Reagan or America.*

Nick knew that what Vincent was disclosing would require the removal of Noriega. That was, at best, a two-year operation with, most likely, an authorized military action.

Vincent stood up and stretched, "Come on. I have reserved a squash court for 9:00 a.m. Let's play before we solve these issues in Central America."

They did just that. Nick was thankful for the exercise. Once back at the suite, they found Richard relaxing with the newspaper and Gabriella reading a new novel, *Wanderlust* by Danielle Steel. She looked peaceful laying on the couch.

Nick asked Gabriella about Audrey Driscoll, the fictional character that always appears in Steel's books. "Does Audrey Driscoll ever have to choose between following her passionate desires or staying true and abiding by her conscience?"

Gabriella smiled and rolled her eyes at Nick and Richard laughed. Vincent left the room to clean-up. Nick followed suit to prepare for lunch.

For lunch, Richard had reserved a private corner table off the patio area overlooking the pool, called the "celebrity swamp." The Beverly Hills Hotel was an electric place to people-watch, no doubt.

It was time for agency work. Vincent led with Gabriella's role. Her objective was to reestablish the rodeo event under the umbrella of USAID. It was also to be facilitated by a committee that would be exclusively selected by Fabio. This gave Fabio oversight of Jaime Leal, who was to manage many of the details of coordinating and providing documentation to local government authorities.

Nick shared his opinion about Leal. "Jaime Leal is a low-level Noriega, working the exchanges to his own advantage throughout Colombia, and—"

Vincent interrupted him. "Nick, Leal is under control for now, and the minute he is not under control, we will deal with it. We will discuss Leal later."

Nick, encouraged by the firmness of Vincent's statements regarding Leal, complied.

After lunch, Vincent asked Gabriella, "Give Nick and I some privacy, okay?"

She took a lounge chair across the pool and began reading her book.

Vincent watched Nick's eyes follow Gabriella's swagger as she walked about the pool.

"Good God, boy. Haven't you gotten enough for the day?"

Nick just laughed. "Let's get on with the steps we need to take."

What Vincent said next would change Nick's perspective going forward.

"You have been identified as Sean Smith, USAID, which is fine, but the intel we have indicates that Nicaragua intel has tied you to the government, possibly our branch."

Nick felt unsure of what that meant. "Am I a target?"

Vincent said, "Of an investigation, yes. But we can use this to our advantage to get closer to Ortega's top people—the ones who are routinely flying in and out of the strips next to our Fun Zone hangar in Panama—"

Nick interjected, "Which are strictly controlled by Noriega."

Nick leaned back in his chair, glanced at Richard, who was observing his every move.

"Are you taking notes? Observing my reactions?" he asked

him. "Measuring my heart rate? Judging my preparedness? Are you evaluating me, Richard?"

Without a break in his gaze, Richard flatly answered, "Yes."

Nick scoffed, "Well . . . How am I doing?"

Vincent and Richard both laughed. "Remarkably well," said Richard, "given the risk. But then again, you are new to the risk." That response did not sit well with Nick.

Vincent reached over and placed his hand on Nick's forearm. "We will never leave you to die if given the choice." Nick looked at his drink.

"That's a helluva thing to say," Nick exhaled.

Richard, seated on the other side of Nick, placed his hand on Nick's opposite forearm. "And I won't let Vincent leave you to die ever. No matter what. I promise."

Vincent sternly looked at Richard, "Don't make those promises, Richard, there are limits to every operation."

Vincent said, "You will do as ordered and you will get the job done."

Nick knew better than to ever question Vincent's word, "So, with these reassurances, how can I say, no?"

"Good," said Vincent. "Let's have an afternoon martini and enjoy ourselves today."

For the rest of the day, Vincent slipped hints about Ortega's operatives in the Panama intel reports that Nick would be authorized to read the next day.

Nick began to understand that Vincent's operation was to be executed "by the book" with more than the usual paramilitary support to control the environment and activities around the CIA-owned Fun Zone, Hangar 63, at the Panama airport.

The hangar got its nickname based on the irony that a custom basement with several interrogation rooms had been built underneath it. If that didn't work to get the desired information from the held target, then they could be flown out, unnoticed, and without paperwork, to CIA black ops sites, where more severe interrogation methods were performed.

The operations involved very few paramilitary affiliates. The op would undoubtedly require a small team of direct operatives to execute flawlessly, as there would always be variables outside their immediate control and often in conjunction with a hostile exchange.

Nick asked Vincent, "Will Jon be leading our special forces team?"

"Yes, he is recovering nearby at the VA Medical Center, West LA, and wants to see you."

Exhausted, Nick decided it was time for a siesta.

Richard agreed. "Good idea. I will be sleeping next to Gabriella."

Vincent and Nick finished their last drink and looked over at Gabriella; she was sleeping like a log. Vincent concurred with Nick's assessment.

"It is time for a rest." Vincent said, "I'm going up to the room to cool off."

Nick replied, "I'll join you."

As they entered the suite, Vincent turned to Nick, "We will receive intel updates tomorrow morning. Let's plan to map out every step with total secrecy and discipline."

Nick was looking deep into Vincent's eyes. "Yes, sir."

Vincent reminded Nick about dinner: "We have 9:00 p.m. dinner plans at The Polo Lounge for Richard's last night in the States."

Vincent started to walk toward their bedroom—and then stopped and looked back at Nick. "This is an opportunity for you to take a risky situation and make a big impact on a high-profile target. You have been trained for this. Because you have been identified, it must be you, you are the bait. Understand?"

Nick nodded affirmatively.

"Excellent. Get some rest, and we will have fun tonight."

Nick turned and walked into his bedroom. *Understand?* he thought. *Sure, I understand. I have been in the Agency one year. High-profile targets, including Ortega's top men from Nicaragua want to kill me—but we can keep it a secret. Let's not forget Noriega, the ruler of Panama, who leaks any and all intel for a few bucks. Sure. I understand. I understand that I must be crazy.*

As he lay in bed alone, he thought long and hard about his role, his training, and what the long-term mission could accomplish. Achieving the greater good was their mission, even though they would be asked to do risky and sometimes horrible acts for the sake of it. He closed his eyes and remembered a quote that was drilled into his memory during training.

Nick whispered the Sun Tzu quote out loud to himself: "It is only the enlightened ruler and the wise general who will use the highest intelligence of the army for the purposes of spying, and thereby they achieve great results."

Nick drifted to sleep, knowing one thing for sure, today he was no longer a career trainee on duty or assignment. He thought, *Now all I have to do is stay alive.*

Chapter 22

Loyalty of Brothers

Nick used the next two days to visit Jon, who was recovering rapidly.

"You look healthy, Jon!" Nick declared, walking into Jon's apartment.

Jon smiled big. "Hard not to be healthy when you have someone taking care of you every day. What brings you by?"

"We missed you at the party. I thought I would bring some party to you." Nick pulled a bottle of Glenlivet scotch out from behind his back. Jon laughed.

"Let's get the party started." Jon rose slowly from his chair to get two glasses.

"Still a bit tender?" Nick asked.

"Yes. But every day it feels better. I will be there with you. Don't worry," Jon offered reassuringly. Nick looked relieved and took seat on the couch.

"How long have you known Vincent?" Nick inquired.

Jon walked into the living room and handed Nick a drink. "Since 1980. Vincent has volunteered for missions to terminate terrorist assassins. And he needed a small team from Special Forces."

"Weren't those handled by Death Squads?" Nick continued questioning.

Jon smirked, "You mean CIA-trained paramilitary units?"

Nick replied quickly out of respect, "Yes. That's exactly what I mean."

"Another round?" Jon grabbed Nick's glass.

Jon talked for the next fifteen minutes about Vincent's first mission in El Salvador, as Nick listened intensely.

December 2, 1980
El Salvador Story

JON EXPLAINED: "Two missionaries based in La Libertad drove to El Salvador International Airport on the afternoon of December 2 to pick up two Catholic Sisters returning from a conference in Managua, Nicaragua. They were under surveillance by a National Guardsman at the time. Acting on orders, five National Guardsmen stopped the four women's vehicle after they left the airport. They were taken to an isolated spot where they were beaten, raped and murdered by the soldiers.

The real story gets worse.

Peasants living nearby had seen the women's white van drive to an isolated spot that night. They heard machine gun fire followed by single shots. They claim to have seen five men flee the scene in the white van, with the lights on and the radio blaring. The van was found later that night on fire at the side of the airport road. The women's bodies were found in a ditch.

Early the next morning, December 3, the peasants were told by local authorities—a judge, three members of the National Guard, and two commanders—to bury them in a common grave in a nearby field. The peasants did as ordered but informed their parish priest and the news reached the United States Ambassador to El Salvador, Robert White.

Their shallow grave was exhumed the next day, December 4, in front of 15 reporters. The U.S. was appalled and demanded accountability."

Nick broke in, "Weren't the policemen charged publicly with U.S. influence?"

Jon held his hand up. "Low-level police were convicted. We killed the men in power."

"How did that go down?" asked Nick.

"Messy. It was bloody and Vincent was on the front line," Jon explained.

"Vincent was shot in the belly that night," Jon said shaking his head. "What should have taken five minutes turned into a thirty-minute gunfight with two of our men dead."

"I'm sorry for that."

"Vincent had passed out. I thought he was dying for sure. But I carried him for nearly three miles to get back to our pickup. We helicoptered out and the team worked on him while we held him together."

Nick remained silent.

"He lived, and the next day he declared me a blood brother." Jon was consumed by his feelings.

Nick could feel Jon's emotion. He realized that these bonds formed during life and death moments were real. He was glad Jon would have his back.

"Let's have one more drink here, then I will take you out to dinner. Okay?"

"Yes," Jon replied.

"Shall we invite Vincent?"

Jon looked serious, "Yes. He was gathering intel from the State Department earlier and he has been way too quiet today. Let's grill him over martinis and steaks."

"Good idea."

VINCENT JOINED Nick and Jon for dinner at Ray's Steakhouse in Santa Monica. It was known for privacy, and they were offered a large corner booth with old-fashioned curtains to draw for enclosure. After the second round of martinis, Jon dove into business.

"Aren't we anxious?" Vincent teased Jon.

Jon shook his head, "Just fill us in."

"Gentlemen, the Department of State believes there is an 'unsub' in their building." Vincent's face turned ominous. "Information about operations is in the target files."

"What is an 'unsub'?" asked Nick.

Jon answered, "It's an unknown subject that is being investigated."

"In other words, someone in our State Department is leaking secrets about operations, and they don't know who it is," Vincent said, irritated.

Nick asked, "How do they find the leak?"

"Counterintelligence and investigation units will build a matrix of profiles using tidbits of intel they uncover from classified interceptions." Vincent explained, "There is reason to believe the link to our operations is the intel between Cuba, Panama and Nicaragua."

"Shit!" blurted Nick.

Vincent offered some action steps: "They will be sharing a list of possible subjects based on a few clues, along with pictures and profiles as soon as possible."

Jon outlined it for Nick, "If intel on us or our operation is being leaked to Cuba by our own State Department, Cuba is either using it to help or selling it to Nicaragua."

Vincent whispered, "We need to be smart. But we can also get creative and shake up the whole mission narrative."

Vincent raised his glass to toast, "Rejoice, and be of good cheer! For THEY are out there, and WE are in here!"

Getting Creative

MOST OF January 1987 was routine. While Gabriella was keeping Fabio, Leal, and Gacha paid off with CIA contingency funds for the USAID rodeo—now rescheduled for April 18 and 19—Sean, Jon, and Vincent were gathering intelligence throughout Central America. Their immediate concern was to reorganize the mission. The plan was to achieve several objectives all at once, pushing the Soviets out of Nicaragua and Central America.

Vincent was privy to President Reagan's efforts over the past couple of years to initiate discussions with five Central American chiefs of state about signing a Peace and Democracy Accord. No material progress was achieved, but Vincent rooted out two leaders, in a couple of less-influential countries—namely, Costa Rica and Guatemala. What incentives or pressure could be put in place to move forward? Vincent designed a new research project, code-named "Turn-About" and tasked several analysts at Langley to search for influential threads throughout Central America to pull on for just the right affect.

February 3
Briefing at U.S. Embassy, Mexico City

JON WALKED into the basement briefing room and poured himself a cup of coffee.

"Greetings," said Vincent.

Nick nodded hello and stay focused on the intel reports.

"Sathya Sai Baba," Jon said ardently.

Vincent looked up. Sean could not tell from his face if Vincent was disgusted at the idea or just upset that he had not thought of it first.

Jon pitched his idea simplistically. "In order to get Ortega in Nicaragua to take notice of U.S. influence, we need to apply pressure to his mobility and financing sources. One material asset is his relationship with Noriega in Panama, specifically the airstrip protection for exchanges."

Vincent and Sean simultaneously insisted, "Get to the point."

Jon smiled. "The point is, by shaking up Noriega's power, Ortega will lean toward signing the Central American Peace and Democracy Accord with the blessing of the U.S. and our reduction in Contra revolutionaries in the mix."

"We know all of this," said Sean.

"But we have not focused on the thread we can pull in Noriega's camp," said Jon. "It's Roberto Herrera."

Sean reviewed the history in his mind. Back in September 1977, President Jimmy Carter and Panamanian leader Omar Torrijos Herrera signed the Torrijos-Carter Treaties. Torrijos dispatched Herrera, Torrijos' own cousin, to many countries, including Cuba, France, and Yugoslavia, as a negotiator of the Panama Canal. Torrijos also served as a political representative in Israel, Algeria, Venezuela, Mexico, and Costa Rica. Herrera became General Chief of Staff to the military, which had been renamed the *Fuerzas de Defensa de Panamá*, or Panama

Defense Forces. At the time, he was second in command of Panama's military under Manuel Noriega.

Vincent spoke up, "Analysts have flagged Herrera as a possible turn."

"That's right," said Jon. "And guess who he follows devoutly?"

Sean said it: "Sathya Sai Baba."

Vincent, now pacing, said, "Sai Baba is a major counter-balancing tool in situations like this. His following has reached the magnitude of a new worldwide religion. Americans make up his most lucrative following."

"Including major business, political, and educational leaders," Sean added.

"And he wants to help us create a new world of peace and justice in Central America," Jon said. "Oscar Sánchez, president of Costa Rica, can get a meeting with Sai Baba to educate him about the Central American Peace Accord."

Sean interjected, "As well as our charitable nature should he persuade Colonel Herrera to turn on Ortega."

Vincent sat back down. "This is so out-of-the-box, it just might work. What's the timing on getting a meeting with Sai Baba?"

"I estimate at least two months, so it doesn't look suspicious," said Jon.

Vincent leaned back in his chair. "We can do this. If we plan everything out, we can pick June or July to provoke a revolution in Nicaragua, with Colonel Herrera leading the charge. We need to expose the nastiest dirt we can dig up on Ortega."

Sean leaned in. "We can simultaneously leverage the Fun Zone hangar at Noriega's exchange lanes within his private airstrip. This will cost Ortega support from everyone—the Soviets and the Cartels."

Vincent was smiling now. "Let's get President Reagan's Peace

Accord signed by all five Central American leaders in time for your birthday, Sean."

Jon asked, "When is Sean's birthday?"

"August 7," Sean said.

Vincent declared, "That will be the day the Central American Peace Accord is signed." Then he changed topics, "Gentlemen, you should all know that President Reagan is planning a nationally televised address where he will take full responsibility for the Iran-Contra affair. The company line will be something like this: 'What began as a strategic opening to Iran deteriorated, in its implementation, into trading arms for hostages. There will be no evidence that President Reagan knew of any arms dealings that involved the Contras."

Sean could tell that Vincent was a little nervous about his involvement and how the allegations would be handled. So, he offered, "This convoluted idea of using Sai Baba just might be a stroke of brilliance. Accomplishing a significant benchmark before President Reagan's term ends will wash away the Contra dealings."

It was already midafternoon, and everyone agreed to break for lunch. They walked briskly to the Four Seasons to eat and continue their planning.

Vincent carried a small satchel.

Sean asked, "What's in the satchel?"

"We have received several dossiers on possible espionage subjects. Maybe you will recognize someone." Vincent pulled five file folders out and handed them to Sean.

Over the course of lunch, Sean poured over the files one by one. After the first four, none of the subjects had recognition value, no one looked familiar.

Then Sean opened the last file. "HOLY FUCK!"

"What it is?" asked Vincent.

Sean stared at the picture, analyzing the man's face, then read his name and profile aloud, including a Professor of Political Science at Columbia University, New York, and his role with the Department of State, Intelligence Collection.

"This man knows Gabriella. They were talking privately at the political conference I attended at Thunderbird—he saw me." Sean was unwinding the moment in his mind.

Vincent asked, "What were you doing when he saw you?"

"Nothing," replied Sean.

Vincent shook his head, "Then what makes you think he identified you?"

"He may have seen me signal to Gabriella—she came to my hotel later that night and left around 4 o'clock in the morning . . . FUCK!"

"Calm down. We will report back and deepen the surveillance on this asshole. Gabriella will prove useful," said Vincent

Jon offered, "It's good. Now that we have a possible lead, we can figure out if Leal or Morales are part of the leaks."

Sean lost his appetite. He retraced his steps and tried to remember if he saw the man at any other time. Nothing came to mind.

THEY BEGAN by laying out a timeline for the new operation.

Vincent in measured voice said, "August seventh is six months away. Jon, we need Sai Baba to begin spinning his influential magic in April. That way, we have two months to coordinate operations in tandem for the highest impact."

Jon thought through the task. "We will make it work, but I will need all of your influence."

Vincent looked at Sean and Jon. "This operation is called Turn-About. We will have weekly briefings in person from now on, so get your personal lives in order. Intel reports will be delivered the same day issued. I expect you to read them, sniff out every opportunity to locate weaknesses in our targets, and apply pressure accordingly."

"One more thing. We have no extra time built into this op. This is our highest priority and, if it works, we will have much to celebrate. We will take significant risks. Details will make the difference. Stay sharp and execute smart."

Everyone concurred and left for the day.

Sean walked back to the Embassy for a ride to the airport and looked for a government-tagged car. He could still make it home in time for dinner with Anna. He understood her new project with McDonnell Douglas was scheduled to start soon, and it would mean she'd need to make frequent visits to their facility in St. Louis. He boarded the plane, closed his eyes, and began developing the lies he would need to explain weekly travel.

Thank God the USAID rodeo event is happening. That will help with the schedule cover, he thought. Between his relationships with Anna and Gabriella, he felt as though he had no relationship at all.

THE GARAGE door opened. Nick was surprised to see Anna's car. She met him at the door and offered a drink.

"Scotch?"

Nick said, "Sure. Are we celebrating?"

"Let's sit down, I will share my big news with you," Anna said smiling.

She made spaghetti, a dinner staple from college days. Steaming spaghetti, garlic bread, and a bottle of wine as a centerpiece. Anna was excited.

"I got an amazing job offer from McDonnell Douglas in St. Louis today!"

Nick reacted, "Wow! That's great, honey."

Anna tried to stay calm. Nick knew she had said yes already.

"It is a big advancement. I am a project lead on a fighter plane tracking system. But I would need to relocate soon, not right away, but within a few months."

He picked up on her slight. *'I' would need to, not 'we' would need to,* he thought.

She continued, "Of course, I told them that we needed a day to discuss it, but they have other candidates and a pretty fast timeline requirement."

Nick offered, "Worst case, you can go there while I try to wrap up the Bogotá USAID projects, and we see each other as often as possible. I'm proud of you, Anna."

Anna did not hesitate, "I knew you would support me!"

Nick raised his glass. "Let's toast to you, the newest project lead for McDonnell Douglas!"

THE MONTH flew by, weekly briefings in Mexico City and Bogotá during the week for Sean, weekends in California for Nick. Sean's attention was completely focused on Operation: Turn-About.

February 27 was Anna's last day at Northrop; she moved right away. McDonnell offered her temporary housing for March, April, and May, which would provide ample time to relocate.

They went out for dinner after work. Nick made reservations at a steakhouse in Palos Verdes called Manny's. Over dinner, they laid out their plans for the next couple of months.

Anna asked, "Are you okay with us living apart like this?"

"I try not to think of it that way," Nick replied.

She reached over to touch Nick's hand. "I miss you."

"I miss you, too. We seem to be chasing our careers before anything else," Nick offered.

"I know. But this is time to grow and support each other, right?" said Anna.

Nick shifted the conversation, "I have to be in Bogotá for corporate relations and promotion of the rodeo event. And you are the project lead at McDonnel Douglas. I don't think your dad believes I have a career at this point," Nick smirked.

Anna leaned back. "Let's try to enjoy tonight."

The next morning, Nick drove Anna to the airport, parking in the garage so he could walk her inside. She liked that. He kissed her goodbye and immediately walked back to the car, grabbed his bags, and walked to the international terminal. His flight for Mexico City departed soon. He had a weekend planned with Vincent and Richard.

When Sean landed in Mexico City, Vincent and his driver were there to retrieve him. They went straight to Vincent's apartment downtown, just blocks from the Embassy. Richard greeted Sean with a big hug and kiss on the cheek. Sean whispered in Richard's ear very discreetly, "You're trying to make Vincent jealous, aren't you?"

Richard leaned back and smiled. "Yes, I am."

Sean laughed. "Well, sometimes we can fool ourselves into believing almost anything."

Vincent had one eyebrow up and a look of disgust, "C'mon. Let's get going."

After settling into the spare bedroom, Sean entered the living room, sat on the couch, and looked at the intelligence reports spread across the coffee table.

Vincent sat down. "Let's begin with our Panama disruption strategy."

Sean leaned in. "We always start with the hard part first, don't we?"

"It's better that way," replied Vincent.

After an hour of reviewing the frequency of flights, predictable cargo, and personnel profiles for each type of cargo flight, something clicked. Nicaraguan officials were aboard these flights twice per month, once near the middle of the month, and once just after the first of every month. Disrupting these exchanges and snatching the personnel would send the right message to Ortega.

Vincent revealed a new negotiation. "Our arrangement with Noriega and his Panama militia involved permission for snatch-and-release operations that would happen without the participation of his uniform militia."

"This is better," Sean acknowledged. He closed his eyes, placed himself on the runway the day he was pulled out of the flight with Jon. Nicaraguan officials profiled him.

He opened his eyes. "Noriega must have the same arrangement with Ortega, that's what happened to Jon and me."

Vincent nodded. "That's why we call it the Fun Zone."

The plan Vincent laid out was simple. Sean would be regularly stationed at the Fun Zone hangar to be a legitimate USAID liaison. The hangar would stock humanitarian and agricultural supplies as part of the cover.

Vincent looked at Sean, "You will need to become recognizable, even boring to watch. Neither Noriega's men nor Ortega's men will be interested. Then, in early June, our clandestine operation will be triggered.

"Sean will snatch top officers from planes headed to Nicaragua. Simultaneously, Colonel Diaz Herrera will launch a revolt against Ortega within Nicaragua. Supplies will be halted, and his own people will revolt."

Vincent went on, "Ortega's country of Nicaragua will be destabilized. They will need to sign the Central American Peace Accord and shut off relations with the Soviet Union."

Vincent's plan assumed Sai Baba, the Guru, would convince

Colonel Diaz Herrera to lead the revolt against Ortega's Nicaragua, all in the name of peace and democracy for Central America—weakening the Soviet presence throughout Central America.

Vincent leaned back into the couch, stared at the ceiling, "Operation: Turn-About is a GO. American critics will be covering these events closely. Remember, this will punish Noriega for his bullying and double-dealing in Panama. Let's think this through, what are the collateral circumstances?"

Sean leaned back into the couch with his eyes closed. He mapped out the entirety of the network they planned to disrupt and spoke, "Do we let the chips fall where they fall? Fabio and the Cartels will be impacted by the shutdowns in Panama."

Vincent sat up. "Let's determine how we handle that tomorrow. I need fresh eyes and a drink."

It was almost 6:00 p.m. Richard stood in the living room, ready for the evening.

"I made dinner reservations for 7:00 p.m."

Nick replied, "Where are we going?"

"To the El Taquito Bullfighting Restaurant, one of the oldest restaurants in Mexico City," Vincent bragged and then disappeared into their bedroom to change for dinner.

Sean replied, "Great. I will be ready in 20 minutes."

Smiling, Richard told Sean, "Dress sharp. We're going out after dinner."

Sean smiled, "Must be a Saturday night," and closed the guest room door.

They arrived at exactly 7:00 p.m. Vincent was always prompt; he always arrived exactly as scheduled. Sean appreciated that.

Richard started telling Vincent and Sean all the facts he had learned about the restaurant. "El Taquito is one of the oldest restaurants in the city. Reason is that it has always been in the same location, it has always been owned by the Guillén family, and it has always kept the same name. It dates to 1923 when the streets were very different, and it claims to be the first restaurant in Mexico City to adopt the bullfighting theme."

Vincent looked at Sean. "Fascinating, right?" as he rolled his eyes.

Richard paid no attention and continued. "The story goes, Grandfather Marcos was friends with meat suppliers, and he met several bullfighters, among them, Rodolfo Gaona, a great bull-fighter in the 1920s. All the recipes were created by Grandmother Conchita famous for the . . ."

Vincent woke up. "Ooooh! Do you have Tampiqueña! Bring me that!"

Vincent had heard enough. "Now, where are our drinks?"

"Now you're in a hurry. . . ." Richard interjected staring at Vincent.

Dinner was fabulous. It was almost 9:00 p.m. when Vincent determined, "We need something sweet before we go dancing."

Sean, showing some desire to call it a night, asked, "Where are we going next?"

Vincent belted out, "Salon Los Angeles. One of the oldest clubs in the city—established in 1937!"

Richard replied, "Another great choice for a night out on the town in Mexico City!"

Vincent winked, "Those who don't know Salon Los Angeles do not know Mexico."

Sean knew when he was beat. "Okay, sounds exciting!" he said with some fervor. Richard and Vincent looked at each other, rolled their eyes, and concentrated on the dessert menu.

The waiter brought complimentary *café con leche* for the table along with three flavors of frozen custard. It was exactly the energy boost they needed. They consumed the custard and caffeine, and single-filed into the car.

The doors were opening for reserved tables at Salon Los Angeles. Richard seemed more anxious than usual.

"Everything okay?" asked Sean.

Vincent answered for Richard: "He just loves salsa dancing,"

Sean perceived this interjection as a signal that something was up.

As they walked into the club, Sean noticed a woman, who, from the back, was the spitting image of—

"Gabriella is here!" Richard proclaimed. He looked at Vincent. "Sean is going to learn salsa dancing!"

Vincent laughed, "Or maybe not. Either way, our boy will be dancing!"

Gabriella swaggered up to Sean. "Hello, good looking. Do you want to dance with me?"

"Yes, you look spectacular!" replied Sean with a hug followed by a passionate kiss.

Gabriella whispered, "One condition, okay?"

"Anything," whispered Sean.

"You have to go home with me," Gabriella said gently kissing Sean's neck.

The night was amazing.

They laughed, danced, and consumed tequila like water. By 1:00 a.m., everyone was exhausted and drunk; it was time to retreat to the apartment.

Gabriella nearly passed out in the car. They made it back to the apartment. The last thing Sean heard before he nodded off was, "What a fun night," from Gabriella as she curled up beside him. Then—just her heavy breathing.

Sunday morning arrived too soon for Sean. He had slept in past 8:00 a.m., but Vincent was awake and drinking his second cup of coffee.

Sean poured himself a cup, "Is Richard still sleeping?"

Vincent replied, "He went out for a run. He peeked in on you to see if you wanted to go, but said you were still asleep."

Sean realized there was still more planning to be done.

"When do you want to walk through the consequential issues list and contingencies?"

Vincent put his newspaper down. "Sometime between your second and third cup of coffee after breakfast."

Richard returned from his run, starving. Vincent made eggs over-easy, toast, and sausage links. They devoured the meal.

Vincent and Richard, fluent in Spanish and German, spoke to each other in alternating languages to annoy Sean. Sean finished his meal, placed the dishes in the sink, and went to check on Gabriella. Gabriella was in the bathroom. He walked into the bedroom, stretched out on the bed, and concentrated on the operation.

Gabriella came out of the shower, a short robe tied loosely around her, smelling more sensual than ever. Sean gave her a kiss good morning. "You smell amazing."

"Stop," Gabriella said, blushing.

Sean disappeared into the bathroom to shower and get ready for the day. They were scheduled to fly to Bogotá together that evening.

Midday, everyone gathered in the living room. Vincent opened the discussion, "Gabriella, can you update us on your plans for the rodeo and be specific about Fabio's involvement and how you see the economics unfolding for all the interested parties?"

Gabriella was pleased to lead the discussion. "Of course, here's where we stand today." She outlined the dates, sponsors, and promotional calendars for USAID, discussed public relations and where the committee was useful. The rodeo event was working out to be a great PR move for USAID and Sean's cover. Gabriella proved to be more than capable.

"Fabio is terrific. Every request we make, he delivers," Gabriella declared.

Vincent warned her, "Be cautious with Fabio. The Cartel gangs are dangerous."

"Be careful with Leal and Gacha, too. The committee is not to be trusted," Sean added.

"Any intel on our 'UnSub Professor' in the State Department?" asked Gabriella.

Vincent offered, "Nothing yet. He's being surveilled and they believe they can catch him in the act of espionage—so it may take a while."

Vincent liked to summarize Gabriella's intel, as if he were testifying to Congress. Sean often thought that could happen, given the money laundering.

Vincent began, "Fabio is the invisible head of the rodeo economics. He provided access to his relationships for money raising sponsorships totaling more than $1 million."

Gabriella interrupted, "—and he expects to keep a third of it for himself."

Vincent stated, "There are eight major bull riders entered so far, expected to draw 10,000–25,000 visitors for the weekend. Leal and Gacha are satisfied and able to make some profit from the event or raise political monies due to Leal's push within the UP political party, yes?"

Gabriella admired Vincent's attention to detail. "Yes. You are correct."

"Where will the friction come from? How are we handling security?" asked Vincent.

Gabriella glanced at Sean for help. Sean responded assertively, "Friction points are being analyzed. I have a sit-down with Fabio planned this week. We will provide clarity after that meeting."

Vincent looked at Sean intensely, "Be sure to get it settled. We need a plan for security and any on-site activities that represent USAID."

Sean acknowledged, "Consider it done."

Vincent and Sean exchanged looks. Without a single word spoken, they communicated visually with a growing confidence.

Vincent leaned back. "This rodeo event could bring Escobar out."

Pablo Escobar was quietly cutting deals with Ortega to hide his operations and money in Nicaragua. Escobar's operation included frequent stops for fuel and other exchanges in Panama, made possible by bribing Noriega.

On the other hand, Sean pointed out, "Escobar's violent nature is not something we could manage at the rodeo."

"Find out some intel from Fabio on this subject," Vincent told Sean.

It was lunchtime. Vincent suggested, "Let's all walk to the Four Seasons Garden Patio for a nice lunch."

Richard agreed, "Yes, we can continue our updates and get some fresh air."

As they walked, Vincent held onto Sean's arm, and they allowed Richard and Gabriella to walk ahead.

Vincent spoke softly. "Are we on the same page?"

Sean replied, calmly and quietly, "If you believe we can leverage our relationship with Fabio to stir up Escobar and create havoc for Ortega's Cartel monies by June—then, yes, we are on the same page."

Vincent placed his hands in his pockets, an affirmative sign that the plan was a go.

Sean expressed one question, "How much do we have in our contingency funds for the Bogotá play?"

Vincent stopped. He looked at Sean. "You will have to tell me what amount is going to be enough for the new op, and I will take care of that immediately."

Sean nodded, "Suddenly, I am hungry again,"

They walked to the table that Richard and Gabriella claimed and sat down.

Vincent opened up a new topic, "Consequential issues, anyone? Concerns?"

Sean asked, "What if we cannot get Sai Baba to convince Herrera to turn publicly and start a revolt?"

"We will. Meetings are being arranged and I will personally assure success," Vincent replied without hesitation.

Gabriella asked, "What if Sean is discovered to be CIA?"

"What have you heard?" Vincent interrupted.

Gabriella declared, "Nothing really, I just know he was profiled in Panama."

"There is always a risk undercover. Precautions are being taken. We need Sean's relationship with Fabio, and his knowledge of the Fun Zone operations," Vincent replied flatly.

Richard looked at the time, "If you two are making our flight, you need to pack-up and call for the car."

"Let's call the car. We can be ready in ten minutes," Gabriella spoke for herself and Sean.

Sean was already packed. He used the time to call the number Anna had given him.

"Hello?" said Anna.

"Hi, how's the townhouse?" said Sean.

"It's really nice, fully furnished and even has a garage for the rental car," Anna replied. "How are your meetings going?"

"Very productive. We are on course," said Sean happily. "I am on a quick break between meetings and dinner plans."

"Don't let me hold you up. I do love you, Nick," proclaimed Anna.

That punched Sean in the gut. Suddenly he was Nick. He realized how hurt Anna would be if she knew the lies he was telling, and about Gabriella. Pulling it together, Sean replied, "I love you, Anna. Be safe and I will check in soon."

Gabriella finished packing her bag. "All, okay?"

Sean smiled. Gabriella's instincts were sharp about Anna, "Yes, all is fine."

She walked over to him and wrapped her arms around him.

"Good, because you need to be focused this week. You are entering the dragon's lair and precision, tone, and details will be essential for survival."

Sean pulled her close and whispered into her ear, "Did you have to say survival?"

They laughed, grabbed their bags, gave big hugs to Vincent and Richard, and left for the airport. It had been a great weekend.

SEAN WAS pleased that Gabriella made the trip to Mexico City. It wasn't necessary and he knew she did it to support him and the operation.

They would be together in Bogotá the entire week. They needed their relationship to be healthy, productive, and satisfying with no distractions.

"What are you thinking about?" Gabriella asked. "I can feel your brain energy."

Sean looked deep into her eyes, "I am glad we made a pact to remain professional and to never let our feelings create a dangerous situation."

Gabriella looked down at the floorboard. "Me, too." She paused, "But we're still going to have sex tonight, right?"

They both laughed. "Of course!" Sean replied intently.

Chapter 24

Roadmap

March 2, 1987

IT WAS Monday morning, Sean was tired. Gabriella kept him up most of the night.

"What a beautiful night," Sean thought reflecting on their conversation and lovemaking.

Gabriella slipped out of her night shirt and whispered "I will always be with you . . . no matter where you are."

"Time stops when we are alone together," Sean said as he caressed her body and kissed her passionately. Sean could still feel her skin on his, her breathing escalating with his touch, and their rhythm working in harmony with each penetrating thrust. He loved how they could share their work pressures professionally, and then find such intimacy in their bodies.

The coffee was ready. Sean sat down at the kitchen table with his first cup. The next few months required exact execution in order—if Operation: Turn-About was to be successful.

Sean pulled out his sketch pad. He loved drawing out the plans, *It's like whiteboarding,* he thought. He jotted down bullet point after bullet point along a timeline:

- *By early April, Escobar would sit-down with Fabio and pull support from Ortega to avoid conflict with U.S. interests in the region.*

- *By April/May, President Sanchez of Costa Rica would coordinate support with other countries for the Reagan Central American Peace Accord. Influenced by Sai Baba, he will co-author the plan.*

- *By May/June, the Agency and Sai Baba would persuade Colonel Herrera to publicly denounce Ortega leading a Nicaraguan revolution and possible coup attempt; clandestine assets and operations must in place.*

- *By June/July, Ortega's supplies from the Soviets via Cuba cargo planes will be disrupted. The flow of money, weapons and supplies to Nicaragua will be stopped.*

- *By July, economic pressure and revolution threats will force President Ortega to the Peace Accord table. He will sign and end his allegiance to the Soviet Union. Target date is set for August 7, 1987.*

Sean mentally listed the essential steps for success: Contingency funds, USAID rodeo and Cartel sit-down, Sai Baba influence, Panamanian airport disruptions, riots against Noriega, President Sanchez leads the Peace Accord Plan, and enough pressure on Ortega to join the Peace Accord . . .

Sean closed eyes. His mind shifted to the resources they would need in the field. *This will take serious cash, weaponry, intelligence, and human intelligence strategically placed; Bogotá, Panama, Costa Rica, Nicaragua, Honduras and Mexico.*

SEAN'S PAGER vibrated. It was Anna. He had promised to call her. He peeked into the bedroom. Gabriella was sound asleep. He called Anna.

Anna answered, "Nick?"

Nick responded, "Good morning, honey. Everything going okay?"

"I love my new job! I have three people on my team already, and the project is amazing." Sean could feel Anna's enthusiasm. "That's terrific, I'm so happy for you."

"How is the rodeo event?" Anna asked. Nick knew she was trying to include him.

"It's progressing. We are meeting some interesting people and learning a lot of the Colombian business environment," Nick said, listening to his own lies. His gut was telling him that this relationship was over, things were going to get worse before it ended. For a moment, he thought about what his life could have been like without Vincent attached to it.

Anna said, "I am leaving the house now for work. Just wanted to hear your voice."

Nick replied, "Good luck today. I love you."

Anna responded, "I love you, too," and hung up.

He knew that he loved Anna, but he was not in love with her. Not sure he ever really was. His sense of sadness was overwhelming. He was cheating on Anna. *Gabriella. What the hell am I doing with Gabriella?* Sean tormented himself. He hung up the phone.

He heard Gabriella rustling in the bedroom and walked to the doorway. "Good morning."

"Good morning. Any coffee left?" she said with a warm smile.

Operation: Turn-About required laser focus. Timelines, requisitions for financial support, and coordinating assets filled every day going forward. By the end of the week, Gabriella was prepared for the USAID Rodeo and had submitted all required assistance at the Embassy. Legitimate cover for Fabio and the Cartel affiliates was in place. They were able to hold meetings, and discreetly message all stakeholders, even Escobar.

Sean planned the sit-down with Fabio for next week to update him and agree upon security assurances for the rodeo and Operation: Turn-About.

Jon established a list of preferred paramilitary assets and militia units in Panama, Nicaragua, and Bogotá for training and on-call service missions. It required a briefing with Vincent in Mexico City. Monday could not come fast enough for Jon. He was itching to start the training and whip his team into shape for the operation.

Jon and Sean discussed the details over scotch.

"You won't believe this one." Jon smirked.

Sean could feel his excitement, "What?"

"Sai Baba, all powerful Guru, has already scheduled the meeting with President Sanchez in Costa Rica for April third," Jon proudly exclaimed. "I knew he would take the pay-off."

"Is there still a plan to get Sai Baba and Colonel Herrera together in April?" Sean said, calculating the timeline in his head.

"YES! It will happen fast. Sai Baba agreed to the timeline," Jon confidently replied.

This provided time for the orchestration of three operational elements:

1) Psyops in Nicaragua threatening the civilian population.

2) Public denouncement of Ortega by Colonel Herrera and demand for a coup; and

3) Staged rioting in support of coup.

They toasted with another round of scotch.

Jon leaned back in, "Let's review Fun Zone ops."

"Okay, how are the trainings going?" asked Sean.

Jon, less confidently replied, "We have strong men, but their experience is light. We need more time to train on all aspects of airport militia actions."

"These airplanes and their personnel cannot make it to Nicaragua," impressed Sean.

Jon finished his third scotch. "We will not let that happen. But I will need you to run interrogations and kill orders."

"I'm ready." Sean could hear himself assuring Jon, but inside, it was gut wrenching. Cano's face haunted Sean. The night he assassinated Cano was a recurring nightmare. Sean had dreams of losing his soul bit by bit with each trigger point.

Jon was observing Sean closely. "Do you have any questions?"

"Will you be the team leader on every op?" asked Sean.

Jon replied pragmatically, "That's the plan, Sean, but if priorities send me on other ops, you will have the best op leaders backing you up, I promise. Okay?"

"Okay," Sean continued with another round of drinks, "Stopping these planes. Pulling weapons, supplies, money and some key officials, if we are lucky, will drive Ortega completely mad."

"Here's to driving Ortega completely MAD!" Jon laughed and raised his glass.

"SALUD!" Sean declared anxiously.

Chapter 25

Spring 1987

Monday, March 9, 1987

VINCENT HELD an all-day briefing in the basement of the U.S. Embassy in Mexico City. Jon scrutinized every alternative and mapped out each executional detail of the operation. Vincent focused on the deceptive narrative, critical timing, and the persuasive strategies on foreign leaders, civilian population, and allied forces.

Sean watched closely. *This operation was based on creative lies, artful timing, brutal mind games with force to back it up*, Sean thought. Vincent proved to be a master at the process. In just a few years, he would prove to be a highly regarded station chief in the Agency. Sean was proud to be selected for his team.

Jon loved showing off his tactical expertise. He lived for this type of action, thoroughly enjoying what he called, "The game of military persuasion—all for the greater good." Jon, a warm-hearted soul, woke up every morning, ready to attack whatever might be in the way. His role was well-defined: paramilitary presence, assassin, and field ops leader. He organized and commanded some 150 hand-selected troops throughout Central America that provided the covert operations needed to succeed. Sean absorbed Jon's energy in the meeting, all the while thinking, *Never ever get on the wrong side of Jon.*

Sean chuckled to himself.

Vincent and Jon looked up from their intel reports and planning notes.

"What?" said Vincent.

Sean straightened up in his chair, "Just pleased with the op and impressed with the rhythm of your work ethic."

"Good answer," growled Jon.

Vincent rolled his eyes. "We are done for today."

GABRIELLA SPENT days studying Fabio and the Cartel's business movements, methods and results. She performed well as the USAID representative in charge of the rodeo event, but her most important role was Sean's liaison and interpreter. She read all intelligence reports related to the Cartel and Leal. Sean relied on her to watch his back with the DEA, embassy investigations, Cartel movements, and provide cover. This was critical for Sean to move covertly throughout Central America.

Sean, youngest and least experienced team member, was anxious to prove himself. Gabriella established methods for mission checkpoints and communiques between them. There needed to be trust, loyalty and bravery otherwise this operation would fail.

SEAN CONFIRMED a meeting with Fabio at the Ochoa Ranch, Bogotá for Thursday. It was a clear, beautiful day with a slight breeze and no threat of rain or foul weather. Sean's car pulled into the ranch. Fabio was sitting under the big tree with one empty chair awaiting his arrival. Sean nicknamed it the "Welcoming Tree."

Jumping out of the car, Sean yelled. *"Me encanta este sitio!"* (I love this place!)

Fabio rose out of his chair, smiling. *"Hace mucho que mi amigo."* (It has been a while, my friend.)

They shook hands and gave each other a hug acknowledging their friendship. Sean could feel Fabio's long hug this time—as he checked Sean's body for wires and weapons.

It was necessary, thought Sean, *I would check him if the tables were turned.*

There would be contingency money for Fabio, given the influence he wielded with Escobar. That influence would slow or even stop the profitable flow of cash through Panama and Nicaragua during May and June.

Fabio gravely stared forward, "Sean, if you are unable to demonstrate progress in the plan by the end of June, Escobar will restart his businesses in full favor of Ortega and Nicaragua will be protected territory once again."

"Allowing the Soviets, a stronger foot-hold," Sean interjected with disgust.

Fabio reach over and firmly gripped Sean's kneecap. "It's not about politics for Escobar. It's money-laundering and drug trafficking. It's power."

Sean knew if that happened, significant financial leverage against Ortega would disappear. He turned to Fabio, "Well, we have our work cut out for us then."

Fabio burst into laughter, "That is funny my friend. Who is we? This is your show."

Sean laughed, "I try!"

As the laughing continued, Sean felt strangely uncomfortable, knowing he was at risk.

———

GABRIELLA AND Sean spent the next three weeks promoting the USAID Rodeo inside the Embassy and throughout Colombia. Gabriella brilliantly communicated the good it would bring to the agricultural development efforts throughout the rural areas of Colombia. Newspapers and local government officials bought into the value of the event for improving relations between the city and its rural counterparts. Sean and Gabriella were in lockstep with each other.

Sean routinely checked in Anna. The distance between them was growing. Sean flew to St. Louis to visit with Anna once to discuss plans for the relocation, but Anna seemed strangely settled in her townhome and more content with the infrequent calls and visits. Sean remembered her last comment as he left St. Louis, "Stay focused on your work. It should be the most important thing."

That remark was haunting him as he wondered, *What does that mean? Should I have stayed longer?* Operation: Turn-About was the priority.

Jon provided intelligence and weekly, detailed analysis along with the standard influx of field intelligence reports. Vincent ran the op from Mexico City. A rhythm was developing among the team that Vincent enjoyed watching. He expressed his confidence in them and the op regularly.

Monday, April 13, 1987

VINCENT BEGAN the briefing, "We have good news about Sai Baba's help. Costa Rican President Sanchez has begun drafting the Peace Accord based on President Reagan's goals, including our timeline. Furthermore, there is a meeting scheduled between Sai Baba and Colonel Herrera. It will occur Thursday, May 7, in Panama. Secret communications are set for Herrera and me. I will initiate after that meeting, assuming he is open to working with us."

Sean spoke up, "There should be no hesitation by Herrera. We will have complete leverage over his situation with Noriega."

"One never really knows the intentions of a man like Herrera," Vincent replied.

Jon successfully built squads throughout Panama, Nicaragua, and Bogotá trained to execute loudly or silently upon command. Deadly missions were looming.

Vincent changed the topic, "We need to start making ourselves visible to the Ortega-Noriega exchanges on the Panamanian airstrip. Our teams should be routine visitors in Hangar 63. They will be less suspicious about our plans to strike. Are we ready with the militia presence?"

"Yes, sir. We will station eight men at the hangar, thirty more in hideouts less than a half-mile away," Jon confirmed.

"Well done," Vincent said, smiling.

They devised a plan. Jon and Sean would make five trips into Panama for fake supply drops. These trips would appear normal, non-covert in nature, and timed to be seen by Ortega's squadrons as often as possible.

Sean questioned, "Will that create enough cover?"

"It should, but there are no guarantees," Jon murmured to Sean.

Vincent impressed upon them, "Let's not start the action doubting each other. The goal is to convince Ortega to sign the Peace Accord and disavow the Soviet Union publicly by August seventh."

The USAID Rodeo was only one week away. Gabriella provided the layout, timing, and exact locale for Fabio and Escobar to meet. Gabriella would be available to Fabio as needed to support Fabio's pitch to Escobar for help with applying economic pressure on Ortega.

Vincent told Jon to call Gabriella into the meeting.

While Jon stepped out, Vincent spoke softly to Sean, "You and Gabriella good?"

"We're good," replied Sean.

Vincent poured himself another cup of coffee and turned to Sean. "I'm guessing things are not so good with Anna."

"You're not really guessing, are you?" Sean replied in a flat manner, already knowing the answer.

Vincent went back to business as the door swung open and Gabriella entered. Her stride was strong, meaningful, and impossible to ignore.

Vincent snapped, "Will Escobar shut down exchanges in Panama during May and June?"

"Yes, Fabio assures me," Sean confirmed, but hesitated with a follow-up: "We need to verify that progress is being made in June or he will resume business in support of Ortega."

"That mother-fucking Escobar always has to give a directive," growled Vincent. "Be watchful of Escobar. He will look for weakness as leverage to use against us. He will not honor his word if there is a path to more money and power along the way."

Sean and Gabriella understood. "SURVIVAL comes first."

Chapter 26
Family & Marriage

Thursday, April 30, 1987

SEAN WAS ordered to make time for family. No one really knew how high the intensity level would climb to execute Operation: Turn-About. Sean felt responsible for the violence Gabriella had experienced just ten days earlier. He closed his eyes to avoid showing his pain.

ON APRIL 20, Fabio and Escobar met. Gabriella's instructions from Fabio were to wait for his arrival in the Ochoa Barn.

Sean winced in his airplane seat as he played Gabriella's words in his mind. Laying in the hospital bed she was still beautifully fierce.

Gabriella broke down with Sean, "I was sitting in the loft, when two of Escobar's men opened the door to look around."

Sean held her hand and listened.

"I tried to be still, but I wanted to hear what they were saying." Tears rolled down her face.

"I shifted my position. . . . boards creaked . . ." Gabriella paused to catch her breath. "Some hay floated down from the loft. They saw it and looked up."

Sean held her hand firmly, leaned over, and kissed her fore-head, "I understand."

"They climbed the ladder and saw me, made fun of me. . . . wouldn't listen to what I was saying."

Her anger took over. "The first man said, 'Take your clothes off, bitch.' I told him NO. I told him I was with USAID and Fabio's partner. They laughed at me. They just fucking laughed!"

Sean opened his eyes and looked out the window at the clouds below. There was evidence that her State Department in-telligence files may have been compromised, *There must be a con-nection to Leal and Morale—who else is informing Escobar—why would he attack Gabriella without damn good reason?*

Sean further questioned the leak as his mind white-boarded the connections. *Has Vincent been linked to Gabriella? How much do we think they know?*

Anger filled him as the replayed the hospital visit with Gabriella. She would not look at Sean as she told him what hap-pened.

"He came at me while the other man watched. He grabbed me and tried to push me down, but I wouldn't go down. I rammed my knee into his crotch and pushed my thumbs into his eyes. I could feel liquid . . . it was blood; it was blood from his eyes. I saw the second man coming at me." She breathed heavily. "I pushed the bloody eyed bastard off the loft. I didn't even flinch. I didn't watch him fall."

Gabriella went on with her story. "The second man stopped to watch his companion fall, and I jumped him. I landed on top of him and began to strangle him. After the fall, it didn't take much for him to lose consciousness. He was passing out, but I wouldn't let go!"

Sean closed his eyes again as he recalled her story.

Angrily, Gabriella went on, "That bastard was trying to pull his pistol on me, so, I pulled it for him. Then I looked at his ugly face and I shot him." I shot him in the face!" she cried.

"The first man was groaning and rolling about, blind. I walked over to him and shot him in the chest and then in the head."

Sean could feel her grip tightening around his hand. He stayed still. Then she broke down and cried out for forgiveness.

"Please God, please forgive me," she begged over and over.

Sean could barely take it. He tried to calm her. He whispered, "God will forgive you. You had to defend yourself."

She had run to the car and the driver took her to the hospital because of all the blood. But it was not her blood. She was severely shaken up.

Sean closed his eyes again as the plane descended into St. Louis, *Those men were Gabriella's first kill*, Sean thought. *She will never forget the feeling of those bloody eyes or the power of that shot.*

THE FLIGHT allowed Nick to shed himself of Sean's persona as he gazed down on the shelf of clouds below him. Gabriella was safe and back home in Arizona.

Despite the two dead men who were found, disposed of, and covered up by Fabio, the rodeo event had worked. Escobar understood that the deal with the Agency would make him millions of dollars for virtually no risk or loss. According to Fabio, Escobar left wanting to grant favors to the CIA.

Sean thought, *The clock is ticking.*

NICK DEPLANED and drove to his parents' home for dinner. He relaxed the minute he stepped out of the car. Nick's father inspected him.

"Thanks for everything, Dad. It's good to be home," Nick said.

Paul looked into Nick's eyes. "Starting out with a thank you? Do you need some help?"

"Not yet, Dad . . . not yet," Nick softly replied.

"I love you, son," said Paul.

"I love you, too." Nick was letting go of all the bad feelings and embracing family.

They stepped into the house. "Dinner smells AWESOME, Mom!" roared Nick.

Loretta smiled, "C'mon let's eat while it's hot!"

Nick loved his mom's fried chicken, mashed potatoes, corn, and beans. He missed farm cooking and hearty, fresh flavors. The visit was going fast. He knew would have to get back to St. Louis and make the most of the two nights with Anna.

He was pleased to hear that Vincent called his parents over the past couple of months to inform them that, "his work was valuable to ADM and the world." He smiled inside when his mom said she bragged about it to the rest of the family. He knew that his competitive brothers would go crazy over the calls, so he embellished with stories about Colombia and Central American agriculture and the positive economic impact to rural coopera-tives introducing new farming methods and practices.

The next morning, Nick shared a cup of morning Folgers and a long walk with his dad. Such moments bonded them deeply. It was difficult to mislead his father, but it was to protect his family from possible danger. Nick genuinely enjoyed walking the farm at sunrise. The trip re-energized him and reconnected him to his patriotic spirit. His chosen career path with Vincent was the right choice.

After the walk, they went into the kitchen where the aroma of breakfast filled the air. Nick hugged his mom and let her know how hungry he was. Breakfast was delicious.

"Time to get back to Anna," Nick said, throwing his clothes back into his travel bag.

Paul asked, "How is Anna? You didn't mention her much on this visit."

"I really don't know. Our lives seem to be going different directions," said Nick.

Paul placed his hand on Nick's shoulder. "If you love her, you will find your way."

"I understand, Dad." Nick hugged him tight. "Time to go find out."

"I love you, Mom. I am so full!" Nick hugged her and left.

The drive felt long and lonely. Nick was dreading the visit. His father's voice was stuck in his mind, "If you love her, you will find your way."

Friday, May 1, 1987

ANNA ARRIVED home after work to find Nick napping on the couch. She walked softly past him and went upstairs to the master bath. Staring into the mirror, she wondered how their whole marriage happened, asking herself if Nick felt the same way. She freshened up and decided to change her clothes for the evening, determined to make the most of the evening together.

As she pulled a pretty Ann Taylor dress from the closet, her memories of college days surfaced. Nick would spontaneously show up with a single flower in one hand and a pizza in the other. She missed the simplicity of those moments. She missed that Nick.

She startled when Nick appeared in the doorway with two glasses of wine. "Hello," said Nick.

Anna smiled. "Hello, stranger."

He handed her a glass of wine. "Here's to the project leader," he said raising a glass and kissing her on the cheek. He took a step back. "You look different. Definitely more in charge."

Anna laughed, "Now you're just trying to get on my good side."

They left for dinner. It was a restaurant with a private booth, stellar service, live piano music, and gourmet food.

"I love this place," declared Anna.

"I made the reservation over a month ago. I told them it was special occasion, so let's enjoy."

"Thank you, honey," said Anna. "It's wonderful."

Although they both wanted to be in love, all conversation ended with work. As Nick drove home, Anna decided to ask questions. "Tell me about the people you work with."

"What would you like to know?"

Anna nudged him. "Everything."

Nick laughed, then described Vincent in ways that even surprised himself. "Vincent is kind, caring, smart, multilingual, a strong leader, and gay. His life partner is named Richard."

They pulled into the garage. As they got ready for bed, Anna continued her inquiry. Anna appeared obsessed with Nick's work relationships in Bogotá.

Once in bed, romance was absent. She asked more questions about Jon, USAID, the Embassy, and then it happened. She asked, "Don't you work closely with an interpreter?"

"Yes. Gabriella." He proceeded to describe her talents, her experience, and how helpful it was to have her plan, execute, and promote the rodeo event.

Anna listened and placed her hand on Nick's chest.

She whispered, "Is Gabriella pretty?"

Nick embraced the question truthfully. "Yes, very pretty," Nick replied and waited.

Anna removed her hand. "I figured."

He lay still. Anna asked no more questions.

"Let's get some sleep," she said quietly.

Morning came fast. Nick woke and looked at Anna sleeping in bed and quietly put on his running gear. He missed running in his familiar neighborhood parks. During his run, his mind reeled, thinking about Operation: Turn-About, interrupted by flashes of what Anna was thinking.

When he returned, Nick found Anna at the kitchen table waiting for him. He poured himself a cup of coffee and sat down.

"How was your run?" Anna asked.

"It was great. It's a beautiful day. Want to go to the river boardwalk and take a walk later?" he said, measuring her temperature.

She was not interested. "Do you go out to dinner much with Gabriella?"

Nick leaned toward Anna. "Yes, we have dinner for planning, dinner for promotions, and sometimes just dinner."

Anna's tone revealed some anger. "Is she married?"

Nick lied. "Yes. She's been married for about five years."

Nick's answer stalled her line of questioning. The anger left Anna's face, but it was replaced with a look that Nick did not recognize. She seemed genuinely sad. Nick decided this was his opportunity to speak up.

"What is wrong?" Nick asked.

"I feel alone. You're never home," she said quietly.

Nick knelt on one knee. He could feel her pain. "I know this is a hard time for us."

"I just feel like you have more reasons to be in Bogotá than to be here with me."

Nick knew that the statement was the absolute truth.

As he consoled Anna, he realized that this was it. Their relationship was breaking. Then Anna dropped an unexpected blow.

"I met someone," she confessed.

Nick stood up. "What does that mean?"

Anna's eyes filled with tears. "I am sorry. Nothing has happened, but I do go out with him for company and—"

Nick stopped her. "It's okay. I understand."

His reaction seemed to surprise her; her guilt turned into rage. "You are sleeping with that woman, Gabriella!"

Nick decided he had better get control of the situation. "No, Anna. But maybe you are sleeping with this man? What's his name?"

Anna screamed, "I am not sleeping with anyone!"

Nick, irritated and upset, believed that was probably true. "So . . . What is his name?"

"Dan."

Nick forcefully asked, "Dan what?" Her hesitation to provide his full name told Nick everything he needed to know. Nick didn't let her answer, "Fine. Don't answer. Protect him."

Nick took a breath, thought about his circumstances, and realized that he was being given an amazing gift. He needed time away and this was his opportunity to make that easy for both. He knelt and reached for Anna's hands.

"Let's take a break. Figure out what we really want."

Anna, crying uncontrollably, said, "You want to end it?"

Nick held her hands tightly. "No, honey. It's just that we are both under a lot of pressure, we are working so hard."

Anna began to calm down, so Nick went on. "My internship will be up in August. Let's not put any more pressure on our relationship. We can take that time to focus on what we need, what we want and then share it with each other."

Anna leaned into Nick. "I love you."

Nick embraced her. "I love you, too." It was an unspoken agreement. They'd take a break for three months.

Nick approached Anna, "We have tonight. Want to take a walk later, get some take out and open a bottle of wine and just relax?"

Somewhat distraught, she answered, "I think you're right, Nick. We need a break to figure things out."

"Okay," said Nick.

Within minutes, he had packed his bag. He knew he had offered the olive branch, and she had refused it. It was his chance to leave and be able to focus entirely on Operation: Turn-About.

He walked down the stairs with his travel bag in hand. He leaned over to Anna and kissed her on the cheek—then passionately on the lips.

"Stay in touch, so I know you are safe, and I will do the same," he told her.

Anna started crying, but she didn't try to stop him. He walked out the door, determined to drive straight to the airport. As he drove, tears welled up in his eyes, yet he knew he had done the right thing by leaving. He knew that he had betrayed her, broken his vows, and now could not see how to fix it. The relationship with Anna could be a distraction from the operation and he could not allow that to happen.

It was for the best, he thought.

He arrived at the airport and changed his Bogotá flight ticket. Then it dawned on him—he had sabotaged his marriage. Stopping at the bathroom, he looked at himself closely in the mirror, his heart was hurting. He told himself, *You are a bad person. You cheated on your wife. You lied to your father; YOU ARE A KILLER.*

Chapter 27

Setting Up "The Turn"

Sunday, May 3, 1987

SEAN WOKE up at dawn, put on his running clothes, and left the Bogotá apartment for a five-mile run to shake off the family trip and his separation from Anna. In just four days, he would meet Colonel Herrera, Noriega's former #2 man in the Panamanian military. *Why did Vincent invite me?* thought Sean as he broke into full stride. The meeting objective: Convince Herrera to publicly shame Ortega in Nicaragua, and to start a revolt against Noriega in Panama.

When Sean returned to the apartment, there was a slew of intel reports waiting for him. Herrera, Noriega, and Ortega were all persons of interest. Jon managed to provide a great deal of detail regarding the Panamanian airstrip traffic and Ortega's militia schedules. Interestingly, there was always a top aide for Noriega present when Ortega's exchanges occurred.

Sean looked at the ceiling. *The night Jon and I were stopped and held at gunpoint, it was Ortega brass and Darryn Morales, a top aide for Noriega.* Puzzle pieces were still missing. Sean made

Panama his focus; disrupting the relationship between Noriega and Ortega was a core tactic of Operation: Turn-About.

Days were flying by.

"It's Wednesday already." Sean sat in the empty apartment while he waited for Vincent and Jon to arrive. They arrived at noon. They worked at the kitchen table and laid out the Herrera visit. A safe house was arranged in the Old Quarter, Casco Viejo, the historic district of Panama City, about 20 miles outside of downtown. Heavily patrolled, it was a safe place if you kept to yourself. The plan involved moving Herrera into the house under cover and back out under cover in a single morning.

Vincent, prepared to entice Herrera with U.S. protection and extraction as needed, was armed with dirty intel on both Noriega and Ortega. He held sufficient proof of the many evils that Noriega had committed against Panama and even Herrera's own family. Vincent put a dossier together on Ortega that would convict the Pope. Herrera would believe it.

At one point, Jon spoke up, "Where did you get this Ortega dossier?"

"Why?" asked Vincent.

"His crimes are perfectly documented; it's hard to imagine getting this close in real life," said Jon.

"I wrote it," Vincent proclaimed.

Jon kept looking at it, "How?"

"Simple. I made it up." Vincent smiled.

Jon and Sean laughed in amazement at Vincent's admission. They wrapped up the plan, feeling confident in their preparations. Jon had to leave immediately for other ops meetings. Vincent asked Sean to sit and have a drink. He poured two glasses.

Vincent asked, "Do you know your contingency plan, should things go bad?"

"Yes," replied Sean.

Vincent said, "Walk me through your schedules and targets."

Sean outlined the schedules and identified and listed top aides as targets for interrogation. "Ortega and Noriega will be pissed and full of vengeance," Sean added.

"That's the idea," said Vincent. "Make it appear brazen and sloppy, Noriega will think it's the Cartel or El Salvador."

"Jon wants to smuggle me into the hangar by hiding me in an arms box on the plane in the dead of night," Sean said.

"Yes? Is there a question?" prodded Vincent.

"They will place me in the basement quarters unseen." Sean was measuring Vincent's reaction as he poured another drink. When any exchange between Ortega and Noriega occurred, Jon's squad would intervene and grab the targets.

Sean looked at his drink and peered at the golden colors shimmering through the ice. He asked, "My orders are to terminate all hostages posing a danger to the op?"

Vincent sighed but said nothing.

"Am I being ordered to kill everyone we stop?" Sean said in disbelief.

Vincent proclaimed, "You will terminate all hostages, because they represent a clear and present danger."

"Can't we hold them or relocate them?" asked Sean.

"No, you're not thinking this through," replied Vincent.

Sean acknowledged, "Maybe not, but I am thinking about how to live with it."

"Follow orders and run the op. You can write your own ticket." Vincent looked at Sean for any sign of uncertainty.

Sean snapped back, "My ticket doesn't mean shit, if I can't live with myself."

Vincent raised his voice, "You won't mean shit to me if you can't follow my orders. You belong to Clandestine Services, and I am your SUPERIOR. You will not place this op in danger!"

"I value the op. I value you and our entire team," Sean replied compliantly.

"Then do your duty." Vincent exhaled to let go of the anger.

"Let's call it for now. Tomorrow is critical," Vincent declared.

"I understand my duty. I will get some rest," offered Sean.

AT 5:30 A.M., Vincent, Jon, and Sean met at the private airstrip just outside of Medellín. Their plane into Panama City was refueling. Jon's squad in Panama awaited the signal for transport Herrera from his home to the safe house. Vincent and Sean were positioned at the safe house in advance of his arrival.

In no time, Colonel Herrera was seated in a high back chair, drinking coffee, and looking Vincent in the eye. After the usual polite gestures, Vincent went straight for the jugular. "You will accuse Noriega of drug trafficking and of planning the assassination of Omar Torrijos Herrera, Noriega's predecessor. YES?"

"Yes," said Herrera.

Vincent continued, "You will claim that Noriega planted an explosive in Torrijos' private aircraft, and you will declare that Noriega ordered the killing of your friend, Hugo Spadafora. And, lastly, you will declare that Noriega orchestrated fraud in the 1984 presidential election with the help of Daniel Ortega. . . . Making secret deals to smuggle arms into Nicaragua."

Herrera calmly said, "This will ignite protests and riots throughout Panama."

"Yes, it will. Lastly, you will demand that Noriega be removed," replied Vincent.

Herrera listened intently. Sean watched. Herrera hated Noriega deeply and wanted to hang him—but his actions were dangerous and traitorous—on behalf of the people of Panama.

After what seemed like an eternity, Herrera tapped his fingers on the table and said, "Let's talk about me."

"What about you?" Vincent asked with a slight grin.

"I need protection, real protection. I need extraction guarantees, payment in advance. My family is to be relocated to America now, and I will join them, alive," Herrera said, resolved.

Vincent started negotiations. "How much?"

"One million dollars now in a secure offshore account." Herrera reached into his pocket and slid a folded piece of paper to Vincent. "Two million more if I die. I need that in writing and signed right now for my wife, or this doesn't happen."

Vincent leaned back and crossed his arms. "Is that everything?"

"Yes," replied Herrera.

"Well. . . . I guess we better keep you alive." Vincent smiled and held his hand out.

Herrera shook Vincent's hand and gripped it tightly, "Can I trust you?"

"Yes," replied Vincent.

They released their handshake.

Vincent said, "Paper on this will be ready in one hour, funds will be wired today, and Jon will coordinate your security and protection. Did I miss anything?"

Herrera smiled for the first time. "Make that happen, and we will rain down on Noriega and Ortega."

The meeting was completed before noon. Herrera returned home; Jon remained in Panama to coordinate necessary ops. Vincent and Sean flew to Mexico City, and walked into Winston Churchill's Restaurant for drinks and an afternoon meal.

Vincent was pleased with the meeting, "This is the beginning of the end for Noriega. That little bastard doesn't have a clue."

"Noriega thinks he owns Herrera and his family," Sean smirked.

"We will stop Ortega's arms and money. Any fucking plane that has a hint of Soviet smell coming through Panama will be destroyed. Fuck Castro and Cuba." Vincent was on a roll.

Sean listened and watched Vincent's energy spill out of him. It was new to Sean, the excitement in his voice. It was contagious.

Vincent raged on, "We will punch Ortega in the face. He will go broke defending communism against the freedom fighters. That motherfucker will sign Reagan's Peace Accord and denounce the Soviet Union. OR HE WILL DIE."

Sean looked at Vincent, raised his glass. "To Operation: Turn-About!"

They drank well into the evening.

FRIDAY MORNING: Sean still tasted scotch from the night before.

Vincent called Sean at his hotel. "Get ready, get dressed, let's take a walk."

Vincent enjoyed downtown Mexico City. He particularly loved City Square and would frequent the hat shops and tailors. As they walked, he shared intel with Sean.

"We have confirmed a high-level exchange of money and arms will occur near the Fun Zone around the first of June. There may be smaller loads before and after as well. But a top official was expected to be at that exchange."

Sean understood. "We are ready."

Over lunch, Vincent updated Sean: "Tuesday, you will be smuggled into the Fun Zone where you will remain until the revolt occurs. We anticipate Herrera's statements to go public on June seventh."

Sean finished his food. "Are we conducting psyops?"

Vincent laughed, "Look at you, all grown up."

Vincent continued: "Radio recordings and propaganda. Everywhere we have influence in Panama and Nicaragua. My personal goal is 100,000 people rioting against Noriega in downtown Panama City."

Sean processed the intel. "Noriega will have his hands full that week."

Vincent pressed Sean. "Your mission, Sean, is critical to the op. You must follow orders and Ortega will sign—otherwise we're fucked."

Sean leaned in, "I won't let you down."

Vincent said gravely, "Don't get caught and don't get killed."

Panama Heats Up

Tuesday, May 12, 1987

SEAN LAID still, crammed into a 6-foot by 3-foot gun box. Small air holes were drilled into one end of the box. He could hear the men on the plane talking but couldn't make out what they were saying. After an hour-long flight, his box was unloaded, and carried into the basement of the hangar. As the lid was pried open, Sean climbed out and felt fresh air rush into his lungs.

Sean was smuggled into the Fun Zone. His living quarters consisted of an 8-foot by 8-foot room with a small bathroom. It was built to maintain detainees and prisoners, making it an ideal spot for Sean's clandestine activity. Equipped with surveillance video monitors showing all angles of the hangar, Sean could see movements and listen in as needed. Intel indicated a possible flight from Cuba in the next 48 hours. Sean was ready.

Sean replayed his orders over and over in his mind. He trusted Jon and his paramilitary squad, so, he waited. Jon stocked the room with all of Sean's requested staples: large jars of peanut butter, bread, honey, water, and a coffee maker, along with a small refrigerator for fruits and dairy. Napping, exercising, and reading intel reports filled Sean's first two days.

Thursday afternoon, there were no updates from Jon. At 6 p.m., Jon knocked on the door briskly and opened it without hesitation. "No exchange tonight," he said. None of the target planes had taken off.

In the morning, Sean needed a cardio workout. He stretched and started jumping jacks. He started counting, but after two hundred or so, he lost count. He kept going for another twenty to thirty minutes, did fifty push-ups, and fifty sit-ups. Satisfied, he started his coffeemaker.

My one luxury in this shitty little cell.

After his third cup, he repeated his workout. He remembered his training from The Farm in Virginia, "The waiting is the worst part of the op. Knowing what you will do and being forced to think about it without knowing when you will do it. . . ."

Sean, addicted to peanut butter for breakfast, waited on the delivery of intel reports. He brushed his teeth, looked in the mirror, and left the light beard on his face alone. He showered and dressed just in time to receive the intel under the door. *Another day in paradise.*

Intel indicated activity—mostly Jon's teams reporting on movements in the region. Progress toward the Central American Peace Accord included commitments from Guatemala, El Salvador, and Honduras. Costa Rica and U.S. led the drafting. Nicaragua was the sole target country in question.

Escobar honored his word. Funds from drugs and money laundering in Nicaragua had stopped flowing. Sean read on. There was plenty of political conflict in the U.S. Congress; Senate leaders hassled President Reagan about Contras in Nicaragua. Sean closed eyes. *The pressure is high on Operation: Turn-About.*

Panamanian psyops were in place. Psyops against Noriega would launch inside Panama in next ten days. Colonel Herrera would publicly denounce Noriega and Ortega. Psyops, acts of civil unrest, and social propaganda would drive the narrative in both countries. Sean laughed, *Take that, you bullshit bureaucrats in Congress.*

Vincent deployed a team of radio spokesmen in Panama and Nicaragua. They pre-recorded news about the riots that were yet to occur. And they planted editorials about the corruption of Noriega and Ortega, all to be published by credible sources.

Sean thought about the op: *Ortega must turn by July, if he is to sign the Peace Accord. He must abandon his alliance with the Soviet Union.* The clock was ticking, and it was Sean's job to apply pressure on Ortega. Convinced he was fighting for the greater good, Sean prepared himself to do whatever was necessary to complete his op.

Night came. Jon entered Sean's cell, "It's happening. A plane from Cuba suspected to be carrying weapons is scheduled for a refueling stop/drop less than 300 yards from the Fun Zone."

"Do we have intel on the passengers?" asked Sean.

Jon shook his head. "Negative."

Sean paused. "Well then, we will just have to wing it."

Sean and Jon knew their orders: "DO NOT KILL TOP AIDES FROM NICARAGUA" without a verification order. All others were classified as "KILL AS A CLEAR AND PRESENT DANGER." Jon trained his team of twelve Special Ops and paramilitary soldiers who occupied the hangar barracks and another thirty-six surrounding the airstrip.

10:42 p.m.: Jon's team waited alongside the airstrip. Armed for a flanking attack capable of overpowering any flight crew or militia force, Jon kept Sean updated on radio.

11:53 p.m.: the plane had landed, taxied to the refueling station and stopped. The boarding door opened; two pilots stepped out with only one guard in tow.

In just seconds, Jon's squadron surrounded the plane, shot the guard, and received fire from within the plane. In less than three minutes, the guards in the plane surrendered. Jon ordered the pilots back aboard, then directed them to the Fun Zone. The squad opened the hangar door, and the plane pulled in quietly.

Loaded from top to bottom with Soviet weapons, ammunition, and cash, the plane was searched for any intel. The two pilots and two guards were hooded and awaited Sean in the interrogation room. Sean let them sit in silence for 20 minutes while he studied their identification, documents, and the cargo. It was apparent that all cargo was Soviet sponsored covered with obscure Cyrillic writing. Jon and Sean relayed their findings to Vincent for cross referencing on the pilots.

Sean took a shot of scotch, as he waited for Vincent's intel on the pilots.

Vincent signaled a GO.

Jon approached Sean, "The two pilots are in the Sandinista forces under Ortega."

Sean started interrogating the guards.

"Who do you work for?"

"What is your rank?"

"What country do you belong to?"

"Do you report to Castro? Is Cuba your home?"

Sean knew the answers. When they lied, he beat them with strikes to the face. The pilots watched in horror.

Without notice, Sean reached his trigger point. He stepped outside himself, pulled his Walther PPK and shot both men in the head. As the men fell to the floor, Sean stood over them and shot them in the chest. The pilots were screaming for mercy and praying to God.

Sean holstered his pistol, turned to the pilots, "Are you ready to tell us the truth?"

For the next several hours, Sean combined physical and psychological harassment. He was trained to perform these tortures, using what the CIA called "persistent manipulation of time"—each time the pilots passed out, Sean woke them up with ice cold water and face slapping, further disorienting them.

Sean maintained his composure by focusing on his training. The Agency taught interrogation methods that would drive the target deeper and deeper into themselves until they were no longer able to control their responses.

4:30 a.m.: Sean retrieved a potentially valuable name from one of the pilots. The other pilot, clearly the superior, remained resistant.

Sean took a break, ordered the men to be stripped naked and chained to metal chairs placed side by side. An electric generator attached to clamps was brought into the room. All soldiers were ordered out of the interrogation room.

5:00 a.m.: Sean re-entered the interrogation room. The men were hooded, exhausted, and frail. Sean loudly pulled a metal chair across the floor and stopped it right in front of them. He whispered, *"Si no respondes a mis preguntas . . . sientiras dolor durante días."* (If you don't answer my questions, you will feel pain for days.)

The pilot screamed, *"NO, NO, NO."*

The junior pilot cried and begged, *"NO, POR FAVOR, YA NO!"*

Sean stood, pulled his Walther PPK, and shot the crying pilot in the head and the chest. The pilot slumped in the chair, bleeding out.

The pilot, shocked at the killing, snapped and began to plead for his life. *"POR FAVOR, SEÑOR, NO QUIERO MORIR!"*

"Who do you work for?"

"Who are your superiors?"

"Where do the weapons come from?"

The pilot repeated the same answer, "I don't know!"

Sean leaned in and whispered, *"No hay respuestas, siente el dólar."* (No answers. Feel the pain.) He calmly turned the generator on, turned the setting to a four, placed the clamps on the pilot's feet. The pilot convulsed, squirmed, and screamed for mercy. Sean removed the clamps.

"*Quieres mas?*" (Do you want more?)

The pilot cried and begged, "*Ya no, ya no.*" (No more, no more.) Then he broke down. "Ortega!" The pilot cried out, "Ortega, I work for Ortega!"

Sean, pleased inside, leaned down to look eye-to-eye with the pilot, "*Has hecho lo correcto.*" (You have done the right thing.)

SEAN PRESENTED a form to the pilot, stating the pilot's agreement to cooperate with asylum and protection. In exchange, he would disclose upcoming strategies, routes and schedules, intel on Nicaragua, Cuba and the Soviet Union. The pilot signed. Jon removed him and prepared him for transport.

Sean left the room to convey his findings to Vincent in code.

"Excellent," replied Vincent. Vincent ordered a debriefing with Sean. "Jon will coordinate transport of Sean to the black site offshore."

Jon informed Sean that during the interrogation, his squad unloaded the plane. The Agency pilot ditched the plane in the jungles of Panama, blew it up as if it had crashed after refueling. The team returned without drawing any unnecessary attention from the Panamanian authorities.

Impressed with the tactical performance, Sean climbed into a supplies bag customized with air holes and an AK-47.

Jon spoke to Sean through the bag, "Don't fall asleep and shoot yourself."

"Good advice," replied Sean.

The squad loaded the bag onto the passenger plane for a direct flight to Mexico City.

This first strike of Operation: Turn-About set the stage with Noriega and Ortega. Soon forces will be organized. The op was live and more dangerous every day.

Sean, curled up in the supply bag, recorded his movements in his mind. Reality was setting in. He closed his eyes to rest, knowing, *There will be more killing, evil fights. . . . don't lose yourself, Nick, just do your job.*

Chapter 29
Mind Games

SEAN ARRIVED in Mexico City, checked into the Marriott, showered, and dressed. As he took the elevator down to the lobby, visions of the men he killed scrolled through his mind. The elevator bell rang, its doors opened, and the crowded lobby bar was in plain sight. Vincent was seated at the bar, and Sean could tell from his posture, he was well into this third scotch or more. Taking a deep breath, Sean walked calmly across the lobby. Vincent noticed him, smiled and signaled to join him.

Vincent waived the bartender over and order two scotch—rocks.

"Sean, that was excellent work with the pilot," affirmed Vincent.

"He had that look about him. He was holding back secrets," Sean replied.

They received the drinks and raised their glasses without a single word.

Vincent couldn't resist poking at Sean, "I guess the other three had no secrets to tell."

"Fuck you," Sean enunciated slowly under his breath.

Vincent leaned toward Sean, "Don't say things like that. You're letting your emotions get the better of you."

Sean looked at Vincent. "Are we going to explore my feelings now?"

Vincent scowled slightly. "Jon mentioned that you seemed robotic, outside yourself, disconnected from what was happening."

Sean paused. "I followed my training; each kill was necessary to the op. I remained focused on the interrogation."

Vincent agreed, "You can't argue with the results."

Sean smiled in an evil manner. "That's right."

"Still," said Vincent, "I want you to go back to Bogotá tomorrow after the briefing. Rest, decompress for three days."

Sean interjected, "How is Gabriella doing?"

"She is healthy, mentally strong, but on leave for now."

Sean asked, "Is she seeing a therapist?"

"Yes, Sean. All you need to know is that she is safe and improving, okay?"

"Okay." Sean was satisfied and agreed to rest in Bogotá.

Over dinner, they discussed new intelligence and agreed that their strike on the Nicaraguan plane already caused strain and paranoia. Both Noriega and Ortega were talking and taking action to investigate.

Vincent offered an update on psyops: "Radio reports are ready. The largest federal stations have been covertly opted in to run the reports. Dissidence and widespread distrust of Noriega and Ortega will be released on command."

Sean just listened.

Vincent continued: "Colonel Herrera's declarations will be a devastating blow to Noriega's credibility. They will create a political hit against Ortega."

"It's happening," acknowledged Sean, as he raised his glass.

Monday, May 18, 1987

THE MEXICO City briefing began at 9:00 a.m. sharp. Vincent, Sean, Jon, and an agency recorder were present. They opened the briefing by rehashing the details from beginning to end.

Jon provided a review and analysis regarding tactics and methods used to take over the plane. One soldier was killed in the operation.

Sean discussed the interrogation methods deployed. His rationale for valuing the detainees, and decision to utilize psychological tactics against the pilots.

Vincent interrupted Sean's presentation, "Two soldiers were executed in front of the pilots. Why?"

Sean answered, "My orders were clear, sir—"

Vincent vehemently interrupted, "My QUESTION was not about YOUR ORDERS."

"I determined both soldiers to be a clear and present danger to the op," replied Sean.

"Go on," said Vincent.

Sean continued: "The junior pilot clearly had no value to the op. I executed him in front of the senior pilot, for psychological impact. I then rested and allowed the senior pilot to think about his options. Upon my return, I proceeded with enhanced interrogation methods, including controlled electrical shock. The pilot gave up his employer as Ortega and begged for asylum and cooperation. He is being held at an undisclosed location, a black site off the coast, deep into international waters."

Vincent declared, "That's it. Good job. Hold tape, hold transcription."

They were finished. The debriefing took less than an hour.

Vincent whispered to Jon, "Stay in touch, don't take offensive actions unless threatened." Jon nodded, said his goodbyes, and left to oversee his squadron. He knew he was walking into a whirlwind of investigations, militia seeking answers about the Nicaraguan plane crash, and the lack of weaponry found.

Vincent turned to Sean. "Why don't you take off now and catch the next flight to Bogotá?"

As they hugged goodbye, Vincent spoke softly, "These killings, this op is about keeping communism out of Central America. Embrace your feelings, talk about it, and stay focused on the greater good. Okay?"

Sean whispered in response, "When will Richard be back for a visit?"

Vincent smiled, "The week of the Fourth of July. We will get together, no doubt."

SEAN LANDED in Bogotá just after 4:00 p.m., called a car, and headed for the empty apartment. He knew it would be safe, he could relax. Sean thought to himself, *It's the closest thing I have to a home at this point.*

Vincent was right: his mind was replaying the executions of every man. Sean asked himself, *How could I be so disconnected?* He had no answer.

The car arrived at his apartment building. Sean found himself dreading the idea of spending the next three days alone, forced to look at himself, to reflect on his actions.

As he entered the apartment, something was different. Sean pulled his gun and crept through the living room peering about, listening for any noise at all. Then his senses picked up on a fresh scent, one he recognized.

"Gabriella?" he shouted.

Gabriella appeared in the bedroom doorway, still wet from a shower, and dressed in a robe. She spoke slowly and lovingly, "Don't shoot me. I heard you had enough this week."

Nick, no longer Sean at that moment, embraced her. Their bodies were drawn like magnets.

"I thought you could use some friendly fire," whispered Gabriella.

Nick was so happy to have her close, words were difficult.

"C'mon," said Gabriella, "let's heal each other."

They lay in bed, shared stories of their families, work, fears, things they had done that they were not so proud of, and things they were proud of.

They shared intimacy, not sex. Nick admitted his mixed emotions about the op and so many killings. Tears came and went throughout the night. He needed a respite, time to reflect before going into the next phase.

Gabriella asked him about his marriage.

"It's coming to an end." Nick replied. "We've separated, until August. Then we will decide what we want."

Gabriella was not surprised. She empathized with Nick, more than she cared to admit. Nick did not tell her that he had lied to Anna about their sexual relationship, and Gabriella didn't press.

They slept in after the long night of talking. Nick could not believe how late he had slept. His only orders were to remain in communication and read daily intel briefings.

AN ENVELOPE was waiting for him just inside the door. He opened it, saw the cover message from Vincent. His fingers ran along the bottom right-hand corner and felt Vincent's embossed code. The cover message simply read: You have stirred Winnie the Pooh's honey pot. Sean knew this meant that Panama and Nicaragua were upset and soon Colonel Herrera would be on center stage causing a shitstorm. The message closed with Investigations will find nothing.

Sean took the intel package into the kitchen, looked out over the park paths below, and began to read. Gabriella sauntered in, poured herself a cup of coffee, admired the beautiful spring day, and kissed Sean on the neck. "All good?"

"All good." Sean looked at her. "Let's take a walk today, find a place to eat outside." Gabriella loved the idea. "Give me an hour to get ready, okay?"

"Excellent," replied Sean.

The day was relaxed. Gabriella was in Bogotá to wrap up her role with USAID at the Embassy. She worked on closing reports. Then she shifted her attention to Thunderbird University, preparing to instruct classes in the summer. Sean studied the intel reports.

Cocktails and dance music were in order as night fell. Sean offered to go out, but Gabriella responded, "Let's stay in and have our own party."

Sean made very dry gin martinis, "Shaken or stirred?"

Gabriella belly laughed, "I love those movies!"

"Me too," declared Sean.

"But he's not real; he's a bit like a cartoon, don't you think? Gabriella asked.

"I suppose you're right," Sean reflected on the movies.

Gabriella said, "I'm making beef and cheese empanadas."

Sean smiled. *"Suena delicioso!"* (Sounds delicious!)

Gabriella flirted in response, *"Tu español es bueno, quien es tu profesor?"* (Your Spanish is good, who's your teacher?)

Sean walked over to her, *"Tengo un professor incredible."* (I have an amazing teacher.)

They kissed deeply. There was no stopping their attraction.

"Take me now," gasped Gabriella.

They flung their clothes to the floor. The dim lights allowed Sean to see Gabriella's sensuous curves and skin. He firmly gripped her right hip with his hand, and slowly touched her opposite knee caressing her thigh upward, then kissing her neck sensuously. Her body shivered with anticipation. His hands explored every inch of her until he reached the small of her back. Pulling her closer, their bodies touched, breast to chest, and hip to hip. Sean wanted her, she needed him. She could feel his growing passion and she was ready.

They made love all night, orgasm after orgasm. Insatiable for each other until they were breathless. Drinking martinis, eating cheese and crackers when necessary—and sleeping only when they could take no more.

Morning light penetrated the bedroom. They could barely open their eyes.

Sean whispered, "I can feel the blood moving through my head—and it hurts to breathe."

Gabriella laughed, "Stop, it hurts my head to laugh. I think we overdid it."

Sean gently rolled out of bed, found some aspirin, and walked to the kitchen to get two bottles of water. He brought everything back to the bed, holding out the aspirin in one hand and the bottle of water in the other as if he were a nurse tending a patient.

Gabriella took the aspirin and gulped down the water. They rolled back under the covers and went back to sleep.

At 8:30 a.m., Gabriella's awoke. She needed to attend meetings at the Embassy. Sean continued to lay still and let his body coax itself back to life. Gabriella leaned over the bed, dressed and ready for work, and gave him a kiss on the forehead, "See you later, okay?"

"Okay, be good today," replied Sean.

Sean took the rest of the day to rest. Gabriella returned from the Embassy around 5:30 p.m. They ordered pizza, stayed in, and watched movies.

As they relaxed, he revealed to Gabriella his plans, "By this time tomorrow, I will be in the Fun Zone."

She asked, "Do you get scared?"

"Yes, but just enough," replied Sean.

She kissed him. That night, they fell asleep on the couch in each other's arms.

SEAN WOKE up early, tucked Gabriella in, still laying on the couch. He quietly made coffee and mentally reviewed the plan for his reentry to Panama.

His extraction team was scheduled to meet in Medellín at 10:00 p.m., where they would pack him into a large supply bag with air holes and fly him into Panama. Once unloaded in the Fun Zone hangar, Jon's team would place him back in his private cell.

Vincent wanted one more solid strike or intercept of a plane prior to Colonel Herrera's public denouncement. The next few weeks looked brutal to Sean.

Today is my last day with Gabriella, Sean thought. He would make the most of it.

Gabriella rustled about on the couch, so Sean sat next to her as she woke up.

"What time is it?" she asked.

Sean whispered, "Almost 10 a.m."

Gabriella smiled, "No wonder I'm so hungry. Now I feel like one of those beef and cheese empanadas."

"You mean the ones we never got to the other night?" goaded Sean.

Gabriella sat up and kissed Sean good morning, "Yes ... Those!"

She prepared beef and cheese empanadas with fried potatoes. Sean was pleased.

Gabriella said, "This will provide you with comfort and energy tonight."

"Yes, you can take care of me anytime you like," Sean said lovingly.

"Then I choose to take care of you today. I will always have your back," Gabriella affirmed with her most loving smile.

After the empanadas, they walked through the park, shared their thoughts, and reflected on their first meeting as Spanish teacher and student. It was a beautiful day.

As night drew close, there was angst building. Gabriella cried a little, "I hate saying goodbye under these circumstances. I need to be there, to watch your back."

Sean smiled, "You have my back, Gabriella. You make me strong and give me resolve in ways I never expected."

"That makes me happy, Sean."

"Good, it makes me happy, too."

They kissed and hugged until it was time for Sean to leave.

"It's time to go," Sean whispered.

Gabriella spoke gently, "Be careful and remember, you are still Nick, the agency cannot take that from you. It's your secret weapon in life."

Sean looked into Gabriella's eyes, "Thank you for that, I will."

Sean walked out of the door.

Gabriella sat down on the couch, holding back the tears, and said a prayer for Sean.

As the car drove Sean to the extraction point, he could still feel Gabriella's touch and knew she was praying for his safe return.

Tension Mounts

HIDDEN FOR five days straight, Sean was isolated from the team, the sunlight, and decent food. The Fun Zone served as his prison.

Sunday, May 24, Vincent paid a visit.

"How are you holding up?"

Sean sighed. "A little stiff, what the hell is going on?"

Vincent told him, "Do your calisthenics. A shipment for Ortega is being tracked for touch down either Tuesday or Wednesday."

"Same tactics? What's the intel?" Sean was anxious.

Vincent outlined the intel: "The size and load are expected to be the same. Two pilots and two specialists. Ortega will be watching. It will be a risky intervention; we have alerted Jon and his squad leaders."

Sean interrupted, "We snatch the plane, interrogate the crew, ditch the plane."

Vincent nodded affirmatively. He stood to leave. "One more thing. On Friday, you will accompany me to a meeting at Herrera's office at the Panamanian Administration Building."

"Is it time?" Sean asked.

Vincent replied, "Yes. Sai Baba has convinced Herrera to go

public. On June second, he will be interviewed on a television newscast, and he will denounce Noriega, list his crimes, name Ortega, and accuse him of total corruption."

Sean smiled. "Noriega will be pissed."

Vincent looked deadly serious. "The word to Noriega from the U.S. Government will be that Colonel Herrera is untouchable."

"Won't that implicate us?" Sean asked.

Vincent shrugged. "Sometimes it's the only way to play the game. We must convince Herrera to do it, and he demanded the assurances. He needs the protection more than we do." Leaving the room, he said, "Good luck. See you Friday."

Motivated, Sean completed 45 minutes of rigorous calisthenics in his tiny cell. Jon stopped in with supplies and a fresh Sunday dinner.

"Did we target another flight?"

Sean dug into the warm roasted chicken and rice, "Yes, I am ready. Are you?"

Jon replied, "Same team. No surprises. I do expect Ortega and Noriega to position hardcore soldiers and more of them."

Sean looked up. "What's your plan?"

Jon concluded, "Watch the intel, generate some of our own, beef up the exterior perimeter, and when it happens, strike hard and fast."

"Okay," said Sean, satisfied.

Monday morning there was a delivery of over 300 pages of intelligence reports. Sean gleaned the reports for pertinent details:

President Sánchez of Costa Rica was developing a peace plan designed to put an end to the cruel civil wars devastating Central America. The Peace Accord targeted Costa Rica, Guatemala, El Salvador, Honduras, and hopefully, Nicaragua. It aimed at free elections, safeguards for human rights, and an end to foreign interference in the country's internal affairs.

The Freedom Fighters had caused material damage to the

Soviet-backed Sandinista regimes in Nicaragua. Ortega expressed concern to inner circles of influence.

This is good, thought Sean.

The U.S. State Department, and more importantly, the Executive Branch, were growing tired of Manuel Noriega's games and his constant betrayal of the rules established under his payment agreements.

Colonel Herrera, according to Sai Baba intel leaks, declared his loyalty to the Clandestine Operation: Turn-About. It designated "the beginning of the end" for Noriega's reign over Panama and corrupt connections to Ortega's Nicaragua.

Back in Bogotá, Escobar held true to his deal to halt all monies and drugs moving through Panama and into Nicaragua. Ortega visited with Escobar. According to intel, Escobar told Ortega to "straighten out his affairs with the U.S. Government or things would end badly."

Sean laughed out loud.

"Escobar must be jerking Ortega around good," he murmured to himself.

Top-secret stats revealed over 100 hours of pre-recorded radio programming, ready to play across Panama City radio stations. Colonel Herrera's accusations, along with his hard-hitting charges of murder, corruption, and criminal behavior of the Noriega regime, would undoubtedly fan the flames of revolt and cause riots in protest of Noriega throughout Panama.

Sean noticed his secret interrogations mentioned in the intel: "One remains alive at the black site in international waters; the others were terminated." His pilot capture was the source of intel for the next flight intervention planned in Panama.

Sean paused, "It was worthwhile. The op now has a credible lead on the next flight capture and disruption of supplies to Ortega."

The Leak Report caught Sean's eye. "Jaime Leal" was placed

at the top of the report identifying potential Soviet assets. His movements were being tracked in and out of Medellín, and most trips included stops in Panama.

Sean jumped to his feet. "Who the fuck does he think he is? Rat bastard Leal is going to get us all killed," he vented out loud.

Sean closed his eyes, determined to tie Leal to the situations he and Jon had lived through at the airstrip near the Fun Zone. He tried to picture the soldier that had held Jon and him at gunpoint. The soldier looked Sean over that night, as if he had seen him before. The more Sean thought about it, the more his suspicions grew.

Where is the connection? Or am I just being paranoid? he wondered.

Tuesday, noon. Sean worked out, ate a light lunch and inspected his gun.

He picked up the Leak Report. There was something in the works with Jaime Pardo Leal; he could feel it. Sean drew matrix after matrix, searching for the connections between Leal and the op. Nothing had materialized as nightfall came.

Jon knocked on Sean's cell door and swung it open, "The flight is scheduled to land approximately 10:35 p.m. Good to go?"

"Confirmed."

Jon gave him a thumbs up and left.

Jon's squadron of twelve highly trained men took their positions in the dark, surrounding the airstrip near the fuel station. For the next ninety minutes, they waited.

"Right on schedule," Jon spoke softly into the radio.

An unmarked plane, fitting the description of the intel report, landed. As it slowed, the plane turned toward the fuel station. The squadron moved in closer. The pilots shut down the engine. The door of the plane swung open, exit stairs were kicked down, and two armed guards hustled out to view the area surrounding the plane.

Gunfire ripped through the air and both guards were killed. Blind gunshots rang out from just inside the plane's door while four of Jon's men closed in from the opposite side.

They ordered: *"Baja la pistola! Sal del avion!"* (Put your gun down! Get out of the plane!) A third guard appeared atop the exit steps, and he drew his AK-47 to fire. He was shot and killed. Both pilots began screaming, *"No dispares! No dispares!"* (Don't shoot! Don't shoot!)

The squadron boarded the plane, held the pilots at gunpoint, and directed them to taxi the plane to Hangar 63—the Fun Zone. As the plane approached the hangar, Jon's team opened the hangar door, and closed it just as quickly as the plane pulled inside. Jon pulled the pilots out, handcuffed them, placed hoods over their heads, and ordered guards to escort them to the interrogation room. They were strapped to the metal chairs, where the two pilots pleaded for their lives. Jon watched them for a moment before he left to get Sean.

Jon knocked on Sean's door. "The pilots are ready."

Sean stood up. "Let's go."

Jon touched Sean's arm, "I don't think the pilots are military. I think they are contractors who had no idea of what they were getting into."

Sean paused, "Really, you got all of that while putting a hood on them?"

"It's called experience, Sean, someday you might have it, too. Who knows, pay attention and you might even stay alive!" Jon pushed back.

"Go inspect the load now, let me know what you find." Sean knew better to pick a fight with Jon's gut instincts.

Sean took a deep breath, left his cell, and entered the room quietly. Both men sobbed and begged beneath their hoods.

"No quiero morir, mi familia se quedara sola!" (I don't want to die; my family will be alone.) They claimed to be hired to only

fly the plane. Sean watched them while Jon inspected the load. Shaking in their chairs, unable to collect themselves, they were scared for their lives.

Jon returned with an estimate. Sean stepped outside the room to confer with him.

"About one hundred guns—mostly shitty ones at that, no ammunition, and supply bags full of trash inside," said Jon. "The plane is a throwaway, and I am surprised they even made to Panama. This is a test. We are being watched right now."

Jon started running through potential scenarios.

Sean looked down as he thought, *Calm down*. He said, "Wouldn't we already be under fire if there were orders to capture or kill us?"

Jon replied. "Yes, but we are exposed."

Sean agreed, "Right. Have your team ditch the plane as planned and clean up the three guards. We have to appear normal and unphased."

Jon confirmed, "All is in process now."

Sean, trained for this false flag op, ordered his extraction, "Excellent. Now, arrange my plane. I will be in my room ready to be bagged in approximately five minutes."

Jon confirmed with a nod and ran to ready the team for extraction.

Sean walked into the interrogation room, unhooded the men still crying and begging for mercy.

Sean asked, *"Quien te contrato?"* (Who contracted you?)

The men cried out simultaneously, *"No lo sé! No lo sé!"* (I don't know! I don't know!) Sean looked at them closely. *"Te creo."* (I believe you.)

Sean looked at the ceiling, "Fuck it."

He shot both men in the head and belly in a matter of seconds. He turned to the squadron soldier manning the door, "Dispose of the bodies."

Within five minutes, Sean was placed into a travel supply bag, then loaded onto the small King Air propeller jet.

Landing in Mexico City after midnight, Sean climbed into his car, and sped to the Marriott. He showered off the stench of the Fun Zone and laid down in his bed, his mind reeling.

"Two more assassinations . . . for the good of the op." Sean said aloud, frustrated with the set-up by Ortega. "Those pilots had no clue. I hope their families were paid in advance by Castro—FUCK THE BEARD!"

Sean looked at the minibar in the room. Two scotches later, he told himself, "Communism killed those pilots tonight. I just pulled the trigger."

He looked at the clock radio next to his bed, 2:23 a.m.

Put it away Nick, do your job, fight the Communists. It's your job . . . do your duty . . . , he repeated over and over until he passed out in exhaustion.

AT 7:30 A.M., the front desk operator awakened him, "Good morning. This is your wake-up call."

Wednesday, May 27, he was due at the U.S. Embassy by 9:00 a.m. for a briefing and recording of the events. He ordered room service and dressed for the day. Sean noticed his face in the mirror. *What's different?* he asked himself. He looked long and hard. *"You are getting used to the killing."*

Was this part of his training, part of paying his dues to move up the chain of command or was this the norm for every mission? Sean searched for rational answers.

None came.

IT TOOK three hours to brief with recordings—Vincent hated briefings when he looked bad.

Sean handily laid out the situation: "It was a false flag. The pilots and guards were used by Ortega to trick us into plain sight. They knew we had a valuable pilot and had no doubt turned him to provide the next flight intel. So, they sent a shit plane, full of shitty guns and contracted unsuspecting civilians to fly to their death."

"Do you have to be so melodramatic? Vincent asked.

"I'm sorry," replied Sean, "For the record, it was not melodramatic at all. Jon's team executed the guards on the strip, and I shot the pilots in the interrogation room as ordered, under the clear and present danger designation."

"We're done here," proclaimed Vincent.

Sean left the room, walked directly back to the Marriott. Instructions awaited him at the hotel to meet Vincent at Winston Churchill's at 7:00 p.m.

Great, thought Sean, *more bullshit intel.*

He arrived at Winston Churchill's restaurant at 7:00 p.m. sharp and was escorted to a table in one of the small private rooms. Much to his surprise, Richard was there.

"Greetings!" exclaimed Richard. He stood to give Sean a big bear hug.

Vincent was clearly agitated. "Sit down you two and stop making a spectacle of yourselves." Richard and Sean looked at Vincent, rolled their eyes, and sat down.

Vincent continued, "I thought you could use a new perspective on the op, Sean."

"The bitterness you displayed today is not healthy," Richard attempted to show care.

"Is this a friendly intervention?" asked Sean.

"No intervention needed!" demanded Vincent. "Right, Richard?"

"Right." replied Richard, "But you do have to get your head screwed on straight. This op has calculated risks ahead."

"We cannot have you carrying this Boy Scout attitude around," Vincent said.

"It's going to get you killed," Richard chimed in to warn Sean.

"How?" asked Sean.

"That's the best question of the night!" Richard said smiling. "Yes, how?"

Vincent explained, "We all have to compartmentalize. You must learn to do it subconsciously, like breathing. It has to happen within yourself, without thinking about it."

Richard further explained, "Compartmentalization is a mechanism. It doesn't make you evil or uncaring. It doesn't strip you of who are inside, it protects who you are inside."

"Does this make sense?" Vincent asked.

"Yes, it does make sense. I will let that happen on the inside," Sean professed.

"First missions of this magnitude are rare, your role is invaluable, and when the real evildoers throw men at us to kill—there are few options available to avoid the killing. Understand?" said Richard.

Vincent's eyes were locked onto Sean. "Yes, I understand," Sean said.

"Excellent. Now that this portion of the discussion is over, let's get some drinks and good food." Vincent said with satisfaction.

Much was discussed throughout the evening.

Sean tried to make the case that Jaime Leal was shadowing their efforts in Panama to double deal with the Soviets. Vincent acted unconvinced and dismissed Sean's theory. Richard wanted to believe but called it "factually shallow."

The night concluded with a toast to their brotherhood just after 11:00 p.m.

"What a great surprise seeing you, Richard," Sean said.

The three men walked out of the restaurant. Vincent offered Sean a lift so he would not have to wait for a second car.

In the car, Vincent spoke up, "We will investigate Jaime Leal."

Sean pointed out the latest intel: "Leal is in the Leak Report, but nothing of substance was included?"

Vincent explained, "He's included on the Department of State matrix. He's one of twenty-seven espionage ring suspects uncovered in their search for the "UnSub" (Unknown Subject). The ring is leaking secrets through Cuba to the Soviets."

Sean reacted, "Holy shit."

"Exactly," replied Vincent. "Everyone is watching him so we can catch him in the act of espionage."

Sean said, "How?"

"Maybe he will sell information or leak intel—maybe even about you, maybe me, maybe pieces of our op? In the interim, we must let it play out, understand?"

"Yes, I think so." Sean's mind was again reeling.

"We will be okay. This is all need-to-know and frankly, I'm sure you needed to know," shrugged Vincent.

"Thank you," said Sean.

Vincent laughed. "You're welcome. Go get some rest. I will call you if I need you."

THURSDAY MORNING, Sean slept in until 9:15 a.m. After a full workout and a three-mile run through downtown Mexico City, Sean relaxed in the room and waited for instructions. At 12:30 p.m., the hotel room phone rang. It was Richard.

"Let's have lunch at that restaurant across the street, behind the Marriott."

Sean walked over to the café. Richard was seated at a table near the corner window.

"Where's Vincent?" asked Sean.

"In meetings," responded Richard. "I thought it might be nice to have lunch together."

Sean smiled curiously, "Absolutely."

During lunch, Sean realized why Richard had invited him. Richard observed him and asked questions related to his training and mental health. He shared experiences he had during his first year in clandestine services.

"Many things can wrong," said Richard, "Never get caught and if you do get caught, never lose faith in your handlers."

Sean asked, "Why are you telling me this?"

Richard leaned in. "So, you will understand, and more importantly believe, we will always look out for you. That's how Vincent builds his teams."

Sean looked into Richard's eyes. "I want to believe."

Richard laughed, "That's a good step."

Richard continued, "Do yourself a favor, never let on that you have doubts. Vincent does not protect doubters for very long, do you understand that?"

"YES! That I completely understand," Sean assured Richard.

They finished lunch and Richard left. Sean walked back to his room to find new intel reports at the front desk.

Sean read the reports. "It sure seems quiet—no real chatter of interest and no material updates."

He strolled down to the lobby bar for a drink. It was approaching 5:00 p.m. He looked across the lounge and saw Vincent and Jon. Vincent spotted Sean and waved him over to their sitting area.

"We were just about to call you," Vincent said in a serious tone. "Tomorrow is particularly important. Herrera has learned that Noriega is leaving the country this Saturday for at least ten days. We have arranged for Herrera to be interviewed on Panama's largest radio station and television station on June second."

Jon chimed in, "The campaign will start on that date. A revolt will spring up against Noriega."

Sean sensed something wrong was happening.

"Let's order another round of drinks," said Vincent. After the waiter took their order, Vincent continued, "We suspect leaks about our involvement—identifiably—within the Panamanian regime and possibly the Nicaraguan government."

Sean had to ask, "When you say 'identifiably' what exactly do you mean?"

Vincent explained. "There is a possibility that someone has made the connection of your USAID work, your Panama presence."

Sean was angry, "Jaime Leal."

"No. It is not Jaime Leal," said Vincent, "but we are gathering more intel every day." Sean accepted Vincent's word.

Jon added to the conversation, "We think it might be one of Noriega's men or that soldier that looked you over on the airstrip."

Sean took a stiff drink. "Well, that narrows it down. It could be anyone in the Panamanian or Nicaraguan forces. What do we do now?"

Vincent said, "We follow our plan. You are the show leader. We will get Ortega to sign Nicaragua into the Peace Accord."

Sean nodded in compliance, but deep down, he had a bad feeling in his gut about going into the open to meet with Herrera.

FRIDAY, MAY 29, Jon, Sean, and Vincent climbed into the King Air and flew into Panama City at 7:45 a.m. Jon coordinated a three-car escort to a restaurant that was located two blocks from the administration building where Colonel Herrera maintained an office.

The restaurant was not open yet. They entered through the back. Jon planned with the owner, who ensured it was accessible, that no employees would be around. Colonel Herrera arrived promptly at 9:45 a.m. He explained everything he was prepared to say.

Sean watched and could feel Herrera's conviction. It was his duty to make these statements and go on the record, despite the danger.

He stated his readiness to accuse Noriega of drug trafficking, and Noriega's assassination of his predecessor, and Herrera's own cousin, Omar Torrijos Herrera, who had negotiated the return of the Panama Canal with Jimmy Carter. He claimed Noriega had planted an explosive in the private aircraft of Torrijos and orchestrated fraud in the 1984 presidential election. He named Ortega as part of the Noriega mafia moving drugs, money and weapons through Panama illegally. His allegations would soon lead many people in Panama to protest, no doubt.

The meeting was expeditious and positive until Herrera informed them that someone in his building broke into the offices the night before.

Vincent asked, "What did they find?"

Herrera responded, "Nothing except my appointment book. They didn't take it, but they undoubtedly reviewed it." Herrera handed Sean the book for inspection.

"Today's meeting is in there—with no names or addresses," admitted Herrera.

Vincent opened a harsh line of questioning: "Where have you been in the past five days? Walk us though the timeline," he demanded. "We need to understand everything prior to the break-in."

Vincent demanded a list of all office and building personnel, clerks, maintenance, and other officials who visited or maintained keys to offices.

Herrera stumbled a bit, but then offered, "I can get that list today."

Vincent instructed Herrera to get the list, and then meet Jon at the abandoned warehouse near the coffee hut at 2:15 p.m. sharp. "And Colonel, don't make it obvious," Vincent added.

"What are you going to do?" asked Herrera.

Jon replied, "Fix it, sir. We will fix it."

Vincent ordered Jon and Sean: "Find them, interrogate them, and terminate them."

Vincent left the meeting for the airport.

Sean went straight to the Panama safe house, only eleven miles away. By 3:30 p.m., Jon's squadron had seven of the nine men identified by Herrera as prime suspects for the break-in to his office. Jon locked the men in the interrogation room.

A squad leader handed a message from Jon to Sean. "In search of final two on list. Suggest you begin interrogation of the first seven."

For the next several hours, Sean grilled each man separately and then in groups. He watched their stories change, noticed when they tried to blame each other.

Waterboarding was the next step.

The last two suspects were caught and on the way to the safe house. He took a break and awaited their arrival.

"Who do you work for? Why did you break into offices? What did you find?" he asked them. All of them appeared guilty at times.

The nine men were standing in a row, looking at each other in bewilderment, crying about their children, their lives as hard-working family men.

Sean water boarded the weakest ones first. After the first three torture sessions, not a single suspect broke, or maybe they were just innocent.

Sean and the squadron repeated the questioning and the torture, one by one, over and over. They strapped each suspect to the gurney, tilted their head down, placed a wet towel on the suspects' faces and poured water onto their nose and mouth.

Sean was growing tired of the process when Jon interrupted the sessions. He whispered in Sean's ear, "We've been ordered to terminate the suspects now. The real thief has been shot and killed by Herrera. He showed up at Herrera's house demanding information. Herrera reached into his desk drawer, pulled his gun, and shot him dead."

Sean replied, "How do we know?"

Jon interrupted, "His fingerprints matched those found on Herrera's office desk taken this morning."

"Okay, good enough for me," said Sean compliantly.

Sean pulled his Walther PPK and pointed it at Number 9 in line, screaming, *"Para quien trabajas?"* (Who do you work for?)

Number 9 cried out, *"El encargado del edificio!"* (The building manager!)

Sean shot him in the head and then the belly.

The other eight men began to cry and plead for their lives. Sean compartmentalized the situation that he was not in control of and proceeded.

Sean asked the men, *"Quien es el encargado edificio?"* (Who is the building manager?)

Number 3 yelled, *"Soy el gerente."* (I am the manager.)

Sean grilled him for nearly 20 minutes. Number 3 had no value. Sean drew his pistol and executed him.

The capture of these men was based on the suspicion detailed by Colonel Herrera. With each kill, Sean began to realize that Herrera's suspicions were hurried and far-reaching. He executed nine men—only to protect his team's identity. Sean stopped seeing the men as "suspects," he compartmentalized them as a known "danger."

He asked each the same question, shooting each man in the head and chest, pausing only once to reload. Without hesitating, he stepped in front of the last man kneeling. He couldn't hear his own words, the room seemed deathly quiet. Sean aimed the gun at his head and pulled the trigger. As the man collapsed, he took the second shot into the man's chest and then watched the breath leave his body. He looked at the clock. It was 11:11 p.m.

It was done.

He noted to himself, *At 11:11 p.m., you assassinated nine men under order of the CIA.*

Jon instructed the safe house team to clean the room. He escorted Sean to a guest room on the second floor.

"You okay?"

Sean looked at Jon, drained of all emotion. "I didn't expect that."

Jon placed his hand on Sean's shoulder. "That was tough, my friend. Rest for a moment. We fly back to Mexico City in thirty minutes for a briefing tomorrow."

Sean sat still as the bodies were being removed two floors below him. He closed his eyes to escape, only to be shaken awake by Jon.

"Let's go. It's all cleaned up." Sean nearly jumped out of the chair. They made it to the hangar, boarded the plane. It was 2:33 a.m. Saturday morning. Sean was shaking and did not even dream of sleep. Sean knew that the nightmares would come and never leave.

SATURDAY, MAY 30, 11:00 a.m., Jon, Sean, Vincent, and the recorder started the briefing.

Vincent paused the briefing and asked, "Sean, are you okay?"

Sean knew he wasn't, but answered, "Just walking through timelines in my mind."

"Don't show weakness or doubt in the op. I followed orders." Sean repeated this to himself throughout the briefing.

Vincent and Jon wisely kept the brief narrow in discussion and short in length.

Afterward, Vincent told Sean to take the rest of the weekend off and to report back to duty, Tuesday, June 2, at 9:00 a.m. Mexico City.

"We will need you in the game—and sharp. Go to Bogotá and chill out."

Sean agreed, "You can send reports to the Bogotá apartment."

Sean got up to walk out of the meeting; Vincent stopped him. "Listen up. Herrera will denounce Noriega and Ortega. A protest of over 100,000 civilians will begin. This will be a landmark moment; we will see it through together."

Sean confirmed his understanding with an affirmative nod.

Vincent continued, "I will be back in Mexico City for dinner on June 1—should you decide to join me. Then we kick off the campaign. Ortega will align with the Reagan's Peace Accord, shutting the door on the Soviet Union."

Sean looked at Vincent, "Operation: Turn-About will make history. We will have made the U.S. safer in the process. That's why I am here."

"Yes, Sean, that is why you are here."

Chapter 31

A Turbulent June

Saturday night, May 30, 1987

THE BOGOTÁ apartment had become home to Sean. He arrived 9:35 p.m., poured himself a stiff drink, and sat on the couch near the phone. He stared at it, and it seemed to stare back. He imagined it talking to him, telling him to call his family. But it was too late to talk with his parents, too late to talk with anyone—least of all talk about the truth.

He picked up the phone and dialed Anna's number in St. Louis. It rang three times—but no answer. Sean hung up the phone, leaned back, and stared at the ceiling.

She's either at her parents' home or with another man, he thought.

He left a brief message, "Hi, it's Nick, just checking in as promised."

He drank his scotch and poured another. Then another.

The bottle is not the answer, he told himself.

Sean laid on his bed, still fully dressed. He could not bring himself to look in the mirror. He tried to focus on the ceiling in the bedroom and eventually passed out. His sleep was not peaceful. He had horrible dreams: victims crying for mercy, bloody floors, and dead bodies surrounded him.

Sunday afternoon, Sean managed to eat his first meal. He jogged a slow three miles, collecting his sanity, all in an attempt to gain back his inner perspective.

Gabriella said, "They can't change Nick, no matter what Sean does."

Sean is the soldier, he told himself, determined to justify the killing.

Back in training, Vincent told him about the risks about pulling the trigger upon orders and not getting caught.

"I followed orders," Sean consoled himself as he looked in the mirror.

Sean looked at the phone, thought about his parents; *It's probably close to supper time—and it would be easy to keep the call short, questions to a minimum.*

He made the call.

His mom answered, "Hello?"

He smiled. His mom spoke with a "hick" accent.

"Hi, Mom. Just checking in—"

Loretta interrupted him. "David? Bradley?"

"It's Nick, Mom," he said, laughing to himself.

"Oh, hi! Is everything okay?"

Nick updated her on his whereabouts and made-up stories about ADM–USAID projects. Loretta was lost listening to the update and was obviously preparing supper.

"Dad, Nick is on the phone from Bogotá! Come talk to him!" she hollered.

Nick took a deep breath and waited for his dad to take the phone.

"Nick?"

"It's me, Dad. Just checking in." Nick's heart was sinking.

"We've been thinking about you. How are you?" said his dad.

Nick pushed his heart aside and repeated the stories he had just told him mom.

"Sounds like a pretty big deal," replied Paul.

"It's a learning experience," said Nick.

"Just come home safe," ordered Paul.

"I will. Love you, Dad," Nick replied softly.

His dad replied in a comforting tone, "And we love you, too, Nick. Mom's putting supper on the table, so bye for now."

"Tell mom I love her too, bye." Nick hung the phone up.

Nick closed his eyes; he could smell supper on the farm. He imagined himself running in from the barn, washing up and sitting down for a giant meal, a home-cooked supper.

No one can take my roots, he told himself.

Sean opened his eyes, dismissed his thoughts about Anna, and refocused on his own situation. He concentrated on tomorrow, *Operation: Turn-About must be my sole purpose.*

Monday, June 1, 1987

SEAN HAD to be in game condition. He woke up early, ran five miles to clear his mind and release the toxins in his body, and ate an early lunch.

Like clockwork, a courier delivered the intel reports. He read all the updates, keenly reviewed the Leak Report, and started his own analysis.

Routes for incoming Nicaraguan planes were laid out in detail. Herrera's public appearance was on schedule. He would fully expose Noriega's Panamanian and Ortega's Nicaraguan corruption, along with many murderous acts.

President Reagan's Peace Accord was on track for being signed by early August.

The Leak Report revealed recent intelligence leaks indicating that counter espionage efforts had not worked, at least not yet. Noriega and Ortega had both been heard expressing suspicions that the CIA was using the Cartel, responsible for the capturing of planes and pilots and disrupting the weapons supply. Sean dissected the reports but could not find anything that pointed directly at him, at least not personally.

His flight to Mexico City was smooth. He checked in at the Marriott and waited for instructions from Vincent. A message was delivered at 9:15 p.m.

    No dinner tonight. Come early tomorrow. V.

Sean laid in his bed, ordered room service, closed his eyes, and played operational scenarios in his head. The next day, Herrera's radio and television interviews denouncing Noriega and Ortega would play across Panama and be picked up in Nicaragua. Jon would lead security and transport Herrera to the safe house. Everything was set.

VINCENT AND SEAN met in the lobby at 6:00 a.m. They flew to Panama City, then were escorted to the safe house by Jon's squad. Vincent remained in the control room. Sean and Jon picked up Colonel Herrera, surrounded by their team. The live television interview started at 11:00 a.m., followed by a radio interview at 11:45 a.m.

Herrera accused Noriega of drug trafficking; of planning the assassination of his predecessor Omar Herrera, who negotiated the return of the Panama Canal with Jimmy Carter. He also ordered the killing of Herrera's personal friend, Hugo Spadafora; and orchestrated fraud in the 1984 presidential election to privately strike deals with Ortega, causing political unrest throughout the region.

Sean looked at Jon, "This is going to break Ortega's alliance."

"Let's get Herrera back to the safe house, we have orchestrated riots happening everywhere," said Jon.

Panamanians began protesting immediately as the news

broke, resulting in a suspension of constitutional protections and austere measures by the Noriega regime, including arrest and detainment of protestors and opposition party leaders, government seizure of local television stations, and teargassing of students. The police were accused of brutality against the local citizens for using batons, rubber hoses filled with sand, and shotguns filled with rock salt.

Jon and Sean escorted Herrera to the safe house for a debriefing with Vincent. Herrera was too hot to transport out of the country.

Vincent spoke softly to Jon and Sean, "The whole country is rioting, and the news is spreading across Nicaragua."

"Now we wait and see," Jon added.

For the next 15 days, Vincent ran psyops across Panama, applying pressure on Noriega and Ortega. Noriega returned to denounce Herrera and wanted to imprison him. But the damage was done. Nearly every radio station throughout Central America was playing the 100+ hours of prerecorded propaganda, including fake interviews, all condemning Noriega.

The revolt was out of control. Jon was ordered to deploy instigators, pay off trusted community leaders, and supply them with financial support for protesting, printing propaganda, and marching against Panamanian military stations to keep them occupied.

The country erupted and Herrera's extraction was terminated. Vincent ordered the abandonment of Herrera: "He is caught in the middle and we're not blowing our cover."

Jon asked, "What's the plan? He's furious and threatening the op."

"He's still worth more to us alive, for now," Vincent concluded.

Sean asked, "What makes you think he won't talk?"

Vincent answered sharply, "Herrera's a lifelong soldier and he loves his family. He'd rather die a hero in their honor, than be a rat in his country—and we are his only chance of returning to his family."

Vincent laid a revised plan to maintain eyes and ears on Herrera, to watch for opportunities to extract. But that was a double-edged sword. If he lost his nerve and implicated the CIA, Herrera was also on the kill list.

Jon returned Herrera to his home, where a few loyalists as guards would protect him.

Vincent and Sean left Panama and planned a rendezvous with Jon in Mexico City.

FIFTEEN DAYS LATER, June 17. Intelligence reported that Ortega's Nicaraguan funds were beginning to dry up. The op was working.

Noriega placed Herrera under house arrest. Many people were going to Herrera's home to shake his hand and show their support. The street to his house was often lined with the cars of his supporters. The whole Spadafora family secretly went into hiding at Herrera's home. The CIA had relocated Herrera's family to the U.S. He would not talk—or it would jeopardize the arrangement and safety of his family.

Sean thought, *This may be his last refuge against Noriega's soldiers.*

"Ortega needs support from the Soviets—and soon," Vincent declared. There was a rumor of a Soviet-sponsored flight originating from Cuba that was to be loaded with money and supplies on or about June 25, but it might fly directly into Nicaragua."

Vincent ordered Jon and Sean to develop a plan for a covert mission to intercept the plane either way. There was no turning back on Operation: Turn-About.

Jon replied, "That will take local cooperation, money, and training. It is damn near impossible. Is it worth the risk?"

Vincent paused to assess before answering, "Yes. This is the opportunity to force Ortega to the table."

Three days later, Sean and Jon presented a plan, a resource list, and a mapping of the mission.

Jon suggested, "We will jungle drop sixty soldiers, combined with advanced training, and coordination with trusted resources in Nicaragua."

However, he felt strongly that he would need two weeks to properly prepare.

Vincent smiled. "Well then, we are a go. We just confirmed delays in weaponry and cash from Cuban handlers; the flight is delayed for at least two weeks. Pack your bags, make it happen."

Sean watched Jon and he could feel his adrenaline surge. It was electric and contagious. For a moment, Sean thought about volunteering for the ground mission but immediately thought better of it. Jon was made for these gambles and he loved it. Getting paid to fly into the jungle, covertly train a special operations task force and command a strike—it was Jon's dream.

Jon looked at Vincent with pride. "Yes, sir."

Action ramped up. The targeted outcome: Force Ortega to the Peace Accord signing table. Vincent was sending cryptic messages to Noriega: "The killing of Herrera will result in the death of Noriega." Noriega's actions were off-balance and Ortega's network was in trouble.

June 26 news reports stated that 100,000 people—that is, approximately 25 percent of the population of Panama City—marched in protest. Riots continued; shootings were rampant. The country was out of control. Noriega charged Herrera with treason and cracked down hard on the protesters. The U.S. Senate passed a resolution demanding Noriega step down until Herrera could be tried, and, in response, Noriega sent government workers to protest outside the U.S. Embassy. As a result, the U.S. suspended all military assistance to Panama, and the CIA stopped paying Noriega a salary.

"Finance is a gun," said Vincent, "and politics is knowing when to fire."

Sean replied, "Where do you think Ortega will turn for support?"

Vincent responded, "Nowhere. Our Honduras base has contained Ortega. He must try to fly in support from the Soviets and their best bet is through Cuba."

The Senate resolution escalated America's intention to remove Noriega, and Noriega tried to exploit rising anti-American sentiment to strengthen his own position.

Sean noted, "This is the beginning of the end for Noriega."

Vincent smiled, "And Ortega is closely watching his fall from power. But don't fool yourself, these changes can take years to complete."

By the end of June, it appeared that Herrera would not be killed, but most likely arrested and placed in exile.

Jon, stationed in the brush of Nicaragua, trained his squadron for the possible intervention of a Soviet-sponsored flight. Vincent and Sean handled the op, manipulated the communications surrounding Noriega, and kept Escobar and Fabio happy, all while applying economic pressure on Ortega's illegal dealings.

Vincent led the dance: Operation: Turn-About was in full swing.

Wednesday, July 1, 1987

SEAN SAT at the table in his Bogotá apartment. The latest intel report package lay unopened. His mind anticipated July and what compromises were in store for the op to be successful.

He knew a sit-down with Fabio was overdue. The messages to Escobar regarding their progress were satisfactory, but he would be asked for more—much more evidence and money. He was growing tired of the Cartel's greed and violence.

Inside the intel package, he found a letter. It was from Anna. The Agency had placed it in the package. His heartbeat fast, he dreaded the idea of dealing with it.

She wrote,

> *I couldn't seem to leave a message on the foreign number you provided for Bogotá, so I decided to write a letter instead.*

As Sean read, a surprising message surfaced.

> *After this long break, I realized that I don't want a divorce, and I want to make this work.*

Relieved that he didn't have to deal with divorce just yet, he read on.

> *I understand you may be angry because I took so long to communicate with you after your phone messages last month. Please take as much time as you need to decide if we can try to make the marriage work.*

Sean leaned back in his chair. "This is bullshit! She is leading me on, buying time to get herself situated!" He was enraged. *Calm down, let go of the ego,* he thought rationally. *Fine. Two can play that game.* Sean smiled. *Thank you, God.* He needed the extra time for Operation: Turn-About. Intel indicated no chatter and no evidence of a flight out of Cuba for several days or longer. Panama is in turmoil, and Ortega is squirming. There was nothing to do but wait.

Sean said out loud, "Fuck it. What am doing here?"

He called Vincent. "Is the July Fourth party still on?"

Vincent flatly replied, "Your room will be waiting," and hung up.

Chapter 32

Personal Declarations

Thursday, July 2, 1987

NICK FLEW BACK to LAX and drove to his Torrance townhome. His mind, occupied with Anna's letter, her temporary apartment, and her ridiculous attempt to lie about saving the marriage. The more Nick thought about it, the more he convinced himself that she was determined to save her reputation. He said out loud, "Tell Mom and Dad I tried to reconcile and make it work, it's Nick's fault. . . ."

As he pulled into the garage, Nick decided to leave her message. Assuming she would be at work, he called her apartment in St. Louis. Her answering machine said. "You've reached Anna. Leave a message, and I will call you back."

He left a message: "Hi, I am at the townhouse. All seems to be in order. I will be going back to Bogotá for most of July, and I promise to think through everything. We can plan to get together around my birthday. I love you."

He hung up, speaking to himself: "I love you. . . . Take that! You think about having to meet with me in August for a while."

Nick reached his limit with Anna. It was over.

This has got to end, Nick told himself.

He knew she was already spreading the information about his poor behavior. He could hear her voice: "Traveling all the time, and when he is home—he's not present."

He knew that her parents were already spreading rumors. That's how they operated.

It seemed easier to play the break-up game with Anna, buy another month, complete Operation: Turn-About. And then end the marriage.

He packed his clothes, jumped in the car and drove straight to the Beverly Hills Hotel, in desperate need of rest and relaxation. His thoughts drifted Jon in Nicaragua, monitoring the civilian psyops underway and just waiting for strike orders.

Jon is disciplined and rock solid, Nick thought. June was a tough month, but his gut told him the worst was yet to come.

He left his car with the valet, and a woman with a familiar figure captured his attention. She turned and walked inside the lobby. It was Gabriella. Nick felt ecstatic and his body was filled with passionate stirrings.

He walked to the front desk, surveyed the lobby, but didn't see her. He asked the clerk to ring the cottage of Liberace. Vincent liked to use cover names. The phone rang, and Richard picked up.

"*Hola,* Nick! Cottage 14A."

Nick replied, "On my way."

Nicked walked into the cottage, and Richard greeted him with a giant hug, "My brother, Nick! So good to see you."

Nick, immediately cheerful, "My brother, Richard. I missed you."

Vincent walked in, joined in the brotherhood greeting, and grabbed Nick's shoulders, giving him the once-over inspection.

Vincent looked into Nick's eyes. Nick's father flashed through his mind; Vincent knew exactly what Nick was thinking.

"Drinks all around!" declared Vincent. They walked out to the patio. Gabriella strolled out of the adjoining cottage directly toward Nick. They embraced long and tight, but there was no kiss.

She whispered, "So good to see you, and feel you, Nick."

"I'm so glad you are here," replied Nick.

Gabriella didn't let go. "I am only here for one night. We need to talk."

"I'm sure talking will be involved," Nick said coyly.

Blushing, she said, "Oh, Nick, you are bad."

Vincent made Bombay martinis with cocktail onions. Nick knew they would soon be drunk. Gabriella drank the first one down faster than the men. Nick could see her nervousness. Something wasn't right.

"That's all for me," declared Gabriella. "I'm going to let you boys talk while I take a nap."

"Are you sure?" said Vincent as Gabriella stood.

"Yes," she said and hugged Vincent and Richard tightly as she whispered something in their ears. Nick watched intensely.

Nick couldn't resist, "Rest up, we will have fun tonight."

Gabriella smiled and walked into the cottage.

Vincent and Richard made fresh drinks; the martinis were flowing.

Nick had to ask, "What did Gabriella say to you?"

Vincent looked at Richard. "I don't think we should say," he said.

Richard said, "Tell him, or I will."

Vincent shrugged. "She said, we need to always take care of you."

Vincent and Richard placed their hands on each of his shoulders.

"Let it out," said Vincent.

Nick sat down. "We weren't trained to assassinate so many innocent . . ."

"Innocent what! What Nick, what are they really?" Vincent growled.

Nick continued, "Innocent men, only suspected of spying . . ."

"You are trained to live. To eliminate risks, spy and live to report about it. It's what you signed up for, Nick." Vincent was losing his patience.

"Let me add some perspective," interjected Richard.

Vincent could see Nick's resistance, "Go ahead, add some perspective."

Richard touched Nick's forearm, "Whenever we need to attack an army, besiege a city, or kill a person, it's a part of both war and intelligence gathering. First, you must know the identities of their defending leaders, their associates, their visitors, their gatekeepers, and their chamberlains, so we, the spies, find out."

"Do you hear me?" asked Richard.

Nick looked at him, "Yes."

"Good. We deal in foreknowledge, which cannot be gotten from ghosts or spirits, it cannot be had by analogy, or found out by calculation. It must be obtained from people, people who know the conditions of the enemy. These people are part of the mission, nothing more, nothing less." Richard paused and finished his martini.

Vincent watched Nick closely. He decided to summarize for Richard.

"Listen, Nick, there are five kinds of spies: Local, Inside, Reverse, Dead, and Living spies. Local spies are hired from among the people of a locality. Inside spies are hired from among enemy officials. Reverse spies are hired from among enemy spies. Dead spies transmit false intelligence to enemy spies. Living spies come back to report. Understand?" said Vincent.

"I'm listening," replied Nick.

"We don't use spies without knowledge, humanity and justice. To get the truth from spies and the characters surrounding them, we use subtlety, and we use force if, and when, necessary. No one in the armed forces is treated as familiarly as spies, and no matter is more secret than espionage. Still with me?" Vincent was concentrating on Nick's body language. Nick was clearly breaking down.

Nick leaned in, "What will I become in life? How do I compartmentalize the killings? I see their faces, all of them, I don't even know their names. I never really sleep anymore, and when I do—they all come back to haunt me . . . I can't eat—so I drink all the time to dull my feelings . . . I constantly worry about losing myself, I don't want to be Sean, he's not me."

Vincent knelt beside Nick. "You are not Sean inside. Sean is your soldier and killing is something that happens in war because of the mission. You are not a cold-blooded killer; you are a spy."

"I am a killer, Vincent, there's no way to deny it," Nick cried.

Richard gripped Nick's arm tightly. "You are a spy running an operation for the U.S. Government. Your code name is Sean, and you will do what's required to achieve the mission."

Richard raised his voice, "If intelligence is gathered by Agents of the U.S. Government before a spy reports it, it now represents a huge problem. Both the spy and the spy's informant usually die." He took a breath, "Do you want to die Nick? Because your attitude today will get you killed."

Nick accepted that from Richard, "I understand. In the field, on enemy ground, it always comes down to them or me."

Richard summarized, "That's right, you want to be a living spy and always come back to report intelligence."

Vincent stood, "Any more questions?"

Collecting his composure, Nick finished his drink. "No, no more questions."

Richard asked, "Are we making more martinis?"

The afternoon became a drunken blur. Nick excused himself and went to the cottage to lay down. Gabriella was awake and reading on the small private patio. She was beautiful and glowing in the sunshine. Nick saw her noticing him, but she pretended to keep reading.

Exhausted and completely drunk, Nick lay on the bed and fell asleep.

IT WAS just before 9:00 p.m. when Gabriella gently shook Nick.

"Nick, wake up. We have a late dinner reservation in the hotel. Time to get ready."

"Okay, let me shower and dress," replied Nick, sleep still in his eyes.

Dinner conversation stayed lighthearted, until Vincent decided to question Gabriella about her plans for the fall. She clearly became agitated and tried to avoid the questions.

"I really don't have plans for the fall yet. Thunderbird has offered me a full class load if I want to teach again," she replied.

"Okay, be sure to let us know how that goes!" Vincent laughed suspiciously.

Nick left the topic alone and asked Richard how long he was in town.

Richard looked at Vincent, sarcastically, "I don't know—how long am I in town for, dear?"

"Oh, Richard, for as long you desire," Vincent teased.

"Check please," Nick called to the waiter.

Richard looked at Gabriella, "I think we make Nick nervous."

"I'm not nervous, Richard, we just have one night together."

Looking at Gabriella, Nick continued, "And we don't want to get in the way of your night."

"Right. Richard, let's all go to bed," Gabriella replied with her usual charm and grace.

"Well, that's settled. We're going to bed. You pay the tab Nick and enjoy your time with Gabriella." Vincent stood and tapped Richard on the shoulder and walked out.

Richard stood. "You two be nice to each other. Good night."

"Good night," Gabriella and Nick replied in unison.

Back in the cottage, Nick and Gabriella prepared for bed.

"What are your plans for the fall?" Nick asked cautiously.

Gabriella slid into bed next to Nick.

"I love you, Nick, but I can't be in love with you." She touched his face.

Nick could feel her looking into his soul. "What does that mean?"

Gabriella tried to explain: "When we last saw each other, I was falling in love with you. Then you left. All I could think about was losing you. I can't live that way."

"I'm not asking you to live that way," assured Nick.

"You don't have to ask me, it just happens." Tears welled up in Gabriella's eyes.

"I'm sorry," said Nick.

"No, don't be sorry, it's not your fault," Gabriella cried and leaned into Nick's chest.

All he could think about was the secure, trusting relationship they had built, and the lovemaking they had shared. Nick was speechless.

She kissed him on the lips very softly. "Make love to me tonight. Make love like it's the last time."

"I love you, Gabriella."

"I love you, Nicholas."

He gently pulled her sheer negligee off. Their bare skin melded into one being. He looked upon her face, "No matter what happens, we will always have tonight."

They made deep love, holding each other so close, they felt their hearts beat in unison.

Yet morning arrived.

Nick woke and looked around the room. Gabriella had left. She did not want to say goodbye. Nick imagined her quietly easing out of bed, dressing, and leaving.

She left in the middle of the night. . . . no goodbye, he thought. *No—this way it's not over. She wants me to come back.*

Confidently, he spoke aloud: "I will return—I am a living spy."

Chapter 33

Turn-About Is Not Fair Play

THE JULY 4 weekend consisted of reviewing Operation: Turn-About intel reports all day and evening on Friday, and a patriotic end to any rest and relaxation with a fireworks party poolside Saturday night.

They suffered hangovers and flat appetites. The intel report arrived Friday morning. Vincent disappeared into the private bedroom to review it and hold private calls. It was nearly sundown when Vincent reemerged to join Nick and Sean.

He looked at long and hard at Nick.

"One of the UnSubs (Unknown Subjects suspected of espionage) on our Leak List was recently in Nicaragua." Vincent sighed. "They spotted him stepping off a Nicaraguan Beechcraft King Air alone at La Aurora International Airport."

"The unsub they spotted is Leal," said Vincent flatly.

"I knew it," replied Nick.

"Listen, they didn't catch him in the act of selling or leaking intel. They lost him and they're not even sure he has left the country."

Visibly upset, Nick growled in anger, "He's turned. He's blowing our cover. I can feel him telling Ortega everything. He's a two-faced traitor."

"What do we know?" interjected Richard.

"We know that Leal is too far gone. We know that Ortega is near the cliff, and we will be desperate. We know we have shut off all delivery routes except Panama and without weapons and money he will lash out soon." Vincent continued, "What we don't know is where Escobar and Fabio stand, and how long Ortega can hold out."

"We can bribe Fabio and Escobar," offered Nick.

Vincent laughed, "Look at the spy, writing government checks left and right."

"What do you propose Vincent?" asked Nick.

Vincent looked at Richard, shook his head, turned to Nick, "Write the check."

"Bribes are easy. Ortega will play every hand he has left with vengeance," Richard spoke from experience and with warning.

Vincent poured a drink, "Yes, Ortega is weak. His partner, Noriega, will try to help him. There will be an attempt to bring one more supply plane through the Fun Zone, and we will be there. We will be ready."

Monday, July 6, 1987

VINCENT AND SEAN met in the basement of the U.S. Embassy in Mexico City to map out the final weeks of Operation: Turn-About.

Vincent summarized the intel:

Noriega, under pressure, was exploiting the rising anti-American sentiment due to the loss of political support and financial aid. "He is now on the enemy list," said Vincent.

Without U.S. support, Panama would not be able to manage

its international debt. "Its economy is already suffering, and revolts are everywhere," he reported.

Noriega was using his troops to quell the riots, so his capabilities were diminished. "Let's not underestimate his willingness to trade for Soviet promises," Vincent warned.

Strategic in-country strikes were happening all around Nicaragua—key utility plants and communication centers were blowing up. The people assumed it was the Contras, the Freedom Fighters. Vincent, pleased with the progress, said, "It's a real strain on Ortega's resources."

Sean interrupted Vincent's report, "Sounds like Jon is staying busy."

"He is making a real dent in Ortega's infrastructure," Vincent said confidently.

Vincent continued, "He is ready for multiple air strikes as needed."

"We have our own private war waged on Ortega," Sean acknowledged.

Vincent continued his intel summation:

"Fabio delivered our bribe to Escobar. The lack of money flowing to Ortega is like a vise tightening on his throat.

"The Central America Peace Accord, led by Costa Rica, has confirmed Honduras, Guatemala, and El Salvador. Ortega will sign Nicaragua into the Accord after his final demands are settled at a conference scheduled for July 27.

"The Leak Report has one very noticeable piece of activity: Ortega has flown between Panama and Bogotá on at least three occasions. We believe he has been smuggled on flights that disappear into Western Colombia—we suspect to meet with FARC and Soviet representatives."

Sean broke in, "Is he begging for help, a new supply route?"

Vincent replied, "We don't know. All we know is it appears

to be in desperation." Vincent continued with assignments: "Jon will remain inside Nicaragua."

Vincent watched Sean, "Don't look so concerned."

"What's the op?" asked Sean.

"You're going back to the Fun Zone, Sean."

Vincent paused, Sean said nothing.

Vincent continued, "Jon put his best ops leader there and doubled the militia squad."

"Is there flight report in your intel?" asked Sean.

Vincent replied, "We have picked up chatter—but nothing positive."

"What is the order? Should we intercept a plane?"

Vincent continued, "There will be a plane, Sean. BUT it will come with an army. Do you understand?"

"What's our orders?" Sean insisted.

"Take the fucking plane, strip it, and interrogate the crew. If attacked, it's war. Got it?"

"This is fucked. This plan is fucked up. Leal has fucked us, and you want me to be his bait!" Sean said pacing back and forth.

"This is complicated, Sean. We don't know what's going to happen and we need intelligence on the ground, if an exchange in Panama goes down," Vincent said convincingly.

Vincent continued, "On July 26, a personal message will be delivered to Ortega. It will contain an ultimatum—sign the Peace Accord—or lose Nicaragua."

Sean kept pacing, unconvinced.

"Listen, Sean, it's risky. Jon is at risk, Herrera is about to be arrested and held for life or killed, our Contras are bleeding every day, and we need you in Panama to maintain the chokehold for just a little while longer." Vincent wasn't asking—he was telling Sean.

Sean stopped pacing.

Vincent placed his hand on Sean's shoulder, "You can do this, you are ready."

"August 7, the Peace Accord will be signed and announced globally as a victory for democracy and strike against communism!" Vincent shouted at Sean. "Our Commander-in-Chief, President Reagan, will know your role in this successful mission. And we will have made an impact!"

THAT SPEECH by Vincent would play over and over in Sean's mind for the next four weeks. He was taken undercover to a safe house not far from the Embassy, loaded into a supply bag, and taken to Panama. He was unloaded as cargo to the Fun Zone hangar.

He was left inside the bag as it was placed in his basement cell. The soldiers tapped his bag and started the zipper. The men left the cell and Sean crawled out of the supply bag. His long stay and even longer wait started.

He did daily calisthenics, ate efficiently, and reviewed intelligence reports, day after day, night after night. He missed the interactions with Jon. The assigned leader of his squadron, Jack, appeared capable—he trusted that Jon would provide the best available—but he wasn't Jon.

A week into the waiting game, Sean lay in bed. The intel had dried up. It was too quiet. Training and conversations with Vincent were creeping into Sean's mind.

Vincent once told Sean, "You must seek out enemy agents who have come to spy on you, bribe them and induce them to stay with you, so you can use them as reverse spies. By intelligence obtained, you can find local spies and inside spies to use. With more intelligence, you can cause the misinformation of dead spies to be conveyed to the enemy. At that point, with intelligence obtained, you can get living spies to work as planned."

What the hell is the plan for me? thought Sean.

Sean imagined the network of spies in Cuba, Honduras, Panama, Colombia, the fucking State Department in DC and probably every U.S. Embassy trading information between these spies. *Where does my op fit in this intelligence game?* Sean questioned. He fell asleep trying to connect the dots in every intel report. Nothing was materializing.

To KEEP his mind balanced, Sean wrote poetry in a small notebook. Some of his writing referenced the search for true love, some was patriotic with religious overtones, and some was very dark.

He woke early in the morning, tired of the wait. Wondering who to trust, if he was to die, if Jon was dead already.

Sean sat up in his bed and pressed his pen against the paper. He wrote:

> Men have given their lives in conflict
> For reasons they could never understand
> The men who take lives in violent ways
> Believe they are archangels from another land.
>
> Who will go to hell in the end?
> Who will have a true heart?
> The men with beliefs that are immoral
> Or the men that act immorally playing God's part?

Sean read the poem back to himself, *I am an archangel. I am a living spy.*

THERE WAS a knock on the door, Sean's heartrate grew faster as he spoke, "Come in."

Jack, his squadron leader, looked at Sean. "Everything okay, sir?"

Sean smiled. "All is good. How goes the chatter outside?"

Jack set down a food bag, along with a sealed intelligence envelope. "Here's the lunch that Jon usually orders for you, the intel arrived just minutes ago."

Sean dismissed Jack. "Thank you. That will be all."

Sean ate his chicken sandwich, read the report, and then reread it.

A plane was expected to land in Panama from Cuba in the next 10 days.

Here we go, thought Sean, as he took a deep breath.

He noticed a tactical strike on the utility stations servicing Managua. He envisioned Jon penetrating the capital of Nicaragua and starting riots. He missed Jon's bravado, his strategic thinking, and his action plans. He said a quiet prayer for his safety.

Lastly, Sean focused on the Leak Report.

There it was: Jaime Pardo Leal was seen with Noriega only two days earlier.

"That motherfucker is here. He's in Panama, getting paid, sharing secrets, telling lies, trading souls for money and power. Leal will get what's coming to him, I swear to God," muttered Sean.

The next ten days were painfully slow. Each intel report became more and more monotonous, repeating the same chatter and guessing at timelines.

Sean had become paranoid. He assumed his intel reports were being filtered. *It is July 22?* he questioned. *What is happening?*

The day passed. Sean laid in bed, convinced his cell was a deathtrap. It was now well after midnight.

He was awakened by Jack. "Sir, sir, wake up—we have intel. Wake up."

"Okay, okay, give me the report."

Jack handed the intel report to Sean. He immediately opened the envelope and found a memo from Vincent. He felt the bottom right-hand corner for the embossed verification code. Convinced it was real, he read the memo first:

> Your part of the mission is calling: A serious
> military operation is a severe drain on the
> nation under siege. We may keep up a siege for
> as long as necessary for one day's victory.
> Your patience and strength in mind, body and
> spirit will be your savior.

Sean looked away to absorb the message, then continued reading:

> To fail to know the conditions of our
> opponents because of reluctance to give
> rewards for intelligence is extremely
> inhumane, uncharacteristic of a true military
> leader, even uncharacteristic of an assistant
> of the government.

Sean smirked.

> What enables an intelligent government and a
> wise military leadership to overcome others
> and achieve extraordinary accomplishments is
> foreknowledge. We confirmed intelligence of a
> flight taking off from Cuba in the next few
> hours. We have reason to believe it's loaded
> with money and weapons and there will be an
> exchange in the Fun Zone.

Sean's adrenaline ticked up, he felt determined to take the plane and push Ortega over the edge.

The intel report concluded with details about two major utility stations that were shut down and destroyed before dawn the day before.

> Propaganda against Soviet culture is being
> spread throughout Nicaragua.

Sean felt pride in Jon's signature strikes. He picked up the radio and commanded Jack's presence immediately.

Jack knocked on the door, within a minute. "You wanted to see me, sir?"

"Yes, Jack. Sit down."

For the next hour, Sean and Jack reviewed the op strike and all contingencies. Jack concluded the briefing, "We expect a signal when the plane is in the air, and we will position ourselves along the airstrip under cover."

Sean noted the date and time, it was July 23 and a coded message was received at 2:21 a.m:

> Flight is off the ground and en route to
> Panama City.

Sean calculated arrival around 4:30 a.m. His op was a "GO." He missed Jon's presence.

HE RESTED but did not sleep. At 3:30 a.m., he worked out and prepared his weapons, holstering his Walther PPK, three knives and spare magazines on his belt.

"Any minute now," he whispered out loud, just to break the silence in his room.

At 4:41 a.m. Sean heard the hangar doors open and the rumble of a small carrier plane. Within two minutes, squadron leader Jack rapped on his door. "Sir, there were no guards on the plane. Just the two pilots—and they don't seem to be military-trained."

Sean cut Jack off. "It's a set-up! Take a defensive stance now! Protect the hangar!"

It was too late. An explosion went off above them in the main hangar. Sean and Jack ran up the stairs as a flurry of bullets ripped through the entire building.

Jack approached the top of the stairs, surveyed the action. Most of his team in the main hangar were hit or dead. There was hot fire outside the hangar.

Jack yelled to Nick, "The exterior squad is fully engaged! Take cover!"

Jack moved into the fray, shooting three men, then ducking into the wreckage of the airplane.

At the top of the stairs, Sean assessed the hangar. He counted ten armed targets.

He needed more firepower. *The gun rack is in the soundproof room, just off the interrogation room.* He ran back down the stairs, through the interrogation room, and into the soundproof room. He grabbed the M-249 with a 100-round box. He made his way to the stairwell, where he heard men gathering.

The gunplay had momentarily stopped. He ducked back into the interrogation room, quietly laid the steel table on its side for cover and established a line of sight on the door. He told himself, *Breathe, Sean, don't waste ammo.*

Men approached the interrogation room. Sean readied his machine gun and took aim. He waited for the first two soldiers to step inside and fired. They fell in a bloody splatter together. Within seconds, several soldiers opened fire on Sean. He could feel dozens of bullets whizzing past his ears as he was balled up behind the steel table. He concentrated on making himself as small a target as possible.

Sean began praying silently, begging for forgiveness for the killings. Like an answer to his prayer, the shooting stopped. Sean could hear a man shouting orders.

"*Alto el fuego! Alto el fuego!*" (Hold fire! Hold fire!)

Barely breathing, Sean listened for the next order.

"*Sal con las manos arriba, no te dispararemos!*" (Come out with your hands up. We will not shoot you!)

Sean held still, calculating his chances. Would he be better off dead?

"*Sal con las manos arriba, no te dispararemos!*" the man repeated. Sean still did not move. The voice shouted. "*Voy a entrar y si me disparas, mis hombres te mataran!*" (I'm coming in, and if you shoot me, my men will kill you dead.)

Sean heard the man walk into the interrogation room. He thought: *Is this it? Is this where I die?*

"*Sal sin pistola y vivirás.*" (Come out with no gun, and you will live.)

Sean slid his machine gun into plain view. With his Walther PPK tucked in the small of his back, he slowly stood with both hands raised in surrender.

He surveyed at least a dozen men in the room, thoughts of his squadron flashed through his mind. Sean focused on the man walking toward him.

"*Todos están muertos,*" (They are all dead) said the man without feeling.

Sean could feel his hands trembling and tried to stop. He stared at his captor. It was the same man who looked him over at gunpoint with Jon. The man held his hands out as a gesture of openness. He was three feet away now. A dozen guns were pointed at Sean.

A second man came up to the captor and handed him a small nightstick. The man leveraged the nightstick against Sean's throat until he was pinned against the wall. He spoke, "*Tengo la orden de llevarte con nosotros.*" (I am ordered to take you back with us.)

Before Sean could even process the Spanish, two men

grabbed his arms, and the leader jabbed the nightstick into Sean's ribs numerous times. Out of breath, Sean took a beating on his entire body, knees, thighs, and calves, shoulders, chest and back. He tried to stand, but he went down grimacing in pain. He rolled onto his stomach as blow after blow pummeled his body. Two men held him down, prone. The captor grabbed his Walther PPK and held it to Sean's head.

"Quieres matarme con esto?" (You want to kill me with this?) he screamed. *"Te matare con esto en su lugar!"* (I will kill you with this instead!)

The captor pistol-whipped Sean. His vision went black, his body convulsed, and he passed out.

The captor ordered his men to prepare Sean's body for transport. They dragged him across the interrogation room floor, up the steps and placed him in a weapons crate.

His captor muttered to his men, *"Me dijeron que lo trajera vivo pero muerto si fuera necesario."* (They told me to bring him back alive, but dead if I have to.) Then he laughed, *"Veamos lo mal que el hombre de la CIA quiere vivir!"* (Let's see how badly the CIA man wants to live!)

Chapter 34
Captured

SEAN WOKE to the taste of his own blood. He was hooded, barely able to breathe without wincing, his hands tied behind his back, his ankles locked in chains. He tried to roll, but he could feel the wooden crate around him. His ears still ringing, Sean could barely stand the pounding inside his head. He closed his eyes and focused, *Remember your training.*

IT WAS November 5, 1985. Two weeks of hell that Nick would never forget. Field training exercises. He was paired with a female partner and control officer. Her name was Alex, short for Alexandra. Tall, athletic, rugged, and yet beautifully feminine, Alex was strong. Nick and Alex reported to Walter, a middle-aged Agency lifer in the Clandestine Services Operations department.

For two weeks, they were thrust into unknown circumstances to investigate, detect, and uncover information. He stole, bribed, and developed assets. He learned "enhanced" interrogation techniques, also known as torture.

With only two days left in field training, Nick and Alex were abducted and taken to separate lockdown cells. As Alex refused to give any information, her kidnappers waterboarded her twice within the first thirty minutes, at which point she cracked—offering all the information they were seeking.

Nick was another story. Regulations allowed 12 minutes of water-method interrogation along with questioning every six hours. That meant for the next six hours, Nick was waterboarded twelve times for about 20–35 seconds each time. He did not break.

Nick displaced himself mentally. Ever since he was a little boy, he maintained an innate capability to cope with stress, physical attack and fear when threatened. His much older brothers harassed him, locked him in small closets—telling him that there had been other brothers before him—but they misbehaved and were planted in the yard, showing him dead spots in the grass as evidence. As Nick grew a little older, they would push him though barn walls, out of hay lofts, and throw sixty-pound grain bags onto his head. If he ever told his parents, the abuse was even worse.

When Nick was waterboarded in training, he removed himself from the table and straps mentally. Instead, he took himself into the farrowing barn where the large female pigs were housed. The stench was unbearable, hog manure collecting overnight in the small enclosure. He gagged and gasped for air, every morning for several years scraping and shoveling the manure from the stalls. Nick could hold his breath and endure the cold, the heat and the attacks of the angry three hundred-pound hogs.

The interrogation went on for nearly three days, beyond the scheduled stop. Nick finally broke down—he gave away one real name, Vincent—and lied about everything else.

UNEXPECTEDLY, he felt choppy turbulence. Sean knew he was on a plane.

He assessed his situation. He could be on his way to Cuba or

Nicaragua. Was his captor a soldier of Castro or Ortega? Or was there an alternative?

The puzzle pieces in his mind moved around the imaginary white board; Leal was the leak. Ortega was the recipient of the intel. All puzzle pieces pointed to Leal. For a moment, he allowed himself to imagine killing Leal, but he needed to stay focused.

He felt the plane descend. He would know where he was soon enough.

The plane landed and several men spoke quietly around his crate. They pulled his crate out of the plane, bounced it down the steps, carried it for a few feet, then dropped it on the floor with a loud smacking bang. Sean's head swelled in pain.

He knew he would be interrogated and tortured. He laid in the crate for what felt like several hours. He pissed himself at some point, fading in and out of consciousness.

Lay still, he told himself. His headache transformed into an entire body ache. As he assessed himself, he realized that he was savagely beaten. Images of the night stick striking against his body and limbs brought the pain to the surface.

Without warning, men hammered pry bars into the crate and ripped it apart. Sean was overwhelmed by the cracking of wood and banging of hammers. They threw the top of crate aside. He smelled fresh air.

Breathe, he thought, *just breathe.*

Two men pulled him out, dragging him across the floor while they said nothing. He attempted no struggle, dead weight to the soldiers. Sean believed if he played dead, he might get some time to recover before interrogation.

Still hooded, shackled and tied, Sean was dragged around corners, down a flight of steps, and then thrown into some sort of room. He assumed he was in a basement cell. He also assumed his movements were being watched or even recorded. He gradually maneuvered himself into a more comfortable position and tried to rest. All he could do was wait. His mind reflected on his childhood memories.

HE THOUGHT *about the games he played with much-older brothers. They thought they could trick him with hide and seek—send him off to hide but never come to seek him. Nick hid just outside the perimeter of the farmyard they played in and camouflaged himself. He could lay still for hours.*

Nick realized, even at a young age, he was different than his brothers. His family was split into two: The boys—and Nick. He hated that. He spent most of his childhood proving that he could do anything they could do, even better.

SEAN HEARD faint footsteps and low voices. He refocused on his situation and wondered who or what they were waiting for—maybe he would be bound and held for days. His mind drifted back to the ambush.

My team is dead. Fucking ambushed by at least fifty soldiers. Anger swelled inside Sean's gut.

Noriega had to bless it, thought Sean. *The Soviets sent a false flag—a fucking decoy—and we fell for it.* Sean tried to think through the probabilities: Who are my captors? How ugly will this be, avoiding the idea of death? He faded and found sleep. His body demanded rest.

The door to Sean's cell swung open, banging into the wall. He was kicked in the ribcage. He grunted and winced in pain.

"*El esta vivo, coronel,*" (He is alive, Colonel) The guard reported.

"*Prepáralo para mañana,*" (Prepare him for tomorrow) said a second voice.

Sean listened intensely and repeated the words, "prepare him for tomorrow," in his mind. Unsure of how long the flight had taken, and unable to identify his captors, Sean still did not know where he was.

At least two guards firmly held him down and unshackled his ankles. Then they stood him up and cut his clothes off. Stripped naked, but still hooded, with his hands tied behind his back, the guards commanded Sean not to move.

Sean heard a third man enter, a paper bag ripping, then a distinct citrus smell.

Oranges, he thought, *fresh oranges.*

A guard spoke to Sean, *"Quieres un poco de naranja prisionero?"* (Would you like some orange, prisoner?)

Sean shook his head vehemently: No.

"Entonces te vencere con ellos." (Then I shall beat you with them.)

Without any provocation, one of the guards grabbed him from behind. He placed Sean a headlock, twisting his neck to the point of snapping. Sean struggled to avoid being killed.

A second guard rubbed a burlap bag, obviously filled with oranges, all over his body. He methodically battered Sean's body with blows to his chest, stomach, and genitals. The hits were harsh and swift; the impact felt like a series of pressurized punches.

Sean's neck was in real jeopardy, and he had to fight back. In one swift motion, he kicked the guard with the oranges, threw his body weight forcefully into a leap backward that removed the headlock. The men landed on the concrete floor. He immediately attempted to stand, and as he rose, he took a blow to the lower back—he recognized the night stick. The guard whipped the night stick into Sean's lower back again. Sean collapsed in pain and his vision blurred; he was fading fast. He accepted the possibility of death as he lay on the cold concrete floor.

Sunrise, July 25, 1987

SEAN SURVIVED the first forty-eight hours of captivity despite being beaten, dehydrated, and suffering from a brutal concussion.

A guard barked at him, *"Preparada para limpiar."* (Stand up for cleaning.)

Sean, hooded, naked; stood and waited. He smelled his own defecation and analyzed his situation. *These bastards want me clean. I must be meeting someone important.*

Then he remembered what Vincent had said, "Ortega was to get a personal message on July 26—his attendance is required at the Peace Accord Conference on July 27—or his reign over Nicaragua would end."

Surely Vincent has stepped up his communication, given the ambush and my disappearance. Hope emerged. *I'm not alone.*

What sounded like two women came into the room. He could hear them scrubbing the floor, with buckets filled with ammonia, nearly gagging Sean. One left to fetch fresh soapy water, and upon her return she gently washed Sean. Dehydrated, bloody and dirty, the soapy water and gentle touch was healing.

He whispered, *"Gracias por tu piedad."* (Thank you for your mercy.)

Neither woman spoke, but one hand touched his chest over his heart; he could feel her sorrow and care. That touch awakened Gabriella deep in his soul. Her memory and spirit flowed into Sean's heart, lifting him. He told himself, *"I'm not going to die here. I'm a living spy ... I will report back. Vincent will see to that."*

He summoned his will, *"Agua para beber."* (Water for drink.) He demanded it repeatedly. But the women quickly finished his standing bath and left.

SINCE SEAN'S capture, Vincent scrambled communications to every influential chief, politician, and department secretary, utilizing "flash cables" typically reserved for acts of war. He envisioned Sean being interrogated and abused. As he reached out for an approval to extract Sean, his superiors at Langley and at the White House stopped all discussions and shut him down. There would be no extraction plan.

The decision to abandon Sean was a death sentence. The White House was not going to allow anything to get in the way of brokering agreements surrounding the Central American Peace Accord.

Vincent made demands on a call with Secretary Shultz's Chief of Staff, "The life or death of my agent in the hands of Ortega in the bowels of Nicaragua is a national security risk, I need approval for extraction now!"

The Chief of Staff said, "Really, a career trainee on his first assignment. An agent who got caught trying to do God-knows-what in a Panamanian airstrip hangar that does not even exist. It's a NO-GO."

Vincent replied, "Fuck you, you hypocritical bureaucrat. If this were one of Shultz's 'landmark treaties' we would have brought our man home already!"

"Don't you teach your men about the greater good and Rule #1—DON'T GET CAUGHT!" snarled the Chief of Staff.

Vincent lowered his voice, "Why do you want to burn Sean?"

After a silent pause, the Chief of Staff proclaimed, "Because he doesn't count. He's collateral damage, not worth the risk—the Peace Accord is top priority. YOU KNOW THIS."

Vincent hung up the phone.

He decided that there was no way to order an extraction for Sean, at least not on the record. Jon, entangled with psyops in Nicaragua and Panama, an entire special forces militia team dead, and Herrera, a foreign asset being held hostage by Ortega. With no other assets in the region, Vincent said, "Hold on, Nick. You will live to tell this story . . . I swear."

SEAN'S HOOD was lifted from his head. He tried to open his eyes, but it was too bright.

"*Que hora es?*" (What time is it?) asked Sean. He assessed the room. It was much larger than he had imagined. *This is an interrogation room.*

There were three guards with weapons drawn in each corner. Two more guards were positioning chairs and a table. There were thick leather straps, stained with blood, bolted to the top of the table and cuffs attached to one of the chairs. A sixth guard walked in, looked at Sean's face and body without expression. He threw a bag of clothing on the floor.

"*Te soltare las manos para que te viste.*" (I will release your hands so you can dress.)

Sean resisted. "*Sin agua primero.*" (No. Water first.)

This aggravated the guard. The exchange escalated.

Sean tested the guard, determined to find out if he had any leverage at all. The guard threw a fierce right hook across Sean's left jaw. Nearly falling, Sean stayed calm, remaining upright with his hands to his side.

Sin agua primero." (No. Water first.) Sean said with confidence.

The guard called for water. He opened a small plastic bottle for Sean, spit in it, and handed it Sean.

"*Adelante, beberlo,*" (Go ahead, drink it) said the guard, laughing at Sean.

Sean looked the guard in the eye. "*Que te jodan.*" (Fuck you.)

The guard poured the water out.

He turned to the other guards. "*Vistale y encierralo.*" (Dress him and lock him up.)

They dressed Sean in a loose denim shirt and pants. Strapping his wrists to the table, hands facing down, his ankles cuffed to the chair, Sean mentally prepared for questioning.

What felt like several hours later, he heard movement in the hallway. The door swung open. Sean did not look. He did not want to give respect. The man walked to the opposite side of the table and sat down. It was Daniel Ortega, president of Nicaragua.

Ortega leaned in and sized up Sean. Ortega appeared to be determining Sean's fate. Sean remained still, concentrating on his breathing and heart rate.

"Eres un liante. Hablas bien español?" (You are a troublemaker. Do you speak Spanish well?)

Sean looked into Ortega's eyes. "Water to drink first."

Ortega laughed, ordered a new bottle of water and waited.

A guard opened a new bottle, fed Sean the water.

Ortega lit a cigarette and leaned back.

"Estas listo ahora?" (Are you ready now?) asked Ortega. He continued in English, "tell me what you know about the Contras. Where they get their weapons and supplies."

Sean responded, "The Contras are fighting for freedom, I'm guessing they have many supporters."

Ortega leaned in and whispered, "Shall I electrocute you? Then will I get answers."

Sean did not reply, nor did he blink during the stare, each weighing the situation.

Ortega signaled to a guard. The guard placed a small ball-peen hammer on the table. "We know who you are. Maybe you need a reason to remember?" He picked up the hammer, caressed it, "You still don't understand the situation you are in. You think you have value, but you don't."

Without hesitation, Ortega smashed the hammer on Sean's right hand, breaking his palm and pinky finger. Sean screamed in pain and closed his eyes.

Ortega roared at Sean, *"Contestame, tu vida no significa nada!"* (Answer me, your life means nothing!)

Sean managed the pain by escaping deep inside his own memories. He associated it with the pain he felt as a teenager when his hand was brutally broken between a steel wagon tongue and tractor hitch. He slowly opened his eyes, looked at Ortega, and said nothing.

Ortega grew impatient. "YOU WILL FUCKING TALK TO ME."

Sean spoke with courage, "You will agree to sign the Central American Peace Accord. Upon your signing, Nicaragua will cut ties with the Soviets."

This enraged Ortega. *"He oido bastantes chorradas por un día!"* (I've heard enough bullshit for one day!)

Reassuring the guards of his superiority, Ortega stood up, walked around the table, and began beating Sean's face with his fists. Landing numerous blows to his cheekbones and neck. Sean's head fell forward; he tried to stay still. Ortega stopped.

Everything was blurry for Sean; blood crawled down his face.

Ortega ordered Sean to be placed in the hot box and left the room.

Sean knew he had won the first round. As he sat still, blood dripped from his face onto the table. His neck was in terrible pain, but he continued analyzing.

There must have been communiques to Ortega that my death would not be tolerated. Sean grew convinced that Ortega knew who he was and believed he was worth more alive, than dead. *Thank God—but for how long?*

Chapter 35

Brotherhood Tested

GUARDS HOODED Sean, bound his aching broken hands, and shackled his ankles. They dragged him up a flight of stairs. He heard a door swing open and could feel the outside air, thick and balmy. The guards unlatched a door and stuffed Sean into a small wooden box. It was hot, spiders and insects invaded his body.

Hours crept by—Sean told himself that Ortega did not want to kill him—he chose to believe, until proven otherwise. He concentrated on Operation: Turn-About. Vincent and Jon were pushing Ortega from every angle by now. His capture was part of the calculated risk.

ORTEGA COMPLETED a press conference. He declared his intent to reach a settlement with the other Central American countries already committed to the Peace Accord. Vincent manipulated Ortega and discredited Noriega. Operation: Turn-About was in full swing.

Quietly, Vincent requisitioned an extraction team for Sean, but Langley gave direct order not to take any actions that could interfere with the U.S. Government's role. More specifically, do nothing to jeopardize President Reagan's role in advising the Peace Accord to a successful end. The planned date for the official signing by all five countries was August 7, 1987. Vincent's hands were tied—but he continued to influence Ortega at every turn. He made it clear that counter measures would be severe, upon discovery of mistreatment or the killing of any U.S. hostage.

Vincent received intel that afternoon detailing Sean's where-abouts, citing an informant sighting. *It was an American, badly beaten, digging a grave in the backyard of an Ortega safe house.* Once again, he was reminded that Sean had a limited window before his value, and his life, disappeared for good.

THAT SAME day, Sean was fed rice and beans and given water. After he ate, a guard opened the box, pulled Sean's hood off his head, and cut away the restraints.

"*Te cavaras la tumba.*" (You will dig your own grave.)

Sean refused.

The guard swung the shovel at Sean's shoulder and drew blood.

"*Cavar o torturer.*" (Dig or be tortured.)

Sean nodded, "*Si.*"

The guard walked to the middle of the backyard and threw the shovel down.

"*Ahora lo haces!*" (You do it now!)

The guard stepped back, drew his pistol, and pointed it at Sean. Sean scanned the area and spotted seven guards with rifles and machine guns surrounding the yard. He walked to the spot, picked up the shovel, and began digging. He had become numb to the pain in his hand. Gripping his shovel was saving his life. Survival was everything.

He placed the tip of the shovel into the dirt, stepped on the edge to force it into the ground, tilted the shovel back with a large clump of dirt. He tossed the dirt to the side. He remembered digging a deep trench from the house to a gas tank more than twenty yards away just five years earlier on the farm . . .

Sean was pushed by a guard holding a machine gun.

"Sigue cavando!" (Keep digging!)

Sean nodded his head and picked up the pace.

His father had pushed him on that trench—trying to make Nick focus . . .

Sean stood in the hole, shoveling dirt and throwing it up and out of the grave. He paused to examine his grave. It was around three feet deep and close to six feet long and just over two feet wide. Sweating profusely, he begged for water.

"Agua, por favor." (Water, please.)

"Que te jodan, eres un hombre muerto." (Fuck you, you're a dead man.)

Sean cried to the guard, *"Te lo ruego."* (I beg of you.)

The guard walked to the side of the house, filled a dirty bucket with water from the rusty pump and gave it to Sean. He looked at the dirty water, eyed the guard, held the bucket over his head and poured it over his body.

By nightfall, Sean completed the grave. It was six feet deep and six feet long by two and a half feet wide. He stood in the center, and thoughts of his father flooded his mind. He would be proud of the job that Nick had accomplished. Suddenly, tears formed, Sean lost his breath and fell to his knees.

He cried out from the bottom of the grave, *"Dios, déjame vivir para ver a mi padre de nuevo."* (Please God, let me live to see my father again.)

The guards inspected the grave, pulled Sean out, placed constraints on his wrists and shackled his ankles.

One of them said, *"Te gusta mucho un universitario"* (You dig very well for a college boy!)

Sean turned to look into the guard's eyes. *"Soy un granjero."* (I am a farm boy.)

The guards laughed, and, for the first night since being held captive, left the hood off Sean's head and placed him in the interrogation cell.

Exhausted, Sean laid on the cell floor, and fell asleep. Unsure whether he would live or die, he knew he had done his best. All his mind and body wanted at that moment was rest, peaceful rest. He silently prayed the Act of Contrition. He prayed for forgiveness in case he was killed in the middle of the night: *Oh my God, I'm heartily sorry for having offended Thee. And I detest all my sins because I dread the loss of heaven, and the pains of hell, and most of all because I offended Thee, my God, who art all good and deserving of all my love . . . I firmly resolve with the help of thy grace to confess my sins, do penance, and amend my life, Amen.*

Sean drifted into a deep sleep. Exhausted, mentally drained, completely beaten.

3:15 a.m. July 28

Two ATTACK helicopters carrying a special ops squadron flew quietly under radar from Soto Cano Air Base, Honduras into Nicaragua.

"Site 1 is visible," Leader radioed to team.

"Front or Back?" Follower replied.

The helicopters, determined to strike, landed together in the back yard of the Ortega Safe House under fire from the exterior guard. Wasting no time, the elite force took out the guards and blew through the back door of the house. They stormed the entire perimeter in a matter of seconds. Gunfire sounded throughout the house as special ops started their search for Sean.

Sean woke to the sound and listened, locked in the interrogation room, bound and shackled. Adrenaline stimulated every reaction.

A soldier screamed outside his door, "Take cover, Sean!"

Sean rolled to the far corner and faced away from the door.

The door to his cell blew open, and two heavily armed special ops soldiers scanned Sean's cell. A third man followed, directly running at him.

The soldier knelt over Sean. "Let's get out of here, brother," he said touching his back.

Sean turned and grabbed his arms for support. "Thank you."

Once Sean was stripped of his shackles and wrist straps, the team methodically moved him up the stairs and out of the house. They waved to the helicopter and placed Sean in the middle seat as the soldiers filed in around him. It all happened so fast.

Sean watched the soldiers leave the safe house and listened to the pilots.

"All accounted for, sir!" the pilot called back to the team.

The soldier sitting opposite Sean responded, "Let's roll!"

The helicopter lifted off the ground. Sean broke down inside, alive and free.

The lights of Managua sparkled below as the helicopter team watched for enemy fire and planes—but the ride was swift and smooth.

"Nine minutes to drop zone, sir," shouted the pilot.

Sean remained rigid, looked down and thanked God for the rescue. His mind was reeling. And then a hand grabbed his wrists. He looked up.

The extraction leader pulled off his helmet. It was Richard.

Sean's eyes filled with tears. Richard leaned in. "It's okay, you're safe. You're not going to die."

Sean's mind was racing. Why . . . How . . . When . . . ?

"Vincent was ordered not to extract you until after the Peace Accord signing. Fuck it, I don't take orders from the U.S.," Richard told him.

Sean grabbed Richard's hands and held them until they reached the secret jungle airstrip built by the Cartels.

The team carefully unloaded Sean from the helicopter. A small airplane was warming up. Richard and Sean hugged for a solid minute.

"Thank you, Richard," Sean exhaled, "thank you for everything."

"Listen, Sean. You are being flown to the private hangar in Mexico City. Vincent will meet you there with medical attention," Richard said reassuringly.

As Sean neared the boarding steps of the small King Air, Fabio peaked out of the door and waved Sean aboard.

"C'mon, Sean, we will get you to Mexico City safely. Just relax," he said.

Sean smiled, "Thank you, Fabio—thank you so much."

The flight took just under three hours. Fabio provided water and blankets to Sean and encouraged him to try and sleep.

Sean continued thanking Fabio, "Whatever I can do to repay your kindness, I will."

Fabio laughed and hugged Sean. *Esto estoy seguro de!* (This I am sure of!)

Just past dawn, the plane pulled into a private hangar in Mexico City.

Sean spotted Vincent, standing in the hangar with his hands in his pockets. Sean knew that stance. It was Vincent's way of appearing in control even when nerves were getting the better of him. This time Vincent could not hide his anxious feelings.

Sean stepped out of the plane. Vincent grabbed Sean and held him tight.

"Welcome back, brother," whispered Vincent.

Sean cried in Vincent's grip, "Thank you for not letting me die."

Wednesday, July 29, 1987

RECOVERING IN the Embassy's hospital in Mexico City, Sean awoke grateful to be alive. His hand had to be reset and put in a cast, his pain was being managed, and his body was mending. But he still did not have the courage to look in a mirror.

Three days of silence. No visitors, no calls, just nurses and the occasional physician visit.

Every night Sean experienced night terrors while violent dreams invaded his sleep. He knew he must be under observation. He couldn't take the silence in the day; he demanded the nurses to tell him who was watching. He acted paranoid and suspicious of everyone. The nurses tried to calm him and assure him that he was safe.

Sunday, August 1, Vincent sat in the chair next to Sean's bed and waited for him to wake. When Sean opened his eyes and saw Vincent, he spoke first.

"Where have you been?"

Vincent smiled. "Doing your job and covering your ass. I was even threatened by Director Webster. I lied and said your capture was part of the op—it opened a direct line of communication with Ortega that worked in our favor."

"Was it part of the op?" Sean asked with uncertainty.

Vincent shook his head, "From now on—YES, it was part of the op."

"Got it." Sean was in no condition to banter, let alone argue with Vincent.

For the next couple of hours, Vincent briefed Sean about the progress of the Peace Accord. Operation: Turn-About was near completion.

Vincent announced to Sean with grandiose flair, "The formal signing of the Central American Peace Accord is set for August 7. Happy Birthday, my brother—Mission Complete."

Sean experienced a rush of pride in the accomplishment. His mind also listed the turmoil that waited for him in the real world.

"What does Anna know?" he asked.

Vincent stood up. "She knows you were mugged, beaten, and held for days as a U.S. hostage by Colombian FARC forces. Those forces believed America would pay. She also knows you were rescued two days ago and is expecting a call today to get the status about your return."

"Do you think she cares about me?" asked Sean.

"No," Vincent replied flatly. "Don't worry, Sean, if you want out of the marriage, it will happen—we will help you."

Sean analyzed the story. His mind developed a full story around the bed of lies already in place. Vincent placed his hand on Sean's shoulder. "Your parents know the same story, and I have been consoling your mother and assuring your father of your safety."

Thinking of the trauma it must have caused. Vincent said quietly, "It's all going to be okay."

Sean replied, "Maybe."

Vincent leaned over Sean. "You will be discharged in about an hour. I will fly back to St. Louis with you and personally hand you off to Anna. On August 7, we will quietly celebrate our mission . . . in secret." Sean nodded.

The nurse prepared Sean for discharge. He took a moment to go into his bathroom and look at himself in the mirror. Most of the facial swelling had faded, the lacerations were beginning to heal, and his motion felt more normal, even functional, despite all the beatings.

He was told that the nagging pain in his neck and back would persist for years—but he was alive. He stared in the mirror—deep into his own eyes. He did not recognize himself.

What the hell do you want? It's still your life, he told himself.

———

THEY BOARDED a private plane and took off for St. Louis. Anna insisted that Vincent bring Nick to her corporate townhome so they could be close to her parents for support. Nick questioned the story Vincent spread. He was lost in the web of lies.

The plane descended into St. Louis; Nick looked at Vincent. "Thank you for not leaving me in that grave."

Vincent reassured Nick, "I will always look out for you."

The wheels of the plane touched down. The breaks slowed the plane down.

Nick stared into Vincent's eyes. "I am finished with this, Vincent. I'm not coming back."

The plane taxied to the private hangar where Anna was waiting.

Vincent stared back into Nick's soul, "It's not that easy. You really don't believe what you are saying. Besides, we are not finished." Vincent beathed a long sigh. "We know Jaime Leal put you in danger. You will want to see that man brought to justice."

Nick shook his head no.

Vincent acknowledged his torment, "I understand."

The plane rolled into the hangar, Nick looked out the window and saw Anna. He wished he were more excited to see her. But flashes of their broken marriage played out in his mind.

The pilot asked, "Ready?"

Vincent turned to Nick, speaking softly, "Listen to me, Nick, you are brave, strong, smart, and skillful. Take some time to think. You did good work back there. We will talk on your birthday. Love you, brother."

Nick stood to exit the plane, leaned toward Vincent and hugged him.

"Love you, too."

Epilogue

Two months later at noon on a lazy Sunday, Jaime Leal decided to dispatch his security and kept only one of his bodyguards for a trip to his farm in La Mesa, not far from Bogotá.

Sean watched. He had waited for nearly a week in hiding for this opportunity. He followed Leal's car into the country, leaving two to three miles of road between them.

Leal visited his farm more frequently—intel reports provided quotes from Leal telling others that he "finds peace on his farm."

This mission was personal. Sean set aside all morals; this time, he was focused on revenge. He acted with confidence. Leal will be terminated as a traitor—a traitor that got his team killed and nearly got Sean killed.

Walking low and fast along the hedgerows of Leal's farm, Sean moved stealthily through the rolling cattle pastures. Less than three hundred yards away from the homestead, Sean spotted a lone bodyguard smoking a cigarette in the side yard.

Taking the silencer out of his jacket, he eyed the bodyguard, and observed his movements. Sean moved covertly to the corner of the outermost barn of the three on the farmstead. Now, only thirty yards away, Sean's training took over.

The guard paced in the yard, consistently scanning the farm in every direction. Sean waited patiently.

As the bodyguard relaxed, he lit another cigarette and sat down on the front steps. Sean made his move, swiftly running alongside the side yard and then angling toward the front steps. By the time the bodyguard noticed him, it was too late. Sean took the clean shot, firing a single bullet that entered the bodyguard's head. As he fell to the ground, Sean walked past him, firing another shot into his chest.

Sean entered the farmhouse. Leal was in the kitchen preparing sandwiches. He turned. Sean stared at Leal; this was it. There was acceptance on Leal's face, no anger or fight. Sean held the gun on Leal for just a moment, saying nothing. Sean had reached his trigger point.

Leal opened his mouth to speak, Sean pulled the trigger, firing the first bullet at Leal's face, the second bullet at his chest. Leal fell, Sean fired three more bullets at his head on the way down, ensuring that there would not be an open casket.

It was done.

At the time of Jaime Leal's death, 471 members of UP had already been assassinated throughout the country. Leal had received many death threats, and, in the end, it had become a waiting game for him.

His published obituary in the local *Las Mesa* newspaper stated,

> Jaime Pardo Leal knew he would be killed. His family knew he would be killed. Patriotic Union knew he would be killed. Journalists knew he would be killed. The whole country knew he would be killed.

By November 1987, Nick and Anna filed for divorce. The Agency assisted Nick with the application for an annulment, which was granted expeditiously the day before Christmas, that same year.

After Christmas, Nick flew to Phoenix. For the past couple of months, his mind was deciphering all that had happened with Gabriella. He could not trust Vincent's reports. A holiday week, he thought—what better present than a surprise knock on the door.

Unsure if she would be home, he secretly drove to her town-home in Scottsdale. "A nice neighborhood, so normal," he assessed as he found a spot to park with a distant, yet clear, view of her front walk and living room window. He waited and watched people coming and going in the neighboring homes.

A car pulled up and stopped in front of her walkway. "There she is," he whispered to himself. Gabriella opened the passenger doors, then helped her parents out of the car.

Gabriella looked up to survey the street. She looked toward his car for a full second, then back to her parents. Nick could feel her energy and was certain she could feel him. As they settled into their living room chairs, Gabriella served drinks and snacks. Nick started the car, took one last look, then said, "I love you, Gabriella."

By early 1988, Nick focused on a new career as an entrepreneur and investment advisor. He developed business ventures back in Illinois near his alma mater with frequent trips that furthered his interests in Bogotá and throughout Colombia. He invested in coffee ventures that assisted rural cooperatives, especially those oppressed in western Colombia by the FARC. Vincent encouraged the Nick's time away from active duty and declared Nick a "sleeper."

Vincent became a Station Chief for Upper Mid-Level Tactical, Operations, and Management at the CIA. Both he and Richard were thrilled with the promotion. Vincent had taken a secure apartment home in the swanky side of Bogotá, where ambassadors and the ultra-wealthy elite resided.

Nick was not allowed a formal release from his service for clandestine operatives. He was removed and "put to sleep"—there would be no record of any official status at Langley. Nick successfully left the reservation of the CIA.

Vincent declared Nicholas Ford to be a "NOC"—nonofficial cover—with no protection in the field or anywhere. Nick believed he would have more control as a private contractor, but Vincent had other plans.

Vincent's power grab to become the Deputy Director of National Clandestine Services, for the entire Western Hemisphere Division was within reach. For the better part of a year, he dived into operations that would lead to his political rise within intelligence circles.

Sean attended periodic day-long strategy meetings regularly in 1988 in Bogotá and Mexico City. Windowless rooms; classified intel. Discussions of economic, military, social and demographic concerns, all centered around intelligence and political agendas, including Panama.

He stayed in top physical and psychological condition, attending secret trainings with Jon Robinson whenever he was invited. He missed the action.

Plans were being laid to oust Noriega from Panama. The U.S. indicted him in Miami on federal narcotics trafficking and money laundering. By March 1988, the U.S. government entered negotiations with Noriega, seeking his resignation. Negotiations were collapsing after just a few months of lengthy and inconclusive talks; Noriega had no intentions of ever resigning. Things were heating up in Panama.

Sunday morning, August 7, 1988, Nick went for a run in the

park near his home and saw a familiar figure sitting on a bench across the street.

It was Vincent. *Of course,* thought Nick, *on my birthday no less.* . . .

He approached the bench slowly, sat down, and asked Vincent, "What's up?"

Vincent smiled at him. Excitement surged in Nick's chest.

"It's time."

Acknowledgments

This book was originally written in just ninety days during the beginning of the 2020 Covid pandemic. The story has been ruminating in my mind for over twenty-five years, and evolved over time through bar stories, debates, and late-night discussions with friends, colleagues and those who have served in the intelligence community.

Without the prompting and unyielding belief from Cynthia Frisina, I may never have put these stories on paper. She was my original editor and collaborator in the development of story and complex characters. Cindy's boundless enthusiasm, love of reading, and support helped bring this story to life.

Upon reviewing my first draft, Daniel Roth (no relation) told me the good, the bad, and the ugly in a two-page critique. He has been unstintingly generous in sharing his expertise and quickly became my sounding board, teacher, and collaborative editor in the process of finishing *Trigger Point*. Daniel has been writing, editing, filmmaking, and most importantly, serving companies and people as a strategist with keen entrepreneurial spirit for over fifty years. His roots in the publishing industry stem back to the 1970s as an editorial director and then publisher at Simon & Schuster.

Along the way, contributing editors and consultants, such as Diane Eaton and Randy Peyser, Author One Stop, as well as Lisa Towles, author and book trailer producer, all shared their talents with enthusiasm with me as a first-time novelist.

Last but not least, the entire team at Meryl Moss Media Group have done a superlative job working with me and believing that *Trigger Point* is a story worth telling. They have been a rock of support and wisdom for the first book in the successful launch of The Nicholas Ford Series™.

Read an excerpt from Tony Roth's
THE OPERATIVE

Book 2 in The Nicholas Ford Series™
Coming Soon in 2022

NICHOLAS FORD noticed a man following him. Only in Bogota for twenty-four hours under his own name, he felt the ghosts of his past already shadowing him along the street corridors. He walked briskly through Bolivar Plaza while eyeing the man cautiously, crossed between the busy traffic and turned down a side street. Hidden in a doorway, Nick spotted the man at the passage entrance. Just as he drew his gun, the man collapsed to the sidewalk.

"Check the man for vitals!" shouted the voice in Nick's ear plug radio.

"Who is he?" asked Nick as he ran to the man.

"You're being surveilled. Give the man CPR. Our van is less than two minutes away."

Nick knelt and took the man's vitals. "He's dead." He began CPR, compressing his chest and breathing into his mouth. Nick grabbed him by his jacket to prop him up, as if he were still alive. The van screeched to a stop. As the door slid open, Nick pushed the man into the van and pulled the radio from his ear. "What the fuck is going on!"

"Noriega knows about the coup. His spymaster is in bed with the Cartel. We're fucked." The van sped away to evade surveillance, and reach the Medellín airstrip.

Nick glared at the agents. "Not yet. Noriega will go down."

This story, inspired by true events, brings forth the human stories behind covert operations of persuasion by non-official civilians in the attempted coup of Manual Noriega in Panama. By mid-1988, the Pentagon pushed for a U.S. invasion of Panama. Multiple pressure tactics had failed to get Noriega to step down, including the Iran-Contra Scandal and several drug-related indictments. President Ronald Reagan refused to invade due to Vice President George Bush's ties to Noriega, the CIA, and Bush's presidential campaign.

Nick is caught in the middle of military campaigns to remove Noriega and allegiance to his assets within Panama, realizing he's not in control of his mission at all. . . .

TONY ROTH has been a farmer, Eagle Scout, college athlete, musician, and serial entrepreneur. He has flown more than 11 million miles, holds six patents and is the youngest of five competitive brothers. Roth founded a national care management company in 2014 in honor of his late father. Nicholas Ford was inspired by true events and created over many glasses of scotch, blending years of bar stories, long-standing friendships in the intelligence community, and new research. *Trigger Point* is his first novel in the Nicholas Ford Series.